WILDFLOWERS

A TRILOGY

by

ROBERT NOONAN

WILDFLOWERS

While overworked child laborers of the nineteenth century might have created the grist for the Industrial Revolution, even darker abuses were committed against them.

BRIDIE'S DAUGHTER

The Orphan Trains carried homeless children westward, altering their lives and the lives of the people who took them in … for better or worse.

SECRETS

The orphan children, as well as the adults who adopted them, have secrets from their past. Some secrets are revealed; others better left untold.

WILDFLOWERS

The First Story in the Orphan Train Trilogy

A Novel

Robert Noonan
Author of *Bridie's Daughter* **and** *Secrets*

iUniverse, Inc.
New York Lincoln Shanghai

Wildflowers

The First Story in the Orphan Train Trilogy

iUniverse books may be ordered through booksellers or by contacting:

iUniverse
2021 Pine Lake Road, Suite 100
Lincoln, NE 68512
www.iuniverse.com
1-800-Authors (1-800-288-4677)

Because of the dynamic nature of the Internet, any Web addresses
or links contained in this book may have changed
since publication and may no longer be valid.

This is a work of fiction. All of the characters, names, incidents, organizations,
and dialogue in this novel are either the products of the author's imagination
or are used fictitiously.

Author Photo by Matt Stary, Hatfield, Wisconsin

ISBN: 978-0-595-42683-6 (pbk)
ISBN: 978-0-595-68552-3 (cloth)
ISBN: 978-0-595-87014-1 (ebk)

Printed in the United States of America

This novel is dedicated to all the abused child laborers who were victims of the Industrial Revolution—slave or free.

"Robert Noonan has presented us with a gift … three extremely well written novels highlighting a desperate time for children of our past. We may not enjoy reading about some of the challenges they faced but it is important that we learn of them. These books will become memorable additions to your historical fiction bookshelf."

—IP Book Reviewers

ACKNOWLEDGMENTS

I owe much gratitude to many people for their inspiration and faith in me to complete my trilogy—*Wildflowers, Bridie's Daughter* and *Secrets.*

Sylvia Brown—Director of Programs at the Ragdale Foundation in Lake Forest, Illinois. A writer herself, Sylvia gave me the confidence and inspiration to continue my writing of *Wildflowers,* which at that time was, only clumsy paragraphs and dreams of a story. Many thanks Chum.

Arlene Uslander—Editor and author. Her belief in my stories gave me additional encouragement to complete the trilogy. Whenever I was lost in the complicated world of writing, she was there to guide me forward. Many thanks.

Steve Manchester—Editor and author. He gave me strong supportive advice in promoting my trilogy and helped me obtain reviews. He was great at describing my stories with only a few words.

Glenda Bixler—Editor and Professional Book Reviewer. Glenda is the lady that put the frosting on the cake. Her expert knowledge of publishing and strong belief in my work was, for me—significant. She was the right lady at the right time as I prepared for publication. She has gone well out of her way to help me.

CHAPTER ONE

Darkness was giving way to light, as eleven-year-old Hillary Cook entered the prairie. Streaks of pink and blue light glowed across the gray horizon, while black silhouettes of birds swooped overhead for their early morning meal. Loud humming and clicking of machinery from Alton Mill traveled far into the prairie, as the night shift came to an end.

Surrounded by other workers, Hillary continued down the gravel path to the rhythm of a hundred shoes grinding against stones. A carriage rolled close behind, dividing the column of people as it passed through them.

Inside the carriage was the mill's owner, Frank Dragus. He remained hidden behind the shelter of dark curtains, leaning against the window, appraising Hillary while the carriage moved toward the mill. Frank didn't know many of his workers personally, but he was aware of Hillary Cook. She was young, pretty and poor. Frank sat back in his seat and smiled. *Someday*, he thought.

At the mill entrance, two black iron doors were spread wide like open arms, guiding workers inside. A single light bulb hung from a black cord, illuminating the entrance and dew-covered ground before it. The laborers entered, drifting to the right or left into vast rooms of machinery. Hillary worked on the second floor. Ahead of her were thirty-eight wooden stairs, grooved in the center from years of use. To Hillary, it was like looking up the side of a pyramid. She hated the climb.

She counted the stairs backward, concentrating on the diminishing numbers, as she got closer to the top. Her right hand held a handrail fastened to a dirt-encrusted wall, with flaking gray paint and pencil scribbles. The incessant clatter of machines irritated her ears more and more as she ascended the stairs, while the pungent smell of machine oil hung heavy in the air.

Hillary breathed a sigh of relief, resting on the landing. A day calendar that read Friday, September 16, 1898 hung on the wall next to her. She tore off the top sheet because it was a day behind. Hillary never forgot when it was Saturday, because Sunday was the only day of the week she was free to play with her friends.

She turned into the room on her left, almost bumping into Kate Moran, secretary to Frank Dragus. Kate was also the best friend of Hillary's mother, Laura. They only nodded and smiled to each other, the clatter of the machines being so loud that a person had to yell to be heard. Hillary hurried toward her station. The work started at six.

Kate hesitated. With papers cradled in her arms, she smiled fondly, watching Hillary walk quickly past rows of machinery. She loved Hillary and dreamed of having a daughter just like her. Kate admired Hillary's long eyelashes and short wavy, blond hair that swirled randomly about her head. To Kate, Hillary looked like a little china doll. She glanced to her right and left, looking at other children in the room with a sympathetic eye. She knew most had little or no education and couldn't read or write their own names. Many of the children were much younger than Hillary, some as young as seven, operating machines that had the potential to damage them for life. Kate continued to watch Hillary until she reached the other side of the room.

Frank Dragus stood thirty feet behind Kate at the entrance to his office. He, too, watched Hillary.

Kate turned around and saw Frank outside his office. His blue suit coat was unbuttoned, his fleshy waist pressed against his belt. He was forty-three years old, one of the youngest entrepreneurs in Delaware. He inherited the mill from his father, shortly after his 36th birthday. Kate watched Frank with disgust, leering at thirteen-year-old Beth Sawyer walking past him. Kate stepped into the office, past Frank, as though he didn't exist.

Hillary passed rows of rattling spinner machines, operated by children finishing the night shift. She nodded and smiled at those she knew, girls in torn, oil-stained dresses fighting sleep as their shift came to a close. She watched boys younger than ten working as doffers, removing fast-spinning bobbins filled with thread and replacing them with empty ones. Many worked barefoot because it was easier to climb machines and change bobbins. Hillary knew their toes or fingers could get caught in the moving parts of the machines, so most of the time she looked away to avoid getting the squeamies.

At the end of the room, Hillary entered the aisle along the outer wall lined with dirty windows and cracked panes of glass. Spider webs and dry, hollow remains of insects lay in the corners of many. Overhead, a single row of dim, oil-stained light bulbs dangled above the aisle. Hillary placed her coat on the windowsill opposite a tall, vertical knitting machine, not much wider than herself. She took a deep breath, dreading the coming twelve hours standing on a box, making cotton stockings, knowing her legs and back would ache long before her shift ended.

Mrs. Gretsch, the day-shift supervisor, stepped quickly toward Hillary, her flesh swaying with each rhythmic stride. She dropped a wooden box in front of Hillary, patted her on the back and scurried down the aisle past the line of windows. Hillary stepped onto the box, looking between the machines for Vera, one of her two best friends. She couldn't see Vera, so she pressed the start button. Her machine began its monotonous drone.

Hillary heard a muffled scream through the din of machinery. She saw Mrs. Gretsch pinching the back of Vera's arm, while pushing her toward a spinning machine. Mrs. Gretsch bent over and stared into Vera's face, waving her finger back and forth, scolding her. Hillary could see that Vera was frightened, but she didn't cry. She worried about Vera all through the morning, wondering what Mrs. Gretsch had said to her in her thick Prussian accent.

At exactly 12:00 p.m., the loud horns blew for the lunch break. Hillary turned off her machine and snatched her coat from the windowsill behind her, slipping it on while running to meet Vera at the stairwell. Without a word, they hurried down the stairs, hoping to get seats on the bench in front of the building. They raced past the black iron doors and into the sunlight. Finding the bench occupied, they sat on a knoll under two gnarly oak trees.

"What happened? Why were you late this morning?" Hillary asked. "You could lose your job—then what?"

"I forgot my lunch," Vera answered, unwrapping her food from old newspapers. "I went back for it, so I was late." She flattened the newspaper on the grass between herself and Hillary, placing her cheese sandwich, apple and crackers on the paper.

Hillary nodded toward Vera's arm. "Did Mrs. Gretsch hurt you?"

"Yeah, but I wasn't gunna show it," Vera replied, rubbing her arm. "She's a big cow. She likes you, but she don't like me."

"Pull up your sleeve," Hillary said, reaching for her arm. "I'll see if you have a bruise."

Vera lifted the sleeve of her dirty blue work dress. "Do I have one?" she asked, straining to see the back of her arm.

"Sure do," Hillary replied, half smiling. "It looks grayish-blue. Good thing, I have grapes. Want me to rub grape juice on it?"

"What will that do?"

Hillary rolled across the grass out of striking distance, then yelled and laughed, "It'll make your arm sticky!"

"Thanks oodles," Vera whined, releasing her sleeve. "Mrs. Gretsch hurts me; then you make fun of me. Some friend you are."

Hillary was still grinning. "I'm sorry; it was too funny to pass up." She rolled back and put her lunch on the newspaper. Her food was in a drawstring bag her mother had made from light blue curtains printed with small white daises and short green stems. Hillary unwrapped a cheese sandwich, soda crackers, a bunch of grapes and four sugar cookies from a sheet of thin white paper. Laura, her mother, knew Hillary traded a portion of her lunch, so when she included cookies she always gave her an even number for sharing.

"What's your sandwich?" Vera asked.

"Cheese, same as yours."

"Crackers are the same, too," Vera remarked. "Not much trading going on today. At least our fruit is different."

"Want some of my grapes?"

"For my stomach or my arm?" Vera joked. "Yeah. Give me some grapes and I'll save half of my apple."

Hillary plucked the grapes and placed the cluster of stems in the center of the newspaper. She stood, ran to a patch of dandelions nearby and picked a few. When she returned, she stuck them into the web of grape stems, creating a centerpiece for their newspaper table.

"Ain't we the upper ones," Vera remarked, holding her hand delicately over her heart. She began nibbling her cheese sandwich ever so daintily.

"Anyone that looks ovah here will simply die of jealousy," Hillary said, faking a Southern accent and fluttering her eyelashes. "Them that hog the bench will want to eat here with us from now on, but we won't allow it. Riff-raff, you know."

"You are absolutely correct, Lady Cook," Vera joined in. "We mustn't mingle with the wrong type person. It would be scandalous."

"Talk about scandal," Hillary continued. "You've met my pretty house girl from Scotland. Well, that dahling girl is with child. I haven't a clue whether the father is our coachman, gardener or houseman. She refuses to say."

"Haven't you forgotten someone?" Vera insinuated, playing along.

"No, dear, them's the only men we've hired."

"Have you thought of looking in your husband's direction, Dahling?"

"My God!" Hillary gasped, rocking and fanning her face with her hand. "How could you suggest anything so vicious? My dahlin husband has me. What more could he want?"

"A pretty little tart from Scotland?" Vera quipped. "Please, don't get upset with me, my dear. It was only a suggestion. I'm sure he is quite pleased with you. By the way, has the pretty little Scot picked a name for the child?"

"She did confide in me," Hillary replied. "Jacob if it's a boy, and Ellie if a girl."

"Ellie!" Vera shouted, pulling them out of the story. "I saw Ellie Tuzik this morning. She had two big bruises on her ..."

Hillary raised her hand to Vera. "Please! Stop! I get upset when I hear about her. That poor girl has been beaten and abused by her drunken father for so long she has no mind of her own. She's like a leaf in the wind being pushed about." Hillary's voice got louder as she continued. "If nobody helps her, she'll go crazy." She paused. "See! I'm upset again. Let's not talk about Ellie." Hillary liked Ellie and wanted to pretend the girl's life was better than what she had been told.

The girls didn't talk much more during their meal and spent their last few minutes lying in the grass, stretching their sore muscles under a warming sun. Hillary leaned back on her elbows, scanning the prairie. The Alton Mill was at its center, halfway between the edge of town and the Clarion River. The size of it awed her. It was a long, two-story brown brick building, with endless rows of windows and two towering chimneys. To her left, she could see the New York and Midland Railroad tracks glistening in the sunlight, running parallel to the river. The prairie stretched a mile from the town's train station to the woods and farmlands in the west. Hillary estimated that she and her friends walked ten miles on a Sunday, going around town and into the prairie. She thought ten miles in a day was impressive.

"Tomorrow is Sunday," Vera said in a half-conscious state. "What are we going to do with our day of freedom?"

Hillary fell back onto the grass and looked to the sky. "If it's a nice day like today, we should go to the pond. I'll meet you and Iris at Thompson's store about 2:30, after I get out of Sunday school."

"Sounds good to me," Vera replied, rolling on her side to face Hillary.

The horns blew again, calling them back to work. They picked up their garbage and ran into the building.

After Hillary and Vera climbed the stairs, they saw Mrs. Gretsch pacing the oil-stained floor, watching for anyone returning late. The girls detoured around her to get to their machines.

At mid-afternoon, Hillary saw Pina walking through the main aisle with her arms wrapped around a pile of rags and cleaning supplies for the women's washrooms.

Pina smiled as their eyes met, then flashed four fingers, her usual method of waving.

Hillary smiled back.

Pina was slender and as tall as Hillary, with eyes black as tar and straight black hair, cut even with her jaw. She had been working at the mill five months, as had her mother and older brother, Marcello. He did the same work as Pina, cleaning the men's washrooms and mopping floors. It was labor given to people who couldn't speak English.

Hillary and Pina liked each other since they first met. They were determined to be friends, but rarely had an opportunity to be together. Hillary almost laughed out loud, recalling encounters with Pina trying to speak English. Most of her words remained Italian, so Pina would get frustrated and smile at Hillary with a "forgive me" look. Trying to communicate during their brief encounters produced lots of grinning and laughing, but little conversation. One thing they did learn from each other was that neither had a papa.

Hillary longed to go to Pina's apartment in the small Italian neighborhood along Mill Prairie and see what her family had brought from

Italy. She wanted to walk the streets and listen to people speak Italian, examine their foreign clothing and see what they sold in their stores.

Desperate to solidify their friendship, Pina promised to invite Hillary to her apartment when she had a free Sunday, knowing that would never happen.

Chapter Two

Kate dropped the pile of work orders on the desk, gave Mrs. Welesko a friendly smile and headed to the stairs. As she crossed the noisy room, cotton fibers churned around her feet. Kate hurried down the front stairwell, nodding and greeting people along the way. She didn't want to be stopped for conversation that would make her late for her date with John Hanley. She passed between the two iron doors into darkness, relishing the cool evening air as it cleansed her face.

The soft lights of Union Avenue served as a beacon, guiding her through the dark prairie. Kate enjoyed her evening strolls down the avenue, peering at people through store windows and pretending each was a theater performing a play as she created a fitting dialogue.

Union Avenue was Main Street in Alton; a treeless avenue paved with red bricks and sidewalks with gas street lamps that were ten feet tall. The dilapidated brick and frame buildings were mostly two stories high with apartments over stores. Though not fashionable, the south part of Union Avenue was the center of activity for the poor, with numerous pubs and eateries dotting the street. The far north end of the avenue was for the more fortunate who were rarely seen in the Prairie District at the south end of town.

Union Avenue was busy Saturday nights, especially the pubs. Horse-drawn wagons squeaked and rattled, as they rolled in both directions. The sound of horseshoes pounding the red brick street accompanied Kate to Doyle's Pub where she planned to meet John. He worked as a mechanic on a freighter and had been at sea for five weeks. She was glad to have him back. Tonight was the seventh anniversary of their first meeting at the pub.

Kate crossed the brick street in the middle of the block, heading directly for the pub entrance when she heard, "Evenin' paper, Miss Kate?" She turned to find Frankie, a neighborhood newsboy who was a friend of Hillary's. He wore shabby brown knickers and a baggy green sweater. Curly brown hair stuck out from under a gray wool cap that he'd turned to the side, giving Kate a full view of his freckled face.

"Evenin' paper, is it?" Kate asked, in a scolding tone. "Since when does the *Alton Reporter* print more than one copy a day?"

Frankie had three papers under his left arm, with his right thumb hooked into his armpit. "They don't, but it's evenin', ain't it?" He tilted the end of his newspapers toward Kate. "I've got three left and three's an unlucky number. If ya buy one, I'll probably sell the other two."

Kate leaned forward, close to Frankie's face. Slowly and deliberately, she said, "And when you got five papers, you say five is unlucky."

Frankie took a step backwards. "I'm a shrewd businessman," he said, straightening his cap. "I do what it takes to sell papers."

"You needn't give me those sick cow eyes," Kate responded. "I want one tonight anyway." She retrieved a black leather coin purse from her coat pocket, unsnapped the clasp and began picking through the coins with her index finger. Removing two coins, she handed them to Frankie. "Keep the change."

Frankie looked at the two coins lying in his palm. "There ain't no change," he replied, with his head askew.

"What a pity," Kate responded, continuing toward the pub carrying her newspaper. In spite of his arrogant manner, Kate enjoyed her encounters with Frankie. She believed it was his brand of humor. After all, who could be truly arrogant while wearing rags?

Kate entered the smoke-filled pub to a crescendo of laughter and chatter. On her right stood a sturdy oak bar, thirty feet long. Thick round columns at each end seemed to support the ceiling. The mirrored wall behind the bar reflected multiple rows of liquor bottles and a solid line of standing patrons. Three large, dirty chandeliers with amber glass shades hung through the center of the room. Small amber lamps hung on the bare brick walls.

Kate spotted John sitting at a table, looking down at a mug of golden ale. His unbuttoned brown tweed jacket hung straight from his broad shoulders, leaving plenty of space around his narrow waist. He had a devilish smile and green eyes that disarmed her. John was her man. Emil Kurst was leaning over him, talking with one hand resting on the table. Kate smiled and greeted friends, as she passed between the crowded tables. Before she got to John, Emil walked away, drinking from his mug.

A huge smile appeared on John's face when he saw Kate coming his way. "You're a beautiful sight," he said, standing to kiss her. "I missed you."

"I missed you, too," Kate replied, as she sat at the table. She let her coat drop from her shoulders onto the back of her chair. "What's with Emil?"

John signaled Meg, the waitress, knowing it would be a while before being served. "It's his wife's birthday. She's coming later to celebrate."

Kate gave John's hand an affectionate squeeze. "I'm glad you came here to Crossroads Shipping. If you stayed in Savannah, we never would have met."

"I've thought of that many times myself. And if I hadn't come to Doyle's the night you were here, we might not have met." John felt guilty for lying about Savannah, but he had to. He had stopped in Savannah for only a few weeks when he ran from New Orleans.

"Do you want to eat now, or wait?" Kate asked.

John delayed his answer, reaching inside his tweed jacket for her anniversary present. "Let's work up our appetite," he answered, placing his gift on the table in front of her. "Happy anniversary, my love."

"For me?" she squealed. "On our anniversary, you've been gone five weeks, and you love me. What a surprise!"

John stared at her for a moment. "That was quite a mouthful. Are you finished?"

"Yes, just feeling silly," she replied, lifting the package from the table. It was long, slender, and crudely wrapped in white paper. Narrow pink ribbon was poorly tied in both directions. "Who wrapped the package?"

"It's a secret," John replied, frowning at her.

"Sorry, I'll be good." Kate rolled the paper and ribbon into a ball and placed it in front of John. "Here, you might want to use it again."

"That ain't being good," he laughed, pointing his finger at her.

Kate raised the lid to the box and gasped. "John, I'll be *real* good. How'd you get this? It's beautiful!" She paused, staring at her gift, a gold pin of three slender leaves joined at the bottom and flaring out at the top. Eight small emeralds spiraled the length of the leaves. "It had to cost a fortune. You can't afford this." She glared at him a moment. "What have you been up to?" She polished the pin against her coat sleeve and held it to her blouse.

"Remember where you're at," John warned. "I wouldn't be flashing it in here."

Kate took a quick look around the room and placed the pin into the uncovered box. She looked anxiously at John with her eyebrows lowered. "How'd you get it?" she asked again.

He leaned forward, shrugging his shoulders before answering. "We were at a Caribbean port where me and Hackey met up with a couple Chinese shipmates. We were tipping a few when one comes over and shows us a deck of cards. We knew what he was getting at, so we joined in. We couldn't talk to 'em, but we all spoke poker. It was the luckiest I've ever been. They had more jewelry, too. Don't know where they got it, though."

"I've never had anything expensive before," Kate declared, looking down into the box. "When could I wear it? People would think I'm putting on."

"Save it for when we get out of this town."

"I feel guilty taking this," she said, with a sly grin. "But I'll get over it." She reached into her coat pocket for John's gift. "Happy anniversary, John." She placed his gift in front of him.

"For me?" he squealed, impersonating Kate. "I hope it's not a pin."

Meg made her way through the crowd, balancing a glass of port wine and a mug of ale on a tray. Her white apron was stained with food and drink, and a curl of blond hair hung in front of her left eye. "We're a girl short tonight, so service will be a bit slow." She placed the glass of port wine in front of Kate. "Hope this is what ya wanted. Trying to save ya some waiting time." She handed the mug to John, "I know ya want this."

"Thanks," Kate said, "You did fine."

"When you're ready to eat, let me know early," Meg suggested, holding the tray against her chest. "Just give me a—well, look at that pin, will you? I guess someone's getting lucky tonight."

"Don't be imagining nothing," Kate replied, with a smug look. "Even if you're right."

John looked directly into Meg's eyes and placed the lid on the box. "Don't mention this to no one. We don't want to get knocked on the head going home."

"Not a word," Meg promised, then turned and disappeared into the crowd.

John opened his gift and smiled. "It's smart-looking. I sure can use this in my line of work." He examined seven different blades and tools in the pocketknife. The body of the knife was a light brown wood, with a picture of a three-mast schooner burnt into one side.

"I thought it was good looking, too," Kate agreed. "I won it from three Chinese ladies at the laundry."

John leaned against the back of his chair and laughed, his green eyes squinting through a pattern of freckles that matched his coarse red, wool-like hair. He wouldn't admit to anything, but he thought her remark was clever. After composing himself, he leaned toward Kate, nervously sliding his mug back and forth on the table. "How's your little girl at the mill?"

"Hillary?" Kate asked. "A darling, as usual. She's the only sunshine I have at work. She'll be having her twelfth birthday soon"

John was still sliding his mug on the table, as he approached a time worn subject. "If we got married, you could have your own Hillary. You will be thirty soon, so we should start planning."

Kate looked across the table at John. "I knew you were coming to that. When you mention Hillary, I know what you're getting at. We've been through this before. You're at sea weeks at a time, sometimes months. That's no way to be a family. I love you, but that's no way."

He took a swig of ale, looked from his left to his right and whispered, "I've been putting a lot of money away. It won't be long before we can buy us a farm. We can go west and be independent, with grain and cattle. Thing's is booming out west. Besides, I don't want to be going out to sea much longer, either. I'd rather stay put on me own land."

Kate gazed into his eyes to explain her feelings, again. "Having our own place sounds nice, but many farmers are working here in town because they couldn't make farming pay. I don't want to lose our savings. As for going, I sure wouldn't miss Alton and this kind of life." She slumped back in her chair. "Let's give it a little more time." She looked down at her gift on the table. "I wonder how that pin will look on farm coveralls?"

"You'd be the topic of conversation at the County Fair," John assured her.

She sipped her wine and wiped her mouth with a table napkin that was clean, but should have been retired long ago. Kate gazed out the window and saw a woman and a little girl with red hair stroll past. She guessed the child was three years old. Mixed emotions of loss and shame clouded her peaceful mood. She glanced at John, relieved he was completely unaware of her abortion three years earlier.

Kate looked across the room at Meg, the very friend she had confided in to arrange the abortion. She recalled her fear the night it happened, entering a small room with bare walls and a single bed with white sheets. Surgical instruments submerged in a metal pan of yellow fluid sat on a small wooden table near the bed. Meg was with her for emotional support, holding her hand and talking to her through the operation. For obvious reasons, she was never given the name of the doctor or his female assistant, but Meg did tell her the man who arranged the abortion, was Frank Dragus, a wealthy businessman who was aware of almost everything going on in Alton. It was only days later that Meg learned of Frank's need for a secretary and introduced Kate to him at a chance meeting at the Mercantile Bank. Kate thought it was her lucky day.

John looked across the table at Kate and smiled.

She smiled back, keeping her secret.

CHAPTER THREE

It was nearly ten o'clock when a sudden sprinkle of rain chased Laura
and Hillary inside St. Paul's Church. Hillary was disappointed, afraid
the rain would ruin her afternoon with Vera and Iris. They stopped in
the vestibule to straighten their clothes, and wipe water from their
faces and arms with Laura's white handkerchief. Hillary fluffed her
light blue dress and used her thumb to wipe a black smudge from her
white belt.

Laura was an attractive and graceful woman. Her smooth complexion and soft blue eyes gave her an angelic quality. She was wearing a long gray skirt that reached the toes of her black shoes, and a
white blouse with ruffles down the front. Her honey brown hair was
brushed to the top of her head, forming a roll on each side.

St. Paul's was a simple white frame church, with a small bell tower
topped with a white wooden cross. Its barren interior consisted of
plain wood pews and faded blue paint covering the walls and ceiling.
Six tall, slender windows of frosted glass lined each of the outer walls.
Between them were fourteen modest paintings, depicting the series of
events from the judgment of Christ by Pontius Pilate to his resurrec-
tion.

Hillary followed her mother into a pew near the front and looked
about, taking inventory of who was there. Only a third of the pews

were occupied, mostly with families whose children attended St. Paul's school. Hillary's friend Vera was a parishioner of St. Paul's, but her parents rarely attended Sunday mass. Iris and her family were members of a Lutheran church on the east end of town near Delaware Bay, though they hardly ever attended services.

Hillary saw Pina with her mother and Marcello sitting in the front row on the other side of the center aisle.

The organist began playing in a small choir loft over the rear of the church. Father Adams, a robust man, entered from the sacristy wearing a green and gold chasuble. His round, red face was a clue as to why his sermons never covered the ruefulness of drinking. Father Adams turned toward the white altar that was dwarfed under a plain twelve-foot wooden cross and began the mass.

After communion, Laura noticed sunlight streaking through the tall, narrow windows. She looked down at Hillary, nudging her with her elbow.

Hillary turned, waiting for her mother to speak.

Laura smiled and tilted her head toward the windows.

Hillary glanced to her left and realized that the sun was shining. A smile the width of her face appeared. "I hope it lasts," she whispered.

When the mass ended, Laura and Hillary talked to friends in front of the church until it was time for Hillary to go to Sunday school. Hillary walked along the side of the church where flat stones formed a path through a garden of flowerbeds, bushes, and five religious statues. The path led to a one-room schoolhouse behind a row of tall bushes. The white frame structure had a small bell tower without a bell, making it a quiet resting place for pigeons.

Hillary ran up three wooden stairs, past the open door and directly to her seat near the back of the room. Two boys ran in behind her, panting and laughing, as if they had been playing vigorously on their way to school.

Miss McLeen, the teacher, was standing at her desk. She was turning pages of a book, selecting lessons for the day. Behind her hung pictures of George Washington and Abraham Lincoln. Miss McLeen brushed a few tendrils of auburn hair from her chubby face and called the class to attention.

During the next three hours, Hillary constantly looked out the window, hoping it wouldn't rain again.

At two o'clock, the sun was still shining. Hillary left school in high spirits, for it was a beautiful afternoon to fritter away at the pond. She skipped and ran to Thompson's store, hoping Iris and Vera were there. Mr. Thompson had been kind to the girls through the years, giving them candy he knew they couldn't afford. Emotionally, he had adopted them. Not having children of his own, he had enjoyed watching them grow from little imps to bigger imps, accepting them as his delightful trio of shenanigans.

When Hillary turned the corner onto Union Avenue, she saw Darby in front of Thompson's store, hitched to Mr. Brummer's furniture wagon. Iris and Vera were standing on the brick street, petting and talking to her.

The girls called to Hillary when they saw her coming. "Pet her nose," Iris said. "It's so soft and silky."

"I know," Hillary replied, reaching for Darby's nose. "I've petted her many times. Mr. Brummer lets me fill her oat bag when I'm there at feeding time."

"Don't dally," Vera said, "Go upstairs and change into your play clothes."

Within six minutes, Hillary had changed her clothes and was back with the girls. They wore dresses with varying degrees of wear and wrinkles, black high button shoes and black knee stockings. Hillary always covered her play dresses with a full white apron that had two deep pockets. To her, the apron was pretty, with lace bordering the shoulder straps and the top of the pockets. Her mother told her the apron had belonged to a seamstress who needed deep pockets to hold scissors and spools and measuring sticks. Hillary liked the pockets because nothing could fall out.

Hillary and Iris were about the same size, but the similarity ended there. Iris had black curly hair and soft gray eyes that demanded one's attention. In contrast to them, Vera was sturdier and a head taller than the other two. Her eyes matched her brown hair, which was usually combed into one thick braid.

"Enough of this horse," Vera said, waving them on. "Let's head for the pond."

"Look in the store first," Iris suggested, rolling her eyes toward Thompson's.

"Yeah!" Vera responded. "Maybe we'll get noticed?"

The girls spread out, peering through the store window for Mr. Thompson. "I don't see him," Vera said, shrugging her shoulders.

"Me neither," Iris agreed, with her nose against the glass. "If we can't see him, he can't see us. Maybe he's in the back room."

Vera backed away from the window, eager to leave. "Off to the pond!" she shouted, waving her arm toward Mill Prairie.

The girls walked five blocks south along Union Avenue, peering into store windows while avoiding staggering drunks and prostitutes. They ran into Mill Prairie, heading for the Clarion River and the pond. Soon, they slowed to a walk and began singing, "Old Man River."

As they passed the mill, Vera stuck out her tongue. "You ain't got me today," she shouted. Suddenly, the sound of a distant train captured their attention. "I wonder if it's an orphan train?" Vera said, scanning the rails coming into town.

"Might be," Hillary answered, looking off into the distance. "Let's get closer to the tracks."

They ran through tall weeds, dodging airborne grasshoppers leaping from one plant to another. Sparrows and red winged blackbirds resting on bushes flew away and circled round behind them to return to their perch. The girls stopped forty feet from the tracks, as the chugging engine came into town, belching clouds of dense black smoke from its stack. It continued on without stopping at the station, a good indication it was an orphan train. They never stopped in

Alton. When it arrived, the noise was so loud the girls couldn't hear one another talk. They began waving to the engineer who responded with one short and one long toot of the whistle, along with a big smile.

Except for two passenger cars at the rear, the train was all freight cars. As the girls waited for the passenger cars, they were enveloped by a swirling cloud of black smoke. Small pieces of hot cinders blown from the engine's furnace fell on them like rain. The cinders cooled immediately. As the first passenger car rolled by, the girls eyes moved from window to window, studying the orphans' faces. Most of the children were busy talking, sleeping, or walking through the car, oblivious to the three girls watching them.

In the second car, a few children rushed to the windows to see the trio, their presence obviously announced in advance. The girls began waving. Some children responded enthusiastically, while sad faces only stared. Hillary scrutinized the children closely, knowing they were filled with fear and apprehension. A shiver passed through her, realizing she was already half way to being an orphan. *I couldn't take an orphan train to somewhere, then live with strangers. I'd rather join my parents,* she thought.

The girls stood like pegs in a hole, as they watched the train move on. "I wonder why orphan trains are always hitched to freight trains?" Vera asked, picking cinders from her hair.

"My Ma said the fares are cheaper," Iris said, turning to her friends. "It takes longer to get somewhere 'cause freight trains stop so often. Ma said, nobody wants to spend money on orphans."

Hillary would never forget that statement. It saddened her.

The girls resumed walking toward the pond, passing the trestle bridge the train had just crossed to the other side of the river. They continued along the riverbank, brushing tall weeds aside with their hands and watching for rats and mice.

"Damn you, you pest!" Vera shouted.

Iris and Hillary looked back and saw Vera swinging her arms over her head at a dragonfly darting about her hair. The girls ran a few yards, leaving the dragonfly fluttering over tall weeds.

"Talk about pests," Iris moaned. "Look who's at the pond—Tommy Deegan and Adam Bowes. I wonder what they're up to?"

"Just ignore 'em," Vera replied, stepping ahead of the other girls for a clear view. "Maybe they'll go away."

They waited in the shade under three oak trees, hoping the boys would move on. Unfortunately, the girls were discovered and the boys ran over to them.

"What ya gunna do here?" Tommy asked.

"We came to sit and talk," Hillary answered. She didn't trust those two because they usually caused trouble. *The less we say, the faster the boys may leave,* she thought.

"Talk about what?" Adam asked, his hands on his hips. "Girls ain't got nothin' worth talkin' about."

"Why are you here?" Vera asked, gruffly.

"We're trying ta catch a frog," Tommy replied. "I want one for a pet."

"Oh, that's real important," Iris responded, giving them a disapproving look. "I hope ya get warts on your face."

Adam stared at Hillary, as though confused. "Why ya got such deep pockets on that apron?" he asked. "You don't own nothin' to put in 'em."

"Do, too!" Hillary replied. "I've got many nice things." He was right, but she wouldn't admit it.

Adam stepped slowly toward Hillary and jammed his hands into both apron pockets, retrieving a piece of metal from one.

"Give it to me!" Hillary demanded with her hand extended.

"Well, lookie here," Adam said, with a big grin. "It's a medal of the Blessed Virgin. Think I'll throw it in the river."

Vera charged forward, looking down at Adam. "Give it back!" she demanded. "Her father gave it to her and he died. It's special to her."

Adam hesitated, looking up at Vera. "You're lucky I'm in a good mood," he snarled and threw it at Hillary's feet.

"Why you in a good mood?" Tommy asked. "Did you feel something else with your hands in her pockets?"

"Pigs!" Hillary yelled, picking up the medal.

The boys laughed, as they walked away. "Hope to feel you again sometime," Adam shouted.

"He did not," Hillary cried, glaring at Adam. "He's a liar."

"Calm your horses," Vera said. "He's just mouthing."

The girls turned from the boys and proceeded to a large patch of wildflowers just beyond the three oak trees. There were red, yellow, white and pink blossoms the size of ten-cent pieces. One-by-one, the girls stretched out on the ground, looking up at the clear blue sky. They were silent, enjoying the warm sun against their bodies.

Hillary saw two trees on the other side of the river. They were filled with hundreds of small birds that broke into flight together, looking like a cloud of pepper. They darted left and right, then up and down, while completing a full circle back to the same tree. Hillary assumed they were gathering to migrate.

"I wish I had a brother or sister," Vera said, breaking the silence. "I'm always alone when my parents are at work. They work seven days a week and sometimes until late at night." Vera tapped Hillary's arm. "Do you like being the only child?"

"I'd like to have a brother or sister," Hillary said. "But with my father gone, my mother would have to work twice as hard. So, it's good that it's just my mother and me."

"I'm glad I have an older sister," Iris said. "We have our fights, but most of the time we help each other. She teaches me about people, how to mend my clothes, and where to shop for the best prices. When we're older, we'll be able to help each other when need be."

They rested in silence again, watching the river flow by and looking up at birds in the sky. Soon, Iris interrupted their silence to say something important. "Hope I can find a rich man to marry. I'm tired of working all the time."

"We all wish that," Vera said, almost asleep.

Iris jumped up and ran to one of the oak trees where she had seen a square piece of thin paperboard lying on the ground. She placed it on her head, pulling down on two corners to form a bonnet. She began sashaying in front of the other two. "Must wear my bonnet. Don't want to get my skin brown. People might think I'm a working class person." She stopped and pointed toward the trees. "Pretend there's two wealthy men sitting on a bench over there. Watch me and I'll give ya a lesson on how to catch a rich man."

"Walk slowly in front of them swinging your bait a little, while pretending ya don't notice 'em. Are they watching me? 'Course they are. Are they drooling yet? 'Course they are. They desire me intensely. Now drop a handkerchief, or small package. Look! They're leaping to be the one to pick it up. The one that wants you most will get there first," Iris assured them.

"'Why thank you, Sir. How careless of me,' I'll say. Then he'll insist on walking me home, so he can protect me from whatever. 'Such a lovely lady shouldn't be walking alone,' he'll say. That way, he'll learn where I live. You must let him carry your package, so he can be ever so helpful. And remember to keep swinging your bait. Another thing, always breathe deep, so your bust goes up and down, up and down. That way he'll be hypnotized. Now ya got him hooked and soon you'll be a rich lady."

Hillary and Vera rolled among the wildflowers, laughing. "I can't *wait* for the next lesson." Vera squealed. The girls continued to joke and tease about marrying a rich man until they tired, and rested under the sun once again.

"It's so nice here," Hillary said, scanning the surroundings. "I love to look at the wildflowers. They're so delicate and pretty,"

"Yeah, like us," Vera shouted, raising her leg into the air, as if punctuating her statement. "*We* are wildflowers."

"You're right," Iris agreed, looking over at the other two. "We're young, pretty and wild. Why don't we call ourselves 'Wildflowers'? You know, like a private club or secret society. Just the three of us."

The girls looked at one another, each liking the idea. "Let's do it." Hillary suggested. "Friends forever. What do you think, Vera?"

"I like it, too," Vera answered, rising to her feet. "Let's pledge ourselves, eternal-like."

The girls stood in a small circle, holding hands. "I'll say something official," Iris declared, clearing her throat. "Let it be known to all mankind, that from now on, until forever, Vera, Hillary and Iris shall be known as the *Wildflowers*."

Filled with accomplishment, the girls walked home discussing their afternoon activities. The weather had been perfect, they had seen an orphan train, and best of all, they'd pledged themselves as Wildflowers. It was an exciting day they didn't want to end, but it was almost seven o'clock. The girls parted in high spirits, leaving Hillary to walk alone on Union Avenue.

Lights were still on in Thompson's store, as Hillary approached the corner. Darby and the wagon were gone, as expected. The Thompson's owned the building where they lived and operated their business. Hillary and her mother were tenants in a one-room apartment on the second floor. The gritty, two-story brick building housed four stores with eight apartments above. A central staircase led to a hallway running the length of the building, with a bathroom at each end. Four apartments faced Union Avenue, and four faced the rear. Laura and Hillary lived in a front apartment at the north end.

The Cooks and the Thompsons had been good friends for many years. Hillary could remember when she was small and the Thompsons had cared for her, while Laura ran errands or worked on Sunday. In return, Laura would help in the store when needed.

Laura stood at the wood-burning stove, preparing supper, when Hillary walked into their apartment. "Hi, Mom!" Hillary greeted her, with enthusiasm. "We had a great day today." She walked past the stove to the wall-hung, cold-water sink in the corner of the room.

"It must have been," Laura replied, turning toward Hillary. "You seem excited. Tell me about it while we eat."

"What are we having for supper?" Hillary asked, rolling a bar of brown lye soap in her hands.

"Barley and vegetable soup, with warm raisin bread. When you've dried your hands, bring the lamp and raisin bread with you." Laura carried the black cast-iron pot across the wood floor, trying not to spill the soup.

"I already had a great day, and now my favorite soup?" Hillary remarked, centering the kerosene lamp on the table. "God must be pleased with me."

"I'm sure that's the reason," Laura agreed, stirring the soup. "Did you go to the pond?"

"Yes. And today I became a Wildflower," Hillary answered, raising her spoon triumphantly.

Laura couldn't refrain from smiling at Hillary's enthusiasm. "And that means?"

Hillary described their afternoon with the orphan train and the creation of the Wildflower's club. She thought it prudent not to mention the incident with Adam Bowes, or Iris's lesson on how to marry a rich man.

After dinner, they sat on the bed so Laura could brush Hillary's hair. "I can see you girls have been to the railroad tracks. Your hair is full of cinders."

After a long pause, Hillary asked, "Where do all those orphans come from, and where do they go?"

"It depends. The trains come from New York City, but the children come from different areas in the east. There's an organization called, *The Children's Aid Society*. Its purpose is to help children without homes. Some are new orphans and some have lived on the streets for a long time. There are even instances where parents give children away because they don't earn enough money to support them. That has to be the most painful thing a parent can do."

Hillary turned her head slightly to look at her mother from the corner of her eye.

"Don't worry," Laura said, smiling. "I won't be giving you away."

"Do they ever see their children again?" Hillary asked. She held a white porcelain hair receiver at her side, so her mother could stuff hair into it.

"Usually, no. Parents aren't told where their children settle because years later, a parent could go after a child the new family learned to love. Then, there would be a new set of problems."

"Nothing could be worse," Hillary remarked, with deep furrows in her brow. "Never see your family again? I would cry forever, if that happened to me."

"I'm sure many do, one way or another." Laura removed hair from the brush and pushed it into Hillary's receiver. "Every week or so, children are sent to different parts of the country for adoption. Notice is posted in advance when an orphan train is coming, so those who want to adopt are waiting. They choose a child and the adoption is completed there at the station."

Hillary turned to face her mother. "Do children get to say no, if they don't want to go with someone?"

"Not ordinarily. They're should appreciate being adopted." Laura turned Hillary's head to continue brushing. "I heard a story about three brothers—five, seven and eight years old. They were at a train station waiting with other children, hoping someone nice would adopt them. A man stopped in front of the three boys, gazed at them a while, then went to a table to sign papers. He returned to the three boys and picked up the littlest one. The boy was elated. As the man carried him away, he faced his brothers. It was then he realized his brothers weren't coming with him. He began kicking and screaming, but to no avail."

Hillary sat motionless, dwelling on the horror of siblings being separated. She tried to imagine the fear the youngest boy must have felt, as he was distanced from his brothers, helpless to do anything. After a short silence, she asked, "What kind of people adopt them?"

Laura finished Hillary's hair, then handed her the brush to put in the dresser drawer. "Nice people, I would guess. It's a kind heart that will take a child and raise it."

With brush in hand, Hillary stood before her mother. "If you were given to someone you hated, then what?"

"That can happen, too," Laura replied, leaning back against a pillow. "Some make the best of it, and some run away to live on the streets." Laura stood quickly, putting her arms around Hillary. "Enough about orphans. Your birthday is coming soon, so invite the other Wildflowers and we will have a little party." Laura stepped back to look at Hillary and smiled. "If your father could see you, he'd be very proud."

CHAPTER FOUR

The following Sunday, Laura was thinking of Jeremiah as she dressed to meet Kate. She reached for her small brass clock on the dresser and wound it until the mainspring tightened. The clock was designed like a cathedral, with two large doors under thin spires. She raised the bottom of her apron to wipe dust from the round glass window. It was her last Christmas present from Jeremiah, a gift she had requested. Laura rubbed her hand over the clock, recalling the evening they had seen it in a store window. Large snowflakes were falling lazily around them and she was holding Jeremiah's arm, as he liked her to do. She was interested in the clock and decided at that moment she wanted it for Christmas, and it should be a surprise. He laughed and kissed her on the cheek. Snow was collecting on his blond hair and eyebrows. With her gloved hand, she brushed the snow from around his blue eyes looking down at her. Their love was as strong as ever. Although he had now been gone five years, it seemed like less than a year to her. The sound of his voice and the memory of him holding her were still fresh in her mind.

She began feeling melancholy and cheated. The three of them had been happy and life was gradually improving. Laura remembered the unexpected knock on their apartment door when Mr. Caradine brought the tragic news on behalf of the construction company. He was very tactful and sympathetic, but Laura didn't want sympathy. She wanted her husband.

Laura noticed it was almost noon and placed the clock on the dresser. She had twenty-five minutes to meet Kate for their ferry ride. They both enjoyed being on water, so an excursion across Delaware Bay became a tradition after Jeremiah died. The last Sunday in September was the day they set aside, hoping for warm weather and bright autumn colors.

Six years earlier, Laura was with Jeremiah and Hillary when she first met Kate and John at a Fourth of July picnic in Mill Prairie. Laura remembered how Kate fell in love with Hillary upon seeing her, and played with her most of the afternoon. At the time, Jeremiah and John had a casual acquaintance at Doyle's Pub, but had never been formally introduced. After the picnic, they became close friends.

Laura removed the apron covering her long beige skirt and grabbed her brown waistcoat from the bed. Once outside, she knew they would be able to sit on deck and enjoy the sun and fresh air. It was a day that made her feel that even Alton was an acceptable place to live.

After a short walk, she arrived at Kate's apartment. Kate was wearing a red and green plaid waistcoat and a green skirt. She was in front of her building, talking to an elderly lady with her white hair braided across the back of her head. A black shawl covered the shoulders of her black dress. As Laura stepped up to them, the woman moved away from Kate, nodded and smiled to Laura, then walked down the street with great effort.

"That's Mrs. Jass," Kate said, watching her frail neighbor inch her way down the sidewalk. "She said she's going to a wake at Rollin's Mortuary, then sit in a chair and wait for her turn to die."

"It's nice she has a sense of humor," Laura commented. "Does she have a husband?"

"No. He was killed the last days of the Civil War. I can't recall where, possibly Missouri? She was told he was shot by a Confederate raider, while he was sleeping on the ground."

They turned from Mrs. Jass's direction and began walking toward Delaware Bay. "Does she have children nearby?" Laura asked.

"None anywhere. They married in '63, as he was leaving for the war. A few letters are the only memories she has of their marriage."

When they got close to the bay, they could see blue water and small boats rocking in place. Banners fluttered in the breeze crossing the bay. "Which is worse," Laura pondered aloud, "memories of ten years with a man—or just emptiness?"

"Sounds even to me," Kate replied, thoughtfully. "You miss what you had and she misses what she dreamed of having. Either way, you're both alone, hurting in your own way."

"Life shouldn't be this hard," Laura said, brushing hair from her eye. "Sometimes, I wonder whether there is a God, and if there is one, why is life so much more difficult for some than for others?"

Kate didn't have an answer and remained silent.

The sound of gulls and water pounding against pilings and hulls of boats changed Laura's mood. They quickened their steps, so they wouldn't be late. Birds rested on pilings until Laura and Kate came near, then squawked before stroking their long wings into the sky. Most circled around behind them, returning to the pilings.

Two passenger ferries were moored at the south end of the wharf, bobbing slowly in the water. A small white ticket booth with a blue peaked roof stood on the dock in front of them. A sign below the ticket window advertised that the ferry crossing cost ten cents. Round trip was fifteen cents. A middle-aged woman with graying hair waited inside. The nametag on her red sweater read, *Lena*.

"Two round trips," Kate said, handing her three ten cent coins.

"Board the boat on your right," Lena replied, presenting two tickets.

Walking to the ferry, Kate handed Laura a ticket. The lower part of the hull was painted black and the upper portion was white with the name *Lady Bingham* on the side. A short ramp with handrails extended from the pier to the boat. A man in black pants and a black sweater assisted them, as the boat gently lifted and dropped with the waves. The people already on board stood along the railings, looking across the bay at the high ground of the New Jersey coast. Others sat on bench seats inside the cabin, with windows on all sides.

Soon, the engines roared, shaking the ferry until the boat moved forward. Men on the dock freed the mooring ropes and dropped them into the water, while members of the crew hauled them aboard with great speed. Two large propellers churned the water into a frenzy, slowly pushing the boat into the bay.

Laura and Kate sat on a bench on the open deck, enjoying the warm sun and fresh sea breeze. After a few minutes of watching passengers walk the deck, Kate elbowed Laura and nodded her head toward the bow of the boat. Mr. and Mrs. Wooley, followed by three little Wooleys, crossed the bow of the boat from the port side. Mr. Wooley was tall and slender, sporting a short beard. Many thought he looked like Abe Lincoln, saying it was intentional. Mrs. Wooley had a face of someone who had bitten into a lemon. The children, two girls and a boy, followed their parents like ducklings in a row. The parents saw Laura and Kate, but didn't acknowledge them. The Wooleys own a clothing store two blocks from Laura's apartment. They weren't wealthy, but had a nickel more than most.

Laura turned to Kate, forcing a comb deeper into her hair. "Do you ever hear from your sister?"

"Not for about nine months. Jean Ann wrote me a letter six months after my mother died. A little late, I'd say. My mother died the same day my father died, three years later."

"Did you respond to her letter?"

"Within a week. I assume she's still in Richmond, living in the house we grew up in. She and her husband, Harold, moved in with Mother soon after Father died. I don't remember whether I told you this, but if it weren't for Harold, I wouldn't be in Alton. A friend of his was starting an exporting business here and got me a secretarial position at decent pay. Five months later, the company went out of business. Then I met John, so here I am."

"Then I must thank John for keeping you here. If it wasn't for him, I wouldn't have you to cry and laugh with."

"Then we're even," Kate chuckled. "You've been my support, too." She closed her eyes and lifted her face toward the sun.

For half an hour, they sat on the bench, pondering their past and future. There were only a few words exchanged between them. Far ahead, the colorful trees along the New Jersey coast became more visible. They reminded Laura of Hillary's laughter when Jeremiah would wrap his arms around her and they would roll down a hill covered with dry leaves. They called it "crackling" because of the sound it made. In the fall, they liked the smell of burning leaves, and on cold nights, Jeremiah would surprise Hillary with a cup of hot chocolate. Memories of Jeremiah made her smile, then hurt, because she would never share those times with him again. Laura turned up her coat collar and leaned into the corner of the bench. Soon, she was asleep.

Kate noticed and let her be. She watched soaring gulls and black smoke from the boat's stack drift directly behind them. Hatfield, New Jersey, was coming into view and Kate began recognizing boats in the harbor. *Less than a half-hour before docking*, she guessed. Minutes later, the skipper announced their presence to Hatfield by blasting the foghorn twice.

Laura woke abruptly with the heat of the sun on her face. She stretched her arms discreetly and gazed at the passing water. "Sorry for falling asleep. It was rude of me." She looked about the deck. "How long did I sleep?"

"About twenty minutes. Another fifteen and we'll be there."

"Did I miss anything, while I slept?"

"The Wooleys fell into the bay and nobody helped fish them out," Kate joked.

Laura smiled. "They're not that bad."

They waited a few minutes and went to the railing for a better view of the harbor and the colorful fishing boats strung along the bay. Red and white seemed to be the most popular colors for the boats, with blue and white a close second. Crews were washing decks and stretching nets across grassy slopes to dry. Hundreds of seagulls circled above, then dropped onto the water to eat scraps of fish washed from the decks. Hatfield's lighthouse was a tower of peeling white paint standing on a rocky point nearby. Below it, a blue and gray rowboat waited on a small sand beach.

The passengers gathered at one side of the boat, waiting to disembark. The Wooleys, like thoroughbreds standing at the starting gate, were first in line to leave. The ferry would remain in Hatfield for only forty minutes before returning to Alton. The next ferry was scheduled to leave in two and a half hours.

Laura and Kate lagged behind the other passengers to linger on the pier. Sunlight reached the sandy bottom in shallow water, exposing small fish swimming over a collection of weeds, rocks, and a variety of bottles. Two crayfish stirring up sand seemed to be settling an argument. After watching for a few moments, Laura and Kate left for their traditional cup of tea.

They walked up a gravel path, meandering through grass, rocks and a variety of tall weeds. The center of Hatfield consisted of eight frame buildings in desperate need of paint and repair. Some had loose clapboard siding or a sagging roof. Two buildings leaned to the side, squeezing windows out of shape. A small general store occupied one of two corner buildings where two dirt streets intersected. It also served as post office and blacksmith. Across the street, a dirty, nine-table restaurant and pub served as the center of Hatfield's activity. Hot tea was all Laura and Kate were willing to buy there.

The rest of Hatfield consisted of fishermen's cottages scattered among a landscape of tall weeds, boulders, and a mix of pines, maples, oaks and birch trees, displaying a rich variety of color. For some inexplicable reason, Hatfield's trees always changed color earlier than Alton's, the very reason Laura and Kate chose that weekend for their ferry ride. The leaves were orange, yellow, and crimson, each hue excitingly brilliant as the foliage prepared to die. A warm gentle breeze rocked the leaves on the branches. It was indeed, Indian summer.

The rocky ground and weather-beaten buildings gave the town a tough, unfriendly appearance. A large, two-story log building near the lighthouse stood in contrast to the village's smallness. They had ignored the building in the past, but today, were curious about its purpose. As they walked beyond the frame buildings, the street became more like a country road, bordered by tall pines and thick, sturdy bushes. Ruts from horse-drawn wagons marred the surface of the dirt road, and footpaths twisted between the trees and bushes leading to the road or log building. The road began to rise, as it led directly to the log building's door.

Halfway up the street, the door to a small shanty swung open and a slender old black man, standing five and a half feet tall, stepped out. His white shirt and brown pants were badly wrinkled and yellow suspenders hung down from his waist. As he scratched his scalp through a thin crop of tight gray curls, he stepped slowly to the dirt street.

Kate assumed he would know about the log building. "Sir, may I talk to you a moment?" she asked.

The man stopped in his tracks and searched 360 degrees. He looked at the two ladies, then searched again, insuring he hadn't missed someone.

"I called you," Kate said, waving her hand.

"I knows who called," the man said, "but I wasn't sho' *who* you was callin'. Bein' I'm the only one here, ya must a' been callin' me. I ain't never been called "Sir" by nobody." His white teeth gleamed through parted lips. "Things is gettin' better all the time."

Laura took two steps toward him. "Sorry, we don't know your name and we wanted to ask you a question."

"Be glad to help, if I can," the man replied. "As for my name, peoples call me Simon, or boy, or hey you. Not often they call me Simon, but never sir. You the first," he said, rocking back on his heels.

"Then we're glad to be first," Kate said.

His teeth burst forth again, as he pointed to his shack. "See that place there?" he asked. "It's mine. Sittin' on a quarter acre, and tha's mine. When ah make soup or bread, tha's mine. Now you ladies come and call me 'Sir.' I think tha's mo' progress than ownin' all them things I got. You make me feel good. What's the question?"

Laura and Kate were enjoying their new friend and considered the encounter a bonus for their trip.

"We were wondering what that large log building is," Laura asked, pointing up the path.

Simon put his hands into his pockets and turned to face the building. "Tha's a tradin' post. Ain't open today. Just Mondays and Fridays."

"Who uses it?" Kate asked.

"Mostly government agents and Indians," he replied. "Indians bring furs and things they make on the reservation and the agents trade 'em for food, blankets and clothes. They also give the Indians animal traps and things for catchin' fish. Anyone can buy there. Best come another day."

"We didn't come to shop," Laura said. "We're taking a round trip ride on the ferry from Alton."

"You got only fifteen minutes befo' it leaves," he said. "Lessin' you not takin' the five o'clock."

"We want this one," Kate said, looking downhill at the ferry. "Thank you for the information about the trading post."

"Yes, thank you, Sir Simon," Laura said, teasing him. "Maybe we can try your soup and bread someday." Laura extended her hand to Simon, giving him another reason to smile.

Simon held Laura's hand gently, while looking deep into her friendly eyes. Suddenly, his smile faded, like water passing through sand. For a moment he looked confused, then he forced another smile. "It's been a pleasure," he said, softly.

Laura stepped aside, while Kate presented her hand to Simon. He said good-bye to her, holding her hand firmly so she couldn't walk away. "You take care of your friend," he whispered, tilting his head toward Laura. He leaned forward and laughed as the women walked on. "Sir Simon," he repeated, so they could hear. "Tha's double good. Come back soon."

As the wind increased and clouds drifted from the west, blocking the warm sun, Laura and Kate returned to the ferry. The temperature had dropped fifteen degrees before the ferry left the dock. Sitting on deck was no longer a choice for Laura and Kate, so they went inside the cabin. A center aisle separated five rows of benches on each side of the cabin. All the window seats were taken, so they sat next to the aisle. "I don't see the Wooleys," Kate said. "Maybe Indians got 'em?"

The engines roared and the boat shuddered again. As it pulled away from the pier, Laura looked back at Hatfield, imagining what it must be like in the lonely, cold dead of winter. *Even a worse place to live than Alton*, she thought.

Laura unbuttoned her coat and looked at Kate. "Shall we have the tea we didn't get in Hatfield?"

"Definitely. I couldn't go two more hours without it."

In the corner of the cabin, a short muscular man wearing a white shirt and white apron sold sandwiches and beverages. Laura went to the counter and read the limited menu posted on the wall. It listed four kinds of sandwiches, raisin muffins, coffee and tea. When she entered the cabin, she remembered a man buying a glass of beer, leading her to believe there was a silent menu known only to special customers.

A blond-haired boy, about six years old, walked to the counter. His clothes were slightly large for his small frame and the amount of wear indicated he wasn't the original owner. But, they were clean and pressed. It was clear he was poor, but well cared for. He stood on his toes and reached over his head to lay a nickel on the counter.

Laura stepped back and smiled at the vendor, suggesting he tend to the child first. By his appearance, Laura guessed the boy was of Scandinavian heritage.

He stood silent below the countertop, out of the vendor's line of vision.

The man leaned over the counter and looked down at the boy asking for a raisin muffin. Within seconds, the vendor reached down to give him a muffin on white paper, and three pennies change.

The cabin door behind Laura opened and a child's voice began singing, "Old Folks At Home." Most of the passengers turned toward the back of the cabin to see who was singing. It was a girl about seven years old. She was dirty, wearing a tattered, wrinkled dress that appeared to have been slept in regularly. A large, pale blue bow lay limp on her matted hair.

The blond-haired boy watched her with great interest, aware that she was poorer than he. When she finished her song, he immediately handed her his coins. Without any show of emotion, she thanked him and plucked the three pennies from his upturned palm.

Laura reached over the boy and gave her a coin, too.

The girl proceeded down the aisle like a mechanical machine, singing "Camptown Races." She didn't have a good singing voice, but was singing because she had too. After passing through the cabin, she went out on deck without a final glance at anyone inside. The boy returned to his mother, who seemed pleased with his decision to help her.

Laura faced the vendor and requested two cups of tea and the name of the girl.

"Song Girl," he replied. "It's the only name she gives us. Seems she wants to stay private."

"How often is she on the ferry?" Laura asked, stepping up to the counter.

The man poured hot water into two white pottery mugs. "Once a week, she's allowed to ride free. She doesn't get much, but always something."

"Is she the only song girl to ride the ferry?" Laura asked, feeling through her coin purse. She watched him place a tea ball into one mug, then the other, until both waters turned black. Laura had forgotten to ask for weak tea. The strong tea was too bitter for her liking.

"One other girl, but never on the same day."

Laura laid the cost of the tea on the counter and returned the coin purse to the inside of her coat. "Does that girl give a name?"

He looked at Laura and smiled. "Song Girl. I think they work as a team? I'd guess her to be a year or two older than the one you just seen. By their looks, I'd say they were sisters. Definitely, dirt-poor."

Laura thanked him for the tea and information and returned to Kate, careful not to spill the tea as the boat rocked.

"Did you enjoy the show?" Kate asked, taking a cup from Laura.

"In one sense yes, in another, no. My feelings for that girl were so overwhelming, I couldn't enjoy her attempt at singing."

"I know what you mean. She didn't appear to be happy, and I don't think she got much money, either."

They sipped their tea and joked about the Wooleys, wondering where they had gone in that Godforsaken town. They also relived their moments with Simon and decided they would bring him some pastries when they returned. They looked forward to their next visit.

When Kate returned the tea mugs to the counter, the captain blew the foghorn twice. They would be arriving in Alton soon. She was looking out at the waves rolling across the surface of the water, when Simon's remark, "You take care of your friend," echoed in her mind. Kate wasn't sure what he'd meant, but decided to keep it to herself.

Laura looked across the aisle at the boy who had bought the raisin muffin. He was asleep against his mother's breast, relaxed and secure. She pondered the difference between his life and the lives of the "song girls" who worked constantly to survive. She thought of her daughter's life and that of battered Ellie Tuzik, another contrast in fate.

"Time to get off," Kate said, breaking Laura's concentration.

Looking around, Laura saw they were the last two people in the cabin, except for the vendor working in the corner.

As they disembarked, Laura saw the "song girl" walking along the wharf without a skip or hop. She didn't look right or left. She just walked with her head down.

They proceeded to the end of the wharf where Lakeview Street met the bay. A vendor was standing there with a varnished wood cart, touting his cider and hot corn cakes. It was a good location, with considerable pedestrian traffic between the wharf and St. James Park across the street. He also had a tall bag of umbrellas to sell to unprotected passengers leaving the ferry on a rainy day. As Laura and Kate sauntered by, the vendor smiled and tipped his straw hat.

Laura enjoyed her afternoon. When they stopped at the stairs leading to Kate's apartment, Laura turned to Kate. "Thanks for being my friend. You make my life more bearable."

"I appreciate the kind words, but don't forget, you make my life more tolerable, too."

Kate paused and asked, discreetly, "Have you thought of having a man in your life again?"

Laura had wondered when Kate would ask that question. She managed a feeble smile and replied, "I had a good man in my life. Now, I live for Hillary. I'm content with the circumstances. Maybe I'll find someone when Hillary is married?"

Kate walked up the first three stairs, then stopped and looked back at Laura. "You won't find another Jeremiah, but there are desirable men out there."

"I know. I'm not looking, but if a man could make me feel the way Jeremiah did, I'd consider it."

"If a man could make you feel that way again, you'd be foolish if you didn't grab him immediately. Good men don't come in bunches, you know."

"I'm going to change the subject," Laura said.

Kate rolled her eyes. "That doesn't surprise me."

Laura laughed. Kate knew her so well. "Come home with me. Hillary will be home soon. We'll play with her."

Kate raced down the three steps and hooked arms with Laura. "I was going to do some sewing, but it can wait."

CHAPTER FIVE

Kate took the signed contracts from Mr. Kerner and slid them into Frank's brown leather pouch. Mr. Kerner, the vice-president of commercial loans at the Mercantile Bank, was also a friend of Frank Dragus and a player in Frank's monthly poker game at the mill. Kate was pleased when she left the bank. Mr. Kerner had signed the documents quicker than usual. Many times, she had to wait an hour or more before they were returned to her.

She stood at the curb, waiting for a horse and buggy to pass, and hurried across the street to avoid being hit by a coal wagon pulled by two powerful brown horses. The afternoon sun illuminated the hillside next to town. Its brilliant autumn colors taunted her to take a closer look. She leisurely strolled toward the mill, enjoying the plethora of color rising up the hillside. At the base of the hill, a tall white cross in the cemetery loomed vividly against the beautiful colors of maples, oaks and birches. Puffs of pure white clouds drifted overhead toward Delaware Bay and the Atlantic Ocean.

Kate loved walking the mild days of autumn without the need of a coat to keep her warm. She wished John were home more, so they could enjoy a stroll to the river and picnic under the oaks, watching people watching them. She loved him, but resented his being gone for weeks at a time.

Kate heard a clicking noise and the sound of shoes slapping against the brick street. Two boys ran down the center of the street, rolling a metal hoop with sticks. Each boy took a turn stroking the top of the hoop with his stick, keeping it in motion. Kate smiled, recalling her youthful episodes with a hoop.

At the end of the third street, she turned south toward the mill and came upon a grocery store with baskets of fruit displayed outside. She stepped into the shade of its blue canvas awning, hanging over the baskets. Apples were plentiful this time of year, so there was a variety to pick from. A golden apple caught her eye and she wouldn't be denied. While paying the grocer, she noticed a small pendulum clock on the wall inside the store. It was only 1:30 p.m. and she would be getting back to the mill quicker than usual. As she walked back to the office, enjoying her apple and the colorful scenery, Kate continued to dawdle.

She entered the mill and went upstairs, using the rear stairwell rarely used by employees. Upon reaching the landing between the two floors, she saw the side door to Frank's office open. Kate stopped and waited. It was Molly, a sixteen-year-old who worked in the shipping department at the far end of the mill. Quickly, Molly stepped through the doorway, closed the door quietly, and disappeared among the machines, unaware of Kate's presence.

Kate knew exactly why Molly was there. She decided to enter the office through the front door. She proceeded slowly, allowing Frank time to get himself organized. Kate heard the office door unlock, hesitating a few moments before entering. Frank was standing behind his desk, putting on his suit coat. The gray hair at his temples was slightly ruffled and his tie was askew. The sun, now in the west, cast Frank's shadow across the top of his desk. Kate sniffed the air for telltale odors of misbehavior, but the smell of cigars dominated the room.

"You're back from the bank sooner than I expected," Frank said, nervously. "Did you run all the way?"

Kate realized his joke was intended to cover his guilt-ridden uneasiness. "I saw Molly going out the side door," she said, putting the pouch on his desk.

Frank deliberately avoided eye contact by looking at papers on his desk. "So what?" he responded, sharply.

"People usually leave by the front door."

"Yes, they do," Frank responded. He continued to flip aimlessly through his papers.

"Why did she leave through the side door?"

Frank glared at Kate, irritated by her questions. He thought quickly for an answer and pointed toward the side door. "Because, I had her put a box of index cards on *that* desk by *that* door." Figuring he gave a satisfactory explanation, he picked up a ledger from his desk and walked toward the front door. "The boys are coming to play cards tonight, so set up the table and chairs before you leave. I'm going down to the accounting department for a couple of hours."

Kate went to her desk and found Frank's ashtray filled with cigar ashes and a cigar butt. She carried it to Frank's desk, where she saw an old brown photograph lying on a tattered white envelope. Kate picked it up and looked at a slender girl about fifteen years old, standing on her toes hanging laundry on a clothesline. She had curly hair and was smiling at the person taking the picture. Kate was curious who the girl was. She looked at the back of the photograph, and in pencil was the name, Megan. A small heart was drawn at each end of her name. Kate looked at the girl again before putting the picture back on the envelope.

Kate finished preparing for the card game. She grabbed her purse and sweater from the coat tree and locked the door. Halfway down the stairs, she encountered Bernie Kerner, the man she'd met at the bank that afternoon.

"Off in a rush?" he asked, stopping to talk to Kate.

"Yeah," Kate replied, continuing on. "Frank should be back soon. The door is locked, so have a seat on a bench near the office."

By 7:25 p.m., all four men had arrived for cards, drinking and conversation. Frank was getting whiskey and vodka from a liquor cabinet while Paul Martane, the only married man in the room, and George Strattin waited at the table. Paul was tall and slender, and was often teased about his long, pointed nose. He was shuffling the cards, while George leaned back in his chair and lit a cigar. George was short and heavy, with a round face and curly brown hair.

Bernie Kerner, a muscular man with straight blond hair and a pencil mustache, was standing next to the window behind a black leather sofa. He was reading rows of book titles in a slender bookcase against the wall. Bernie removed one volume and began flipping through the pages. "Is this your favorite book?" he asked, holding it high.

Frank was filling his arms with liquor bottles to carry to the table. Unable to turn and look at the book, he asked for the title.

"*Fart Proudly*, by Benjamin Franklin."

"Oh, that one," Frank snickered, walking to the table. "Franklin was an intelligent fellow, but also a bit of a rogue. He would do or say things for shock value. I believe he wrote that book to prove there was freedom of the press." Frank set the bottles on a corner of the table and reached for the cards. "What'll it be, Boys, draw poker?"

All agreed and adjusted their chairs to the table, while Frank dealt the cards.

George took off his suit coat and handed it to Paul. "Would you reach over and put this on the sofa? I need freedom of movement to destroy you guys," he boasted.

"Sofa?" Bernie questioned. "That's not a sofa. It's Frank's love nest. His pleasure wagon."

"I thought it was his leather crib," Paul added.

"Very funny," Frank responded, glaring at the two men. "Keep that kind of talk to yourselves, or lose my business."

"Don't worry," Paul answered. "We enjoy hearing about your conquests. When are you going to give us names, so we can enjoy your stories more thoroughly?"

"Don't hold your breath," Frank replied, while George bet a dollar. "I'll keep my stories a mystery." Frank looked at his cards and tossed a dollar coin into the pot to match George's bet.

Paul and Bernie folded their cards without betting.

"There's an old saying," George said, "Old enough to bleed, old enough to breed."

"That would be right," Frank agreed. "And this should make you bleed." He slammed his cards on the table. "Three queens."

"Shit! Three tens," George yelled, throwing his cards down. "Thought I had you beat."

Bernie gathered the cards from the table and began shuffling them. He stopped momentarily to take a sip of whiskey from a crystal glass. He dealt the cards around the table and the men slid them into their hands.

"I bet two dollars," George said, throwing his coins into the pot. He palmed his cards and looked around the table, waiting for a counter bet.

Paul and Bernie looked at their cards and folded again.

"You must have good cards, if you're starting at two bucks," Paul said to George.

Frank was squinting at his cards, while fingering his stack of silver dollars.

"You in, or out?" George asked, staring at Frank.

"I'm in," Frank mumbled. "I'm deciding how deep to go." He paused and slid four coins to the center of the table. "I'll meet your two and raise you two."

Paul and Bernie sat back in their chairs with their arms folded, waiting for the betting to begin.

Without hesitation, George began counting his coins, so he wouldn't look weak in the cards. George met Frank's raise and added another two silver dollars. "Let's show some guts and not draw—just play with the cards in hand. Agreed?"

"That's a lot of money for a guy with only one hardware store," Frank said, leering at George. "Yeah, I agree. No draw. Here's two to match and I raise another three."

"I'll make you a better offer," George said, sliding his cards together in his hand. "Forget what's in the pot. I'll bet you twenty dollars. If you win, take the money. If I win, keep your money and get me one of your pretty young employees for an afternoon."

"Can't you get your own girls?" Frank asked with a grin.

"Of course," George replied. "But not pretty young girls like you have. I have men and boys working in my hardware store. I have no occasion to meet young girls, and if I tried, my intentions would be obvious to others."

Bernie and Paul continued sitting with their arms crossed, listening to George's offer to Frank. Both were amused and anxious for Frank's answer.

"Would you bet fifty dollars on the same terms?" Frank asked.

"Like you said, I have only one hardware store. Fifty dollars would be too steep for me."

"If I needed the money, I might consider the offer," Frank said, looking at George. "But since I don't, I'm going to refuse your offer. You also know I won't reveal the names of the girls, so your offer was wasted. Let's get back to silver dollars and the cards."

George decided not to raise Frank's bet. He put the additional silver dollars in the pot and waited for Frank to show his hand.

"All spades, king high," Frank said.

"Shit, again," George bellowed. "All diamonds, Jack high." He threw his cards into the center of the table and took a long drink of whiskey.

At Doyle's Pub, Kate sat at a table by the window waiting for John. Unwashed derelicts, beggars and prostitutes walked by, permanent fixtures on the street like lampposts or street signs. In Alton, there was a fine line between existing and living. Kate folded her arms on the table, rocking it to one corner. She could see one table leg was shorter than the others, but it was the last vacant table by the windows. The old wooden table was chipped at the corners and scarred with multiple knife carvings of names, dates and geometric designs. Kate had been there only a few minutes when John crossed the street, waving to her.

He entered the pub, greeting friends at various tables until he reached Kate. "Missed you," he said. "Miss me, too?"

"Of course," she replied, reaching for his hand. "Again and again I miss you. I wish *not* to miss you."

"I know. I know," he muttered. "That may change soon. I got a deal going and I might make some good money, soon."

"What kind of deal?" Kate asked. "Some Chinese business again?"

"Can't tell you now. I don't want to jinx it. I'll tell you when it happens."

Kate studied John's face. She truly loved him and knew that he was reliable and hard working. She believed he would do his best for her. *Maybe it was time for them to marry*, she thought. *Damn seamen!*

Meg came to their table with two menus, a mug of ale and a glass of port wine. "Having supper tonight?"

"In a bit," Kate answered. "We'll have our drinks, while getting reacquainted."

Meg glanced at them. "Here?" she questioned. "We don't allow that. This is a respectable place." She smiled at her joke and walked away.

"She's got the right idea," John said, raising his eyebrows.

Kate reached across the table and held his clasped hands in hers. "Anticipation is half the fun. When do you have to leave again?"

"I'll be here ten days, time enough for a bunch of anticipation."

"It may seem easy to someone at sea all the time," Kate said, "but it's not to me. My life is lonely waiting for you. I'm getting tired of reading the same dime novels over and over."

"Like I said before," John repeated. "Your waiting may be over soon."

Kate handed John a menu, then began reading hers. They remained silent, pondering the same offerings of the past five months. "This menu is getting boring and I'm not very hungry," Kate said. "Why don't we share a cod dinner?"

"Here's what I think. You eat half your cod dinner and I'll have beef stew and the other half of your cod dinner."

"You're that hungry?" she asked, peeking over her menu at him. "Didn't they feed you aboard ship today?"

"At noon. They served chipped beef and collard greens. Don't like 'em." John searched the smoke-filled room for Meg and signaled her to come and take their order.

Tom Knauz, a tall, good-looking man of forty-two, came to their table with a big, friendly greeting. His premature white hair was protruding from under his black fedora.

Kate had a good idea what he wanted.

Tom gave John a hearty pat on the shoulder and invited him to play "monte" with him and the Mertes brothers. He assured John they would start with a sealed deck of cards.

"Skedaddle, I say politely," Kate said, with a smile. "He's home only a couple hours, so he's concentrating on me."

"I can certainly appreciate that," Tom said, winking at John. "If I was in his shoes, I would do the same. Enjoy your evening." Tom walked away, scanning the room for another player. He went to the bar and gave John Broe a pat on the shoulder. A few moments later, he continued his search.

"I didn't get to say a word to him," John said, pointing to Tom. "You did all the talking."

"Good," Kate replied. "Maybe that's the kind of relationship we should have."

"If it was, you'd be a memory in no time," John said, swinging his finger from Tom to her. "Besides, you wouldn't be happy with a rug for a husband."

"You're right. I was joking. I also know you wouldn't leave me."

"What will it be?" Meg asked, approaching the table with pad and pencil in hand.

"I'll have the cod dinner and John will have the beef stew," Kate answered. "You can repeat our drinks, too."

Meg finished scribbling on the pad and slammed a dot at the end. "Back shortly," she said and walked away.

John was glaring at Kate. "What's wrong? Why are you looking at me like that?"

"You did it again. You spoke for me. What if I changed my mind about what I wanted to eat?"

Kate put her hand to her mouth. "I did, didn't I? I'm sorry. It wasn't intentional."

John sat back in his chair and smiled. "You're forgiven. You've never done it before tonight."

Kate thought it wise to change the subject, immediately. "Do you know what your next port will be, and how long you'll be gone?" She sipped her wine, waiting for an answer.

"Probably about four or five weeks in the Caribbean area. But, I'll be concentrating on you until I leave."

Kate gasped, then pointed out to the street. "Someone's in trouble." She leaned closer to the window for a better view.

John looked over his shoulder and saw a dark green, two-seat buggy running out of control. The brown horse was frightened or confused. It repeatedly sidestepped, stopped and started again, causing the buggy to jerk erratically over the brick street. The driver was guiding the horse one direction and then another, using his black whip. People scattered to get away from the buggy, and those few who stayed, shouted advice to help the driver get the horse under control. The problem continued as the buggy moved down the street, beyond where Kate and John could watch it. People stood motionless on the street and sidewalk, looking off in the direction of the buggy. Kate and John listened for a crashing sound that never came.

Meg arrived with a tray of food and drinks, while yelling to some-one to keep his hands to himself. "These buggers will drive ya mad. Some seem ta think *I* come with the drinks."

Kate leaned toward Meg and looked up at her. "Some girls don't get any attention."

"Bless 'em," Meg shot back, walking away. "If they're lonely, they can work here."

Kate picked up her knife and fork and began cutting the fish fillet into equal portions. "Your stew looks good," she remarked, staring at John's plate.

"It is. The meat and carrots are tender."

Kate stopped eating to look at him. "I'm glad you're back. I've been lonely without you and I don't like being lonely."

"I don't get a chance to get lonely aboard ship, but I certainly missed you. If we get a farm, we won't be separated again."

"I admit life in the country sounds nice," Kate said. "But then, any change from Alton would be an improvement."

A roar of laughter resounded from the card table across the room. "It appears the boys are having fun," Kate commented. "Feel left out?"

"Not at all. I can meet with the boys when you're at work."

When John finished his stew, Kate used her fork to slide half of her fish onto his plate. "It's good fish. You'll enjoy it."

A few minutes later, Meg returned to see if they wanted anything else. John leaned back in his chair and looked up at her. "Just the tally," he said, reaching inside his jacket for his wallet.

"How long before you leave again?" Meg asked, placing the check on the table.

"About ten days. Then I have to leave my girl again." He handed money to Meg and signaled with his hand that she should keep the difference.

"She doesn't like it when you leave," Meg said, tilting her head toward Kate. She thanked them and went to the next table.

When they stepped outside, Kate took John's arm for their walk to her apartment. "I don't see that green buggy smashed up anywhere," he said. "The driver must have regained control."

Kate didn't respond. She was examining the squalor and smells she would be glad to leave behind. What bothered her, though, was that if she left Alton, she would be separated from Laura and Hillary. That would be difficult.

They turned the corner onto Lakeview Street where children were hanging out of windows, watching other children playing in the street. Kate commented to John, about the foul language being used by the children.

Three young boys, about ten years old, came storming down the front stairs as Kate and John were going up. "It's almost ten o'clock," John said, "and these babes are still running loose? What are their parents thinking?"

When they got to her apartment, John took the key from Kate to unlock the door. The dancing light from the gas lamp down the hall gave the illusion that the keyhole was moving. He chuckled and opened the door.

Kate lit the kerosene lamp by the door and carried it to the kitchen table.

John followed, holding her apartment key in his outstretched hand. When she reached for it, he pulled her into his arms and kissed her moist, eager lips. "I think of you all the time when I'm away," he said, then kissed both her eyes, slowly and tenderly.

Kate kissed his cheek. "I'll be back in a moment," she said, with a coy smile. She went behind a screen that stood in folds in front of her dresser.

John stood alongside Kate's bed to undress, then waited until she came forward in a sexy, light blue robe. He took her in his arms and they kissed again. John reached for her breasts, finding her fingers opening the buttons to make room for his invading hand. The robe dropped from her shoulders. He gazed at her in the flickering light and pulled her close until her breasts pressed against him. His lips pressed down on hers, revealing the depth of his desire. They sprawled together on the bed, caressing each other with slow fingers. They kissed deeply, confirming their oneness, as they gave and received.

CHAPTER SIX

Hillary raced home from school, eager for her birthday party. Iris and Vera were to be the guests. She unbuttoned her coat, ascending the stairs two at a time. Laura was at the stove with a small birthday cake when Hillary entered the apartment.

"When will Iris and Vera be here? Last year, they came late because someone's dog had a litter of puppies."

Hillary hung her coat on the door. "Soon, Mother. Less than fifteen minutes, if they're on time." Hillary went to the window to look for her friends. Across the street, Mr. Brummer was loading an oak chest onto his delivery wagon, while Darby waited with her face buried in a canvas bag of oats. She watched Darby jerk her knees and swish her tail to chase flies pestering her. There weren't many flies this time of year, but Darby got the attention of those remaining.

Laura looked at Hillary, gazing down on the street. The sunlight illuminated her blond hair and fair skin. She recalled the years when Hillary had been an infant, her first steps, first words, first hugs and kisses. Laura thanked God for her beautiful child. "She is ours," Laura whispered to Jeremiah.

"They're coming!" Hillary shouted.

Iris and Vera were swinging their arms, marching past one store after another, as though they were the only people on earth. Each carried a small white package.

Hillary watched until they crossed to her side of the street and waited by the door.

"Let's pretend we're not here," Laura suggested, smiling.

"Not this time," Hillary replied, looking at her mother as though she were daft. "We did that once before and they were gone before we knew it."

Soon, they heard shoes stomping on the wood stairs, followed by footsteps in the hall. The girls whispered until they knocked on the door.

Hillary hesitated a moment, then yanked it open. "Hurry in," she demanded, while looking up and down the hall. "Don't want my neighbors to think I know you."

"Well, I'm glad to know them," Laura responded, as she approached the girls.

"Thank you, Mrs. Cook," Vera replied. "Then we'll stay."

They turned their backs to Hillary, while unbuttoning their coats, then spun around with gifts in hand, yelling, "Happy Birthday!"

"What a surprise," Hillary exclaimed, holding her hands to her cheeks. "What day is this?"

"Oh, yeah, like our being here is a big surprise," Iris laughed.

"I didn't wear my party dress because I knew we would go out to play after the party," Vera said, with a grin.

"Me, too," Iris said playfully. "Or did we wear these clothes because we don't have a party dress?"

"Black shoes, black knee stockings and a cotton dress are good enough for a party and playing outside," Laura said. "Besides, Hillary doesn't have a party dress, either."

Iris and Vera knelt on their chairs, leaning on the table toward Hillary as she unwrapped the presents.

The gifts were identical in size and shape, but she couldn't guess what was inside. Hillary felt the packages until the suspense got the best of her. With one hard tug, she tore the white paper off the top of the present. A bunch of wild flowers landed in her lap. The small red, white, pink and yellow flowers were tied together with pink ribbon. She thought wildflowers were a clever idea and suggested it become a tradition with them on birthdays. At the bottom of the wrapping paper were a handful of butterscotch candy and a heavily used dime novel. She turned the book around to read the title. "Thank you! Thank you, Vera!" Hillary shrieked. "I've wanted *Black Beauty* since I was nine." Hillary glanced at her two friends. "And your gift has peppermint?" Hillary asked Iris. Iris didn't answer, so Hillary knew she had guessed right. With the peppermint was the book, *Anne*, by Constance Fenimore Woolson.

"What's that book about?" Vera asked.

"A young orphan," Hillary replied. "God knows we have plenty of them around here." Hillary took a few moments to flip through the pages. "Last summer, I told Iris I wanted this book and she remembered. Thanks, Iris."

"Flowers aren't the freshest this time of year," Vera said, "but it represents who we are."

Hillary blew a kiss at both of them. "Thanks, Wildflowers. I'll make a small wreath of them and hang it on the wall."

The flame of a stubby pink candle trailed backwards, as Laura carried the chocolate cake to the table. They began singing, "Happy Birthday."

Hillary sat with her back straight, shoulders back, and a pleased look on her face.

"You only get one candle," Iris quipped, "because you're only twelve once."

Laura enjoyed watching the girls giggle and act silly, recalling parties when she was a girl. She went to her clothes closet next to the bed and removed two presents from under two sweaters on the closet floor. "The pink package is from me, and the yellow from Kate."

Vera and Iris continued to devour cake and tea, as Hillary unwrapped her mother's gift.

Laura stood behind her, smiling, waiting for Hillary's response.

Hillary was obviously pleased, thanking her mother profusely, while displaying her gift to her friends. Laura had knitted a matching set of white gloves and scarf, with little wildflowers on the back of the gloves.

Iris stared at the gloves with envying eyes. "They're beautiful," she commented. "Don't wear 'em. Just look at 'em."

Hillary handed the scarf and gloves to her mother. "Please, put these on the bed, so they don't get spilled on."

Vera looked at Laura with a demure glance. "You'll be invited to my birthday party, Mrs. Cook."

Hillary took two quick bites of cake and carefully removed yellow paper from a hand-knitted white beret. Immediately, she suspected collusion between Kate and her mother. "It's very pretty. It matches the gloves and scarf. Did you tell Kate what you were making for me?"

"Yes. We planned this together. Try them on in front of the mirror and see how you look."

Hillary jumped out of the chair, grabbed her gloves and scarf from the bed and stepped in front of the dresser mirror. "Perfect!" she cried out, adjusting her beret. "Now, I'll have something nice to wear to church."

"You could wear them to a Royal Ball at Buckingham Palace," Vera swooned.

The girls continued eating and singing, with "Jim Crack Corn" and "Buffalo Gals," their favorite songs.

Laura announced it was almost three-thirty, suggesting they go out and play before it got too late. The girls put on their coats and dashed into the hall. Laura heard six feet pounding the stairs, while she cleaned the table.

The girls stopped to look into Thompson's store before moving on. When he saw them, he waved for them to come inside. They ran to the door, bouncing off one another, trying to enter the store at the same time.

"You girls can earn a licorice stick," he said, from behind the counter.

"How?" Iris asked, eagerly.

"Take a package to Mr. Browder, at his furniture store," he replied.

"That's easy," Vera responded. "We know the place."

The trio stepped to the glass candy case filled with a variety of sweets. There were colorful boxes of gumdrops, peanuts, jellybeans and an assortment of hard candies. Pretzels and licorice sticks stood in round glass jars on top of the display case. Mr. Thompson removed three pieces of licorice from one of the jars and handed them to the girls. "Go to him directly, no lollygagging."

The girls thanked him for the licorice, and raced out the door and into the street. Mr. Thompson watched Iris charge into the path of two galloping horses, pulling a coal wagon. He shouted her name like a thunderbolt, hoping she would hear him through the glass windows. Vera saw the problem developing and grabbed Iris's coat, yanking her backward out of the horses' path. Mr. Thompson began taking short, quick breaths, with his mouth open, filling his lungs repeatedly to slow down his heartbeat. He sat down on a cracker barrel to get off his shaky legs.

The girls passed a row of stores near Browder's furniture store when Iris suddenly shouted, "Quick! Look in this store window!" They stood in a row, staring down at hardware items, big and small. "Don't turn around," Iris directed. "Keep looking toward the window."

"Nice hammer," Vera commented.

"Not funny," Iris replied. "Don't move! Now look at the reflection in the glass. See that girl across the street by the tobacco store? That's Sarah."

"Who's Sarah?" Hillary asked, turning her head toward Iris.

"She's the one I told you about a couple months ago. She sells herself to men."

"She's our age," Vera said, staring at the glass.

Iris agreed. "Thirteen, from what I hear."

Hillary stared at Sarah, trying to see her face clearly. "It must be difficult supporting yourself that way."

"I couldn't do it," Iris stated, sternly. "My cousin, Annette, told me Sarah has been coming around since April, and she's seen her leave with men."

"Where does she live?" Vera asked, concentrating on the reflection.

"Don't know. She's an orphan. Annette said she was sent to live on a farm somewhere, probably went on a … look! A man is coming out of the tobacco store." They watched intently at the reflection. A shabbily dressed man wearing a tweed cap stepped down a pair of concrete stairs between two bay windows. Large green letters, outlined in gold, spelled the words, *TOBACCO SHOP*. Sarah stepped forward, looking up at the man as she stopped him. The girls guessed him to be forty-something and certainly one of the working poor. He shook his head and moved on.

"I could never do that," Hillary said. "I'd die first."

"Go on about the farm she was sent to," Vera demanded.

"Annette said the farmer made her sleep with him, so she ran away," Iris added.

"To do this?" Hillary questioned, her face twisted in bewilderment. "She doesn't look like someone who would do that. There must be more to this story."

"I suppose," Iris agreed, "but I don't know it. I'll see if I can get more information from Annette."

The girls arrived at Browder's, still contemplating Sarah's activities. Before entering, Hillary turned for another look at Sarah, trying to understand her existence.

They stepped into a large room, with wicker furniture stacked in all directions. At the end of a long aisle, between towering columns of furniture, an elderly man, very slim and balding, sat behind a large desk, his white shirt open at the neck. The walk toward him was like passing through a canyon. He never looked up, as they approached his desk. Smoke drifted upward from his skinny brown cigar resting on a red metal ashtray. On the wall behind him, a pendulum clock struck four times.

"Are you Mr. Browder?" Iris asked, meekly.

The man raised his head to look at the girls. "I am." He smiled, observing three shabbily dressed waifs standing before him. "Is that package from Mr. Thompson?"

"Yes," Hillary replied. She handed him the package and noticed a man leering at her, while hand-weaving a wicker chair. He was standing behind a worktable, almost twenty feet to her right. He was fat and perspiring, wearing an undershirt that clung to his wet skin. He watched her with great interest, making her feel uncomfortable.

Vera noticed him, too. She leaned toward Hillary and whispered. "Maybe we should send Sarah here?"

Mr. Browder stood and reached into his black trouser pocket. "Good service deserves a tip. Here's two pennies for—no, make that three pennies for a quick delivery."

The girls thanked him and turned for the door. Walking away, Hillary could feel the sweaty man watching her. She wasn't about to look back.

The girls returned by the same route they had come. Hillary looked up and down the street for Sarah, but she was gone. "What'll we do now?"

"It's your birthday," Vera said. "You decide."

Hillary thought for a moment. "Let's go to Krump's chicken store. He might let us play with chicks in the back room."

"It's stinky in there," Iris responded. She immediately realized she shouldn't have said that. It was Hillary's choice. She tried to correct herself. "But he does let us feed the chickens sometimes, so let's give it a try."

"Let's do it," Vera replied. "Krump may even give us an egg to take home. Better than nothing."

The girls walked west to Union Avenue, repeatedly stepping around other pedestrians and coming together again. When they arrived at Market Street, Vera thrust out her arms, stopping her friends without warning. She pointed down the street, with its dilapidated stone and frame buildings, and suggested they walk through the market, if Hillary agreed.

Hillary delayed answering, until she examined the size of the crowd. A horde of shoppers meandered in all directions, stopping occasionally to pick through merchandise on a table or cart, then moving on until they found something to haggle over. Realizing it was the end of the season for vendors, and it may be their last opportunity to walk the market, Hillary agreed.

"It sure is crowded," Hillary said, stretching her neck to see everything. "Some vendors sell things from different parts of the world. Last year, Eugene Pawl bought a dragon kite from a Chinaman. It was huge, with big eyes and scales painted on its sides. It even had long red streamers attached to the inside of its mouth, making it look like it was breathing fire."

"Eleanor Waymoll's mother bought her a beautiful French rosary made of blue glass beads," Iris added. "It was the prettiest I've ever seen."

"Then let's go, but stay away from old ladies in black," Vera said, knowing Iris and Hillary scared easily. "They're gypsy witches."

"I hear gypsies steal children and sell 'em," Iris warned, shaking her finger at her friends. "We'd better stay close together."

"They only steal babies," Hillary said. "Besides, the three of us could make enough noise, so someone in this crowd would help us."

"You lead the way," Iris said to Vera, pushing against her back. "You're bigger and stronger."

"All right, I'll lead," Vera agreed, eyebrows raised and nodding her head. "But you girls stay close to me."

The girls didn't visit Market Street often, but it looked the same today as it had the times before. Vendors lined the center of the street, displaying their same specialty at the same location, with the same vendors surrounding them. Some had new and used clothes draped across tables, or piled on carts. One cart had square compartments filled with buttons, buckles, and spools of colored thread, needles and fancy pincushions. Shoes lay on tables, or hung from rods so they could be seen from a distance. Many carts had canvas canopies, sheltering merchandise from the sun or sudden rain.

Along the sidewalks, under striped and solid-colored awnings, fruits and vegetables were displayed in wooden crates with colorful paper labels explaining the product's place of origin. Most merchants wore white aprons over dark clothing; straw hats were a tradition for the men. Much of their day was spent scurrying in and out of their stores, receiving payment or restocking a display.

The girl's eyes searched Market Street, watching for old ladies in black. As though tied together, they continued down the sidewalk in unison.

"Look at this death house," Vera said, pointing to a butcher shop. In the center of the window, two pigs heads were displayed on a large metal platter. A wooden box of chicken heads and one of chicken feet, sat under a row of plucked chickens that were hanging upside down, their legs tied together. Furry brown and gray rabbits were displayed in the same manner, while flies walked over them undisturbed.

Vera got down on one knee to get closer to the pigs heads. "What do people do with animal heads?"

"They eat them, of course," Iris answered. "I was told people boil them to get meat from the head, or to make soup. Some people eat the eyes and brain."

"Eeewwww," Vera wailed. "I'm gunna be sick." She grabbed her friends' arms and marched them away from the window toward the carts in the street. They passed an elderly blind man, with yellowing white hair and a long scar on his neck that went below the collar of his tattered, blue Union jacket. He was sitting on a wooden crate, singing Civil War songs with his blue military cap upside down on the street before him, hoping people would drop a coin or something to eat. Iris walked close to the military cap to see what was inside. She saw an apple and four pennies.

They came upon a vendor selling religious images painted on wooden boards. Most were lined in rows on the cart, while others were displayed overhead hanging from a wire. Hillary was impressed. The bright gold and red colors illuminated the pictures, as well as Hillary's desire.

The vendor was a large woman wearing a long unbuttoned black coat over a yellow and white striped dress. She looked down at Hillary. "You like icons?"

"They're beautiful," Hillary replied, scanning the large selection. "But I don't have money to buy one."

"Sorry, dah'link. Maybe someday you have money. You come back then." The woman turned away and began speaking a foreign tongue to a man in high black boots.

"She speaks jibber and bad English," Vera said, as they mixed with the crowd. "I wonder where she's from?"

The girls walked arm-in-arm past carts filled with adult clothes and shoes. A woman held a man's brown overcoat, while he tried on a tweed jacket he didn't seem to like. At the next cart, a man with a short white beard was sitting on a keg, reading the *Alton Reporter*. He was selling a variety of used hand tools with spots of rust on the metal. Next to him, a tall slender man with tiny spectacles was selling new and used knives, and sandstones to sharpen them.

The sound and smell of sizzling sausages frying with mushrooms and potatoes began to tease their senses. At the curb, a cloud of bluish smoke drifted skyward from glowing coals and two large frying pans of burning oil. The aroma spread through the crowd, stimulating business from those who could afford to spend a few extra pennies. The girls walked over to watch the man engulfed in smoke.

"I'd like some sausage and bread," Iris whispered, sniffing the air.

"Sausage and potatoes would do me fine," Vera commented, staring at the smoking pans. "Wish we had a nickel."

Hillary was attracted to a cart filled with colorful dolls in ethnic costumes; boy and girl dolls dressed in bright red, blue, and green clothes, some trimmed in gold, silver or white. She walked over for a closer look, leaving her friends behind. Hillary picked up a few dolls to examine the variety of costume designs, colors, and quality of undergarments. She was impressed with the collection, deciding which one she would buy if she had money. A voice speaking jibber came from behind. Hillary turned to see who was talking. It was a woman in black. Pure white hair protruded from a black scarf covering her head. Her face was mantled with deep wrinkles, like a dry riverbed, and seven brown teeth leaned in different directions. They looked into each other's eyes, only inches apart. Hillary was afraid the lady would grab her or cast a spell. She was too frightened to run or speak. She could only stare at the old witch. The woman spoke jibber again and bumped into her. Hillary froze in place, wondering what the witch was doing to her. Her strength seemed to seep out of her body, leaving her legs like pillars of sand, threatening to drop her to the street. As if clouds had just drifted in front of the sun, Hillary's vision darkened. She believed she was going under the witch's spell. She tried to run, but couldn't. The witch's face remained close to hers—staring, staring.

Hillary felt herself being pulled from the old woman, her legs forced to move as the distance between herself and the witch increased. Vera held her around the waist, pulling her back to the food vendor.

The man began to laugh. "Ya look like you was scared,"

Hillary looked to her friends, as she gasped for breath. "I was!" she said, shaken by the experience. She took several deep breaths. "That black gypsy witch was putting a spell on me."

The man laughed again, showing teeth similar to those of the old woman. "She ain't no gypsy or witch," he said, in a scratchy voice. "She's a widder. All the old ladies in black are widders. When their husbands die, they wear black 'til the good Lord takes 'em upstairs ta join 'em. It's the custom with some folks."

The girls turned and studied the old woman again, not fully convinced the vendor was telling the truth. Her back was to them, rearranging the dolls so they would face the passing customers.

"See. She ain't running after ya," the vendor said. "She's someone's Granny."

The girls backed away from him, without saying a word. He continued to chuckle about gypsy witches, as the girls disappeared into the crowd.

"Do you think he's telling the truth?" Iris asked, scanning her friends' faces for an honest answer.

"I know there are gypsy witches," Vera said. "I've heard stories about them from my parents."

"I've heard about them, too," Iris agreed. "Let's move away from here." The girls held hands, as they wandered through the congested street and what seemed to be an endless line of carts. Colorful merchandise was displayed high and low in an attempt to lure shoppers. The girls looked at carts filled with hats, belts, and a variety of candles, pots and pans; then came upon an organ grinder with a monkey on a leash. A man sporting a long, black mustache cranked the portable organ, while his monkey passed through the crowd, presenting his red and gold cap for coins. The girls thought he was cute, enjoying his squeaks and chatter, but backed away when he approached, afraid he might bite with his tiny, sharp teeth.

The concentration of people was so thick, the girls decided to move away. Still holding hands, Vera led the other two through the crowd toward an open area near the curb.

Two girls in their early teens stopped in front of them, blocking their way. Both were wearing a hint of rouge and lip coloring, just enough to give spark to their faces. Their hair was combed up in the back, in an attempt to make themselves look older than they were.

The taller girl examined the trio closely. "Are ya planning on working Market Street?"

"Working?" Vera questioned. "We don't work here. We're shopping."

"Girls that shop here come with their parents," the shorter girl said. "Girls that come alone, come to work."

"Are you entertainers?" Hillary asked.

"Yeah, we're entertainers," the taller girl answered with a smile. She continued to scrutinize the trio with a critical eye.

"You're wearing face color," Iris said. "Do you dance or sing?"

The taller girl stepped forward to examine them again. "You *are* shopping, ain't ya?"

"Of course," Hillary answered, "Why else would we be here?"

The taller girl turned to look at her friend. "'Why else would they be here?' she asks." Again, she looked at the threesome. "I guess you ain't doing our work."

"What do you do?" Iris asked. "We may want to watch."

The two girls snickered, as they turned to walk way. The taller girl whispered back at them, "I don't think ya can watch, my dear," then proceeded to tell them what they did.

The girls stood numb, as the two walked away. Vera turned to her friends, wondering if she had heard correctly. "We're all standing here with our jaws sagging, so I guess we heard the same thing," she muttered.

"They aren't bashful," Iris said.

"Two men are sitting on the steps watching us," Hillary whispered. "Maybe they think we work with those girls."

Vera noticed one of the men start down the stairs, looking over at them. She grabbed Hillary and Iris by the hand and pulled them into the crowd.

After the girls left the party, Laura washed the party dishes and went grocery shopping. She hurried across Union Avenue, toting groceries in her tan canvas bag. It seemed heavier with each step, the frayed straps cutting into her fingers. She glanced up and down the street on the chance of seeing the girls. *Wildflowers,* she thought. *That defines them quite well!*

Laura was pleased with Hillary's choice of friends, for neither Iris nor Vera was troublesome. Their friendship was bonded by a need for a childhood in a world of long hours doing adult labor. Laura made sure Hillary had as much time with her friends, as possible.

She arrived at a bench outside of Lou's Barber Shop and dropped on it, exhausted. She was startled when someone sat next to her. It was Kate Moran.

"You timed it perfect. I just caught up to you, as you sat down. Got time to talk for a while?"

"Absolutely," Laura answered. "I'd love to sit and rest under the sun for a while. There won't be many days like this before cold weather moves in and stays."

"How was Hillary's birthday party this afternoon?"

"It went well. Hillary loved your gift. She plans to thank you at work tomorrow. Anything new with you and John?"

"Nothing's changed. He's gone again. Won't be back till the middle of December."

"Does he still mention marriage?"

Kate rolled her eyes. "Yeah, and I give him the same answer. Said he's been saving and has a good amount, plus he's going to make a lot of money soon on some business deal. Don't know what that is, either. Then he'll have enough money to buy us a farm."

"Does farming scare you?" Laura asked, rubbing her sore fingers.

"Not really, but I reminded him that farmers are working in Alton because they couldn't make a go of it. John says it's different out west, with the population growing and all. I worry about losing our money."

"It's a difficult decision, but the years are ticking on while you're thinking about marriage and a family."

Kate looked down at her hands. "I've thought about changing my answer. Whenever he asks about Hillary, I know he's getting on about marriage. He knows how I feel about her, so he tries to soften me up, first."

"My life would be empty without Hillary," Laura sighed. "With Jeremiah gone, she *is* my life. It's a wonderful relationship you must experience to understand. It can't be imagined. All we have is each other, yet we are reasonably happy. If anything happened to her, I would be devastated. Or, something happening to me would be equally frightful. She couldn't survive alone."

Laura noticed Kate staring at something behind her. "Well, look at this," Kate remarked. "If it isn't himself, coming this way,"

Laura turned to find that "himself" was Frankie. He was walking toward them with newspapers tucked under his arm and hands in his pockets. He was wearing a big smile with a corncob pipe clamped between his teeth. His chin was raised, as he strutted like a peacock down the avenue. Huge amounts of smoke drifted into his face and curled around the peak of his cap before going skyward. His right knee showed through his worn corduroy knickers and half his shirttail hung out of his pants.

"What are you burning in that thing?" Kate called to him. "Kerosene?"

Frankie stopped to face the ladies sitting on the bench. "No, Ma'am," Frankie answered. "Pieces of newspaper. As you know, I've got plenty of that. Makes me look dapper, don't it?"

"I wouldn't say that exactly," Kate answered. "But then, I wouldn't say what you look like. How come it smokes so much?"

"I put a piece of incense with the paper. Makes me smell good, too."

Kate and Laura looked at each other. *Wrong again*, they thought.

"Either of you ladies wantin' a newspaper this afternoon?" he asked, showing them the headline, *Yukon Gold Rush A Success.*

"No thanks," Kate replied. "You're all the news I can take for one day."

Frankie thanked them for their time and turned to leave. He stopped and backed up to Laura. In his formal manner, he said, "Iris told me Hillary had a birthday?"

"That is correct," Laura replied, wondering what he was getting at.

Frankie reached inside his coat to retrieve a small gold and black tin box. "I was fortunate enough to find this box of incense in the ally behind Kane's Drug Store," he boasted. "Please give this piece to Hillary. I think she'll enjoy it." Frankie laid the incense on Laura's open palm.

"Thank you, Sir," Laura responded. "I'm sure she will enjoy it." Frankie took two puffs of his pipe and walked away.

Kate tilted her head and looked at Laura. "Future son-in-law?"

"If that's who she wants, when the time comes," Laura replied. "Remember the story of me and Jeremiah?"

Kate nodded and shifted herself to face Laura more directly. "How is Hillary doing at school? Still a star pupil?"

"Yes. She is doing extremely well, I say proudly."

Kate smiled. "Everyone likes your Wildflower. She's a delight to have around."

Laura laughed. "My Wildflower. Actually, I think it's cute, those three calling themselves Wildflowers." Laura leaned towards Kate. "What I haven't told you yet, is you and I are honorary Wildflowers. The girls decided last week that we were nice enough to be the old wildflowers; they'll be the young flowers."

"Well, isn't that sweet. But, I'm not sure I like the word 'old' in my title," Kate responded.

Laura waved her index finger in front of Kate. "Of course, we can't attend any of their meetings. We're just honorary."

"I would like to know what they do when they're together," Kate said. "I'm sure they'd be fun to watch."

"Maybe, then maybe not," Laura said, rolling her eyes upward.

Kate laughed. "It's a shame your parents never got to enjoy Hillary. They've missed the thrill of being grandparents."

"They weren't dedicated parents, so being grandparents wouldn't have concerned them, either. If they had loved me, they wouldn't have gone back to England without letting me know where they were going. The only relative I know of is my mother's sister and she has never responded to my letters. My mother probably told her not to write me."

"I find it hard to understand how parents can disown their daughter because she married someone they disapprove of," Kate said. "They must have been very strict with you."

Laura nodded. "Oh, yes. Keep the family image, don't disgrace our name, do what is expected of you. Jeremiah was one of the most decent people I've met, certainly nicer than the pretentious people my parents had for friends. He wasn't 'a man of means or station,' they would say. Not good enough for me. I loved him and wanted to be with him, no matter what kind of life we had."

"Your parents weren't wealthy, were they?"

"No. They were upper middle-class, but certainly not wealthy. They wanted to mingle with the rich, but they only had the attitude, not the money. It was important to them that I marry well. When that didn't happen, they were disappointed and angry, so they left me to my fate."

"Does Hillary ask about them?"

"Not often," Laura answered. "I've told her what happened between me and my parents. She said she probably wouldn't like them, if they didn't like her father."

Kate leaned a little closer to Laura. "Don't turn your head, but do you see two men at the barber shop window looking down at us? Just sneak a quick glance."

Without being obvious, Laura positioned herself to look from the corner of her eye. "I believe you are correct. Shall we move on?"

"I'll carry your bag, so you can rest your fingers," Kate insisted.

"Thank you. We can take turns. Let's go north and look in the fancier shops? We haven't done that for some time."

"Why not?" Kate answered, rising to her feet. "Let's go see what we can't afford."

At the next corner, on a vacant lot, vendors sold produce to housekeepers shopping for their wealthy employers. Occasionally, too, a lady in fine clothes examined fruits and vegetables with her charge following behind, carrying the purchases. It was a market of convenience where the rich shopped at lower than store prices, without having to shop with poor people on Market Street.

Open wagons and rickety canvas shelters lined both sides of a central path, fifteen feet wide. Colorful vegetables and fruits, in various stages of maturity, hung from strings tied to nails. Piles of cabbages, yams, potatoes and melons filled wagons and carts.

Laura gave a passing glance into the market, while men touted their produce as the freshest available. They continued along Union Avenue, crossing Perry Street where buildings were clean and smart looking, with window frames and doors richly painted and adorned with polished brass hardware. Brick buildings were nicely tuck-pointed with stone steps that were unblemished and level. Shops advertised with gold letters on clean windows, shaded by colorful awnings. Laura and Kate felt a tad elegant in this part of town.

They stopped in front of Sperle's Shoe Salon to admire the newest in footwear. Kate looked at a pair of black Balmorals next to the open door, examining the front lacing and quality stitching. The heavy aroma of leather coming from the store penetrated her nostrils, reminding her of the cost of such merchandise.

"I like the black shoes farther back," Laura said. "The ones that lace along the side and pearl buttons down the front."

"That's a few months' wages," Kate said, leading them way from the store.

Slowly, they passed a bakery showing cookies, breads and frosted delights. Laura and Kate looked at each other, but continued walking. They passed women shopping in velvet jackets over waist-shirts, flared lightweight overcoats, and fur-topped Adelaide boots. Laura saw a woman wearing a light gray bonnet, with a black bavolet draping the back of her neck. She wanted one.

Laura heard her name being called from across the street. It was Mr. Bittel, the haberdasher, a short round man with red cheeks and white hair. He was standing in the doorway of his store, between two bay windows displaying men's hats, canes, shirts, ties and scarves. Above him was a green sign with gold letters running the width of the storefront. It read, *Bittel's Accessories for Gentleman.* He waved and smiled, as they proceeded down the street.

"Mr. Bittel is one of my clients," Laura said, waving back to him. "I've been doing his bookkeeping for almost two years. He's very nice to work for, always giving me a bit more than what I ask for my services, suggesting I take the extra for Hillary."

Kate grabbed Laura's arm and stopped in front of a photography studio displaying numerous pictures in a variety of Victorian frames. "Let's look in here for a moment." Kate set the canvas bag on the ground and massaged her fingers. She was amused by the pictures of men sitting in chairs, while their dutiful wives stood behind them, symbolic of their obedience. Pictures of infants in frilly bonnets were plentiful, as were images of families grouped together. In the center of the display was a large picture of John Lodge, Mayor of Alton. He looked like a confident leader, standing next to his large polished desk, with fingers of one hand resting inside his suit jacket.

Kate pointed at a picture in the second row. "Look at that man with the long beard, sitting in the high-back chair. Isn't he a pile of agony?"

Laura laughed. She understood the instant she saw the severe expression on his face. "Where is his wife, hiding behind the chair?"

"I would, if I was her," Kate chuckled.

"If we discard our manners, we could have fun with these pictures," Laura said, scanning the large display.

"I agree," Kate said, with an evil grin. "Let's be honest and rude." She pointed to a photo left of center in the display. "See that little monkey in the Christening dress? Can you imagine smiling with pride, while holding that?"

They laughed again and covered their mouths, somewhat embarrassed by their actions. Laura pointed to a photo, but couldn't talk until she stopped laughing. "Look in the back at the man with the bare chest, posed in a boxing stance. Is that picture supposed to show his athletic prowess, or the bulge in his pants?" Again, they laughed, more at their silliness than the photos.

"That one looks constipated," Kate said, pointing at a well-dressed man with beady eyes and a forced smile.

Soon, their sides were aching and their faces were warm and red. "I think it's time to be civil again," Laura said, wiping tears from her eyes.

Kate agreed, still maintaining a smile. "Let's go to the other side of the street to walk home."

Laura gripped the canvas bag and followed Kate to the edge of the street. "Time for us *old* Wildflowers to return to the real world."

CHAPTER SEVEN

Hillary walked amidst a stream of workers, sheltering herself from a bitter December wind. She was wrapped in a long, black wool coat, with a red hat pulled down over her ears. With each step, her white stockings flashed in the early morning light.

Upon entering the mill she opened her coat, eager to absorb any heat available, then stopped by a radiator to warm her hands. At the top of the stairs, Mrs. Gretsch was hanging a Christmas wreath on the wall, so it could be seen from below. Hillary put her hands close to the radiator one more time and started up the stairs. When she got to the landing, Mrs. Gretsch greeted her with a smile and told her she would be making stockings the next two days on machine twenty-five. Hillary was tired, and didn't relish the thought of standing all day.

She crossed the room, trying to ignore the filth floating in the air and cotton fibers tumbling around her feet. Her disappointment was lessened by the fact that machine twenty-five was next to a wide aisle that divided the second floor. From there, she could see a large area around her, making the work less confining. Hillary arrived at her knitter across the aisle from rows of spinning machines lined end-to-end, with double rows of cotton spools, one above the other. A thunderous klakity-klak, klakity-klak dominated the area.

Hillary saw Vera walking to machine twenty-one and waved to her. Vera kicked her machine, letting Hillary know she didn't want to stand all day, either.

Hillary worked diligently through the morning aware that time seemed to pass faster when she was busy. After filling her fourth wooden case with stockings, she looked up at the clock. It was almost noon and her stomach was growling. While closing the box, she noticed a commotion further down the main aisle. Three men were tending to a boy younger than herself. He squirmed and jumped, while moving in erratic circles. His muffled screams and body motion demonstrated that he was in pain. A man in a white shirt lifted the boy into his arms and carried him away, exposing blood on the boy's left hand and shirtsleeve. Hillary watched until they disappeared behind a row of machines. She wondered how bad it was this time.

At twelve o'clock, the powerful electric horns began blowing through the thunderclap of the machines. Hillary grabbed the draw-strings of her multi-flowered lunch bag and ran to Vera who was tugging at her lunch, trying to free it from her coat pocket. The newspaper wrapping tore, spilling peanuts on the floor.

"Yummy. Peanuts," Hillary remarked. "Hope I've got something you want."

"I'm sure ya do," Vera replied, picking up peanuts from the floor. "I don't like peanuts all that much. I'd trade 'em easy."

"Let's eat on a bench near the stairwell radiator," Hillary said, with a grin. "We can keep warm and watch Mrs. Gretsch eat her lunch of pickles, sausage and onions."

"Eeewwww," Vera wailed. "I just lost my appetite."

"More for me then," Hillary said, shaking her lunch bag in Vera's face. "Follow me."

At the end of the aisle, they ran for the stairwell, stopping at a gray wooden bench standing against the wall. "Let me sit on that side of the bench," Vera said, stepping around Hillary. "You can sit closer to the radiator and I won't have to look at Mrs. Gretsch." Vera spread her newspaper and food on the bench.

"Did you know a boy got hurt this morning?" Hillary asked, dumping her food onto the newspaper.

"No. I couldn't see anything except machines."

"He was crying and jumping about until three men took him away. I saw blood on his hand and arm. He must have been hurt bad. Do you want your pickle?"

"Yeah, but you can have half of it. The company will probably pretend the accident wasn't serious, but we'll hear what really happened within a week or two. I'll give ya a piece of cheese for part of your apple."

"Boys like toting scars," Hillary said. "It makes them feel tough and manly. Of course, they don't want to get hurt bad, just enough to get scarred, so they look tough. I'll give you my cornbread for your peanuts."

"Deal," Vera replied. "It's hard to understand boys. They do the dumbest things. Remember last year when Ed Roos was working barefoot on a spinner and got two toes ground in the gears? He went barefoot all summer, showing he had only three toes. Here, take this piece of cheese, too. He never went barefoot before then."

Hillary, the slower eater, finished her half apple and wrapped their garbage in the newspaper. "Now that I finished lunch, I'll enjoy your peanuts for dessert."

"I hate winter," Vera said. "When we're done eating lunch, it's too cold to go outside, so we're stuck looking at the machines or Mrs. Gretsch."

"I could bring a deck of cards," Hillary said, "but the horn would blow before we could finish one game."

"I have an idea! Since I bring my lunch wrapped in newspaper, you can read something to me, or better yet, you could teach me to read."

"Good idea," Hillary replied. She reached for the garbage filled newspaper and stopped abruptly, nodding her head toward Mr. Dragus's office. "Look over there." A girl about thirteen came out of the side door to his office. She stood there a moment and began to cry as she hurried down the rear stairwell.

"I wonder what she did wrong?" Hillary questioned. "Maybe she got fired?"

"Could be," Vera agreed. "I think Mr. Dragus likes boys better than girls. I rarely see a boy going into his office. It's mostly girls."

Late that afternoon, while removing a stocking from her machine, Vera glanced toward Hillary. The girls between them blocked her vision, so she leaned back for a better view. She was surprised to see Hillary standing motionless with her face buried in her hands. Vera continued watching, wondering whether Hillary had an accident. Vera moved toward Hillary and saw she had blood on her stockings. She realized what was happening.

Vera ran to Mrs. Gretsch two aisles over and brought her to Hillary.

Mrs. Gretsch recognized the problem, immediately. Girls nearby watched sympathetically, while pretending to be working. Mrs. Gretsch lifted Hillary from the box, as though she were a statue. Her face was still buried in her hands, crying from embarrassment.

Vera ran to Mr. Dragus's office for Kate.

Mrs. Gretsch guided Hillary to the women's washroom. Pina was inside cleaning the floor when they arrived. With her Prussian accent, Mrs. Gretsch told her to clean the blood from around machine number twenty-five.

Pina didn't understand what she was saying.

When Vera returned with Kate, Mrs. Gretsch had Vera take Pina to clean the area where Hillary had been working.

Kate took Hillary into her arms, trying to console her, but it did little to relieve her embarrassment. Next, they began tearing rags into strips, while Hillary cleaned herself at a line of decrepit porcelain sinks.

Kate told Hillary she would take her home, then asked Mrs. Gretsch to get Hillary's hat and coat, while she went to the office. Kate informed Frank about what had happened and promised to be back quickly.

Frank was pleased by the information. *Almost time to harvest,* he thought.

When Kate returned to the washroom, Pina had an arm around Hillary, telling her in broken English, "You woman now."

Hillary smiled, but wasn't consoled. As Kate led her from the washroom, Hillary looked down at the floor afraid the boys were looking at her and laughing. She wanted to get home.

CHAPTER EIGHT

Ten days before Christmas, Alton was under a blanket of snow and more was accumulating. Hillary and Laura approached St. Paul's with their heads down, protecting their eyes from the gusting wind and snow. The church bells rang, but were muted by the surrounding cover of snow. The garden on the east side of the church held a myriad of snow sculptures, as saintly statues resembled stalagmites and bushes became giant white mushrooms. Children ran around the perimeter of the church, laughing and squealing as they battled with snowballs.

Hillary was excited. Today, she would help decorate the Christmas tree that would stand near the altar. As well as being helpful, she believed it a privilege. They entered the vestibule, stamping snow off their boots and shaking their coats. Vera was waiting for them. Laura led the girls down the center aisle, echos of coughing and sneezing surrounding them. The girls followed Laura into a pew five rows from the front. After they knelt to pray, Hillary and Vera leaned against the seat with their heads together.

"Let's try to find Pina," Hillary whispered. "Maybe her mother will let her help decorate the tree."

Laura nudged Hillary with her elbow and gave her a stern look. The girls slid quietly onto the seat.

Father Adams emerged from the sacristy, as the organist began to play. His black shoes appeared, then disappeared, from front to back under his vestments, giving the appearance of a clapper in a bell. He blessed the congregation and proceeded with the service.

After mass, Laura and the girls remained seated, watching the parishioners pour through the back doors to Howard Street. Again, Hillary and Vera searched for Pina, but couldn't find her. When the pews in front of them emptied, the girls rushed to the altar, anxious to begin decorating.

Mr. Crowley and Mr. Storch carried a long worktable to the altar railing. Women followed with pine branches and all the trimmings for making wreaths and ornaments. Mrs. Crowley had made eight baskets of popcorn for stringing on the tree; double what was needed. She knew a large portion wouldn't survive the volunteers.

Tad Crowley, a slender boy of sixteen, carried a rectangular wooden box filled with cranberries to the worktable. It was obviously heavy for him, but he was attempting to impress Juanita and Arlene, two teenage volunteers. He put the box on the floor with a bang, hoping the girls would notice the weight he had carried. The girls looked at each other, smiling at the performance.

After much deliberation, three women decided where the tree should stand. When Father Adams returned from the sacristy, he disappointed the women by giving Mr. Crowley a different location.

Mr. Storch and his son, Peter, arrived with chairs and stools for the volunteers. Without hesitating, Hillary and Vera hopped onto stools at the table and began stringing cranberries and popcorn. Laura, Juanita, and Arlene sat with four other women, making pine crosses, wreaths and white paper ornaments. They placed red or white bows in the center of the pine crosses, representing the body of Christ.

As the crosses were completed, Tad and his father hung them between the windows over the Stations of the Cross. Tad insisted his father hold the ladder, while he worked from the top. He wanted Juanita and Arlene to notice his daring-do on the tall ladder.

In an hour, Hillary and Vera had completed two fifteen-foot strands of popcorn and cranberries. With pride, they stretched them out to show Laura and the other women. All but Juanita and Arlene, who pretended to be too busy to notice, complimented them on a job well done. Carefully, they carried the strands to the tree and began wrapping them among the branches. When they couldn't reach the higher boughs, Mr. Storch volunteered to finish the task.

"Time for a treat," Hillary declared, wiping her hands on her apron.

"Right, you are," Vera replied, bolting for the food table.

After enjoying a polite amount of cookies, popcorn and apple cider, Hillary and Vera left St. Paul's to meet Iris at Thompson's store. They were grateful it had stopped snowing. It was already too deep for their liking.

The girls plodded along Howard Street in snow as deep as their boots, then turned onto Union Avenue into a stiff wind that sent a chill across Hillary's shoulders. With both hands deep in her pockets, she tugged her coat tightly around herself, trying to contain what body heat there was. She watched the surface snow blow erratically over the street, creating miniature white tornadoes.

Except for a large black sleigh pulled very slowly by two powerful brown and white horses, the avenue was barren. The sleigh was filled with a heavy load of cut logs, explaining why the horses were moving so slow. Hillary braved the wind and lifted her head to look toward Thompson's store. "It looks like Iris's clothes, standing on the corner," she declared.

"Then Iris must be inside them," Vera responded with a laugh.

When they arrived at the corner, Iris announced that there was a large wreath on Thompson's door. The girls stepped up to the wreath, not to look at it, but to look beyond it in search of Mr. Thompson. He was standing near the door behind a rack of brooms and mops, amused by the three faces encircled by the wreath.

They noticed him when he stepped from behind the rack, dressed as always in black pants, black shoes and black leather cap, white apron and white shirt open at the neck. Surprised at finding him so close, they backed away in a hurry, hoping Mr. Thompson hadn't seen them looking for him.

Pretending not to see them, Mr. Thompson casually stepped behind the counter and slipped six pieces of butterscotch candy into his apron pocket. He moved slowly, looking in another direction until he got to the door and yanked it open. "What a surprise finding you girls here!" he said with a grin.

Embarrassed, the girls stood in the doorway like three grinning bowling pins. "We were looking at your wreath," Hillary declared, as they stepped inside.

"Sure you were," he replied, closing the door behind them. "Go over by the stove and warm yourselves for a spell."

The girls walked between shelves filled with canned foods and tins of cereal. In the center of the store, a black potbelly stove stood on a square metal sheet. Flames danced behind a window in the small door that had a silver-coiled handle.

Mr. Thompson suggested that the girls open their coats and let the heat warm the linings. He waited a few moments before stepping in front of them, his two fists extended. It was a game they had played many times before. "Which hand is it?" he asked.

"They're in your apron pocket," they yelled.

He laughed. "Looking at my wreath, were you? I think not." He handed them the candy and wished them a Merry Christmas.

After the girls warmed themselves, they thanked Mr. Thompson for the candy and marched out into the cold. They stood on the corner, braving the bitter wind, watching snow blowing around them. All three were wrapped in layers of clothing, peeking at each other between scarves and hats. Without saying a word, each knew what the other was thinking.

"My apartment?" Hillary suggested, pointing her gloved thumb upstairs. "We can play cards and drink hot tea."

"Sounds good to me," Vera said.

"Me, too," Iris joined in. "If we stay out here, we'll become girlcicles."

The girls climbed the stairs, stomping snow off their boots and pulling their gloves off. When they got to the landing, Tommy Dostle was leaving his apartment, carrying a bag of garbage. He extended it to the girls, wishing them a Merry Christmas.

"I'd take it," Vera said, "but it's not wrapped pretty."

"I'll have to remember that for next year," he replied, flashing a devilish grin.

Hillary stopped at her door and beat her mittens against her leg to remove the snow. She did the same with her hat before starting to unbutton her coat and sweater.

"You got that key down in your apron pocket?" Vera asked.

"Of course," Hillary responded. "I won't lose it from there."

"By the time you undress, we'll have to go home," Iris said.

"I've got the key. Hold your pantaloons." Hillary unlocked the door and stepped into the apartment, with her friends following. They put their boots on a small rug next to the stove, but kept their coats on in the cold room.

Hillary put paper and small pieces of wood into the stove to start a fire.

Iris and Vera were at the window, looking down at Union Avenue and the blowing snow. A loose pane of glass rattled under the wind's force.

"Make it a big fire," Iris insisted. "The wind is still blowing hard."

"While I'm trying to keep a fire going, will someone put water in the tea kettle and get cups from the cabinet?" Hillary asked.

"I'll do it," Vera said, crossing the room.

Iris took a book from the table next to Hillary's chair. "Is this geography book from school?"

"Yes," Hillary answered, adding wood to the fire. "I like reading about different places and pretending to be there. I plan to travel when I'm rich."

"When you're rich?" Vera questioned, filling the kettle with water.

"When I'm twenty and beautiful," Hillary said. "I'll go where rich men are and apply Iris's lesson on how to marry a rich man."

"Don't forget to breathe deep," Iris yelled from the window.

"Yeah! And don't forget to wiggle your bait," Vera added. The girls laughed, as they created more ideas for successful courting.

After twenty minutes, the fire in the stove warmed the room enough so they could remove their coats. Iris carried the geography book to the kitchen table and stood it on end.

Hillary went to the food cabinet next to the stove and discovered there weren't any cookies. She looked at the lower half of the cabinet and found two apple dumplings on a plate. "No cookies," she announced, "but we have two apple dumplings."

"That's a shame," Vera said. "Iris will have to go without."

"Not on your life, barrel britches!" Iris yelled, sliding onto a chair at the end of the table.

"All of us can have two thirds of one," Hillary said. "I'll cut them, so we'll each have an equal amount."

"What's two thirds?" Iris asked. She sat back in the chair, waiting for an answer.

"I'll show you when I get to the table." Hillary asked Vera to pour the hot water into the cups and dip the tea ball, so the tea wouldn't be too strong. She carried the plate of dumplings and a knife to the table and placed them in front of Iris.

Hillary made knife marks on the dumplings, so Iris would understand three parts of one.

"That was easy," Iris said.

Hillary continued to use the knife to show Iris and Vera other portions of one, so they would understand more thoroughly.

"Time to travel," Vera demanded, rapping the geography book with her knuckles.

"Let's hop into our balloon and drift through the clouds to Africa," Hillary suggested.

"Africa has wild animals. I'll stay in the balloon and eat one half of my two thirds of the dumplings," Iris said, proud of her new knowledge of fractions.

"Very good," Hillary said. "You learned fast."

Vera proposed they open the book to any page and pretend to be there, rather than trying to choose a country.

"I agree," Iris said. "Just open the book."

"You do it, Vera," Hillary insisted. "You have the book in your hand."

Vera slid a fingernail into the side of the book and parted the pages. She looked at the name of the country at the top of the page, but couldn't pronounce it. Hillary stepped to her side. "Prussia," she declared.

"Where is Prussia?" Iris asked. "Lay the book on the table, so I can see."

"I'm not sure," Hillary said. "Let's look for it on the map. Kate told me Mrs. Gretsch came from Prussia."

"Eeeewwww," Vera screamed, slamming the book shut. "I'm not going where she came from."

Laura entered the apartment with her coat collar raised and her scarf across her nose. "Hello, Mrs. Cook!" Vera and Iris shouted.

"Are the church decorations finished?" Hillary asked, walking toward her.

"Everything is ready for Christmas. I'm glad you girls are here and have a fire going. It's bitter cold outside."

"We came here to get warm and have cookies and tea, but there were only two dumplings."

"If you girls want to make cookies, I'll help," Laura said. "It's only 4:30 and I have the makings."

Vera dropped the geography book on the table and the three girls gathered around Laura.

"Hillary, help the girls get the pans and ingredients, while I wash my hands."

"I'll make one-third of the cookies," Iris said, glowing with pride.

CHAPTER NINE

At two o'clock in the afternoon, John was below deck getting ready to go ashore. He jammed the padlock shut, locking his tools in a large metal chest welded to the ship's steel floor. He grabbed his coat from the back of a chair and locked the tool room door, then climbed the open metal stairs to the deck, each step echoing off the steel-plated walls. Once on deck, John looked at the sky to estimate the oncoming weather. Puffy dark clouds coming from the west rolled out over Delaware Bay. John was sure it was going to snow. The white undersides of seagulls seemed to shine, as they glided under the dark gray sky.

Gordon Ray, the ship navigator, waved to John from behind a pilothouse window. John displayed a broad smile, because Gordon knew he would be with Kate tonight. A burst of cold December air shot across the deck, sending a chill through his body. He turned up his coat collar and headed for the ramp and solid ground.

John walked along the dock to Crossroads Shipping, a two-story brick warehouse with offices on the second floor. Just inside the entrance door, there was a meeting room where the men gathered for coffee and conversation. The rest of the ground floor was a massive storage area.

To avoid the brunt of the wind, John stayed close to the building wall, walking with his head down and holding his coat collar closed.

He was hurrying to the paymaster's office to get his wages and wait in the meeting room for Karl Polen. Every payday, John and Karl enjoyed a couple of beers together before going home. John arrived at the building entrance, as two men in black jackets and black knit hats walked out. One of the men was counting money in an open envelope. John grabbed the metal door before it slammed shut, then raced up the wooden stairs, two at a time.

Jaymes Mameister, the paymaster, was standing behind his desk, leaning against a row of file cabinets and reading a shipping news magazine. Pictures of cargo ships and tugboats decorated the walls. He saw John through the door window and had his pay envelope in hand when John walked in.

"This is the quickest I've seen you off the ship," Jaymes said, handing the envelope to John. "Count it, and sign for it."

John counted the money. "Didn't have as much to do today. Thought I'd exit fast and beat the crowd to your office."

Jaymes sat in his chair. "That you did."

"The money's right," John said, bending over to sign the pay sheet on the desk. "Enjoy your Christmas and I'll see you soon after."

Jaymes implied the same with a casual salute as John walked out of the office.

While waiting for Karl, John went downstairs to the meeting room for a cup of coffee. It was a large square room filled with tobacco smoke and noise. The walls and ceiling were unpainted plaster, marred with pen and pencil markings, and three bare light bulbs hung through the center of the room. Some of the men stood along the walls, while others sat at two rectangular wooden tables. The laughter and chatter of deep male voices reverberated through the room. John went to a small iron stove in the corner to get warm and have a cup of coffee. A single shelf laden with a variety of coffee cups and mugs was mounted on the wall over a cold water sink next to the stove. John grabbed a cup and looked inside. It appeared to be clean, so he lifted the metal coffee pot from the stove and filled his cup. As he was taking his first drink, he saw Karl Polen enter the building and go upstairs without looking into the meeting room. He took another drink of the bitter coffee before putting his half-filled cup in the sink.

John walked across the room, acknowledging men he knew with a nod, or a wave, then went upstairs to join Karl. As he walked toward Mameister's office, he looked through the door window. Tom Bettis and another man were standing with Karl in front of Jaymes Mameister's desk. John didn't recognize the third man until he got closer. John turned and quickly stepped to the side, so he couldn't be seen from the office. He retreated down the stairs and went out of the building.

"Gotta think," John muttered. "Why is Tyler Sharpe here? Is he visiting or what?" John walked to the end of the building to wait for Karl. If Tyler came his way, he would walk to the back of the building until Tyler was gone. John hoped Karl would come out alone, so he could learn what Karl knew about Tyler Sharpe. He paced back and forth. Men came out of the building at different times, walking past John on their way to town. He chatted briefly with a couple of his crewmen, but always kept an eye on the door. When the men left, John began pacing again. A short time later, Karl came out and John waved to him.

Karl was looking at John in a strange way. "Why are you out here?" he asked in his deep voice. "When I didn't see you in the meeting room, I thought you went home."

"I had to wait for you out here. Let's walk, while we talk." John turned to walk alongside Karl. "Was my name mentioned when you were in Mameister's office?"

"Yeah. Someone asked who is the biggest loafer in our crew, and I mentioned your name."

John laughed. "Thanks for the kindness." It appeared to John that Karl hadn't heard about the murder. "Who was that guy in the office with you? Can't say I've seen him here."

Karl began rubbing his chin. "His name is Tylerrrr ... something or other. I can't recall.

"Tyler Sharpe?"

"Yeah. That would be it." He looked at John, "You know him?"

"Those bushy eyebrows and that scar on his chin make him easy to remember," John said. "Do you know why he was in the office?"

Karl slid his hands into his coat pockets. "He bought a piece of the company. We're going to have another boss."

John's strength drained from his body. He felt weak and disorganized. "A partner?" he repeated. "That means Tyler will be living in Alton."

"To be sure. He bought a house at the north end of town."

"Let's not go to Doyle's," John suggested, pointing in another direction. "I want to talk to you where it's quiet. The Lighthouse Bar is just around the corner. It won't be busy at this hour and we can sit in a booth."

Karl studied John's face. He had never seen John so nervous. "I'm listening."

"What I'm about to tell you is true, and I want you to tell my story to Kate tonight." They crossed the street quickly then entered the small bar, with eight tables in the center of the room and six booths against the walls. Every table and booth had a candle stuck in a liquor bottle, with wax dripping down its side. The only customers were a middle-aged couple sitting in a booth, and two men standing at the bar talking to the bartender. John went directly to a booth in the corner of the room while Karl went for two beers.

When Karl got to the booth, he slid a beer in front of John and lit the candle in the bottle. "On with the story," Karl said.

"It's almost three o'clock. I'll tell you fast, so I can move on." John took a drink from his mug and began his tale.

"Seven years ago, I worked for South Line Shipping, a mid-sized company in New Orleans. They only shipped to American ports along our southern coast, but it made a good profit. It was owned by, Tyler and Jesse Sharpe, two brothers who were never apart at work or play. They were good businessmen, but tough and ornery." John wiped the back of his hand across his mouth.

"I was there only four months when I had my night in hell. It was payday, the 15th of the month. Except for a few dollars in my pocket, I kept my money under my shirt in a money belt tied around my waist. I walked to the Delta Saloon, a popular place for a game of poker. The Delta wasn't fancy, just a beat up old pub. I was standing at the bar, having a private conversation with a tall guy named, Haggar. He wasn't a friend, just someone I had seen in there before. We were talking about women, work, and different ports we had been to through the years. On our left, next to the bar, there was a high stakes poker game with a lot of whiskey drinking. Two of the players were Tyler and Jesse Sharpe. Haggar seemed interested in the game, because he kept looking over at their table. It was Jesse's fat wallet that had caught Haggar's eye. We were finishing our third or fourth beer when Haggar took my cap from the bar and placed it on his head. He liked it and offered me three times what I'd paid for it, plus a steak dinner at a restaurant down the street. I knew I could replace it, so I agreed. That was a big mistake, because my name was sewn inside the cap."

"Right, like most of us do, in case they get lost on ship."

"Exactly." John glanced around the room before continuing. "Our mugs were empty, so Haggar bought two more beers. After a couple of swigs, Jesse Sharpe stood up at the card table, saying he was going to the outhouse, then went out the side door. Suddenly, Haggar said, he was hungry and wanted to eat now. I thought it odd since he just bought two beers, but he was buying, so I agreed and followed him to the front door. When we got outside, it was dark. Haggar suggested I wait for him, while he went to the outhouse. I continued across the street and stood there."

John paused to swig his beer and look around the room. "A couple minutes later, Haggar was hurrying from the side of the saloon. Light from inside the saloon appeared behind him, which meant someone else was going in or out of the Delta's side door. Whoever it was, he started yelling for Tyler. Haggar ran toward me. He slapped something in my hand, hit the front of my shirt with the other hand, and kept running until he disappeared between two frame buildings. I didn't know what the hell he was doing. What he put in my hand felt wet and sticky, so I walked over to the street lamp to see what it was. It was money with blood on it. Then I saw blood on my shirt where Haggar had slapped me. Now, I could hear a bunch of people going out the side of the saloon. Someone yelled to Tyler that Jesse had been murdered. Moments later, I heard Tyler scream, 'Find John Hanley. I'll cut his filthy throat.' I was dumbfounded. Why me? Then I realized Haggar hadn't been wearing my old hat when he ran by me. He must have lost it by the outhouse. Or left it. And Tyler must have seen my name in the hat. So there I was, bloody money in my hand, blood on my shirt, and my cap with the body. I figured my life wasn't worth a clamshell. I knew if I were caught, Tyler's friends would hold me, while Tyler stuck me with a knife or shot me. There wouldn't be any judge or jury, I guarantee you. I slipped between the two buildings behind me and ran out of town as fast as I could. Eventually, I hopped a freight train that took me to Baton Rouge where I stayed a day, and bought clothes and a train ticket. Two days later, I was in Savannah."

"I'm glad that never happened to me," Karl laughed. "I couldn't run fast enough to get away." With only two gulps, he drank the last of the beer in his mug. "Your story made me thirsty." Karl slid out of the booth, picked up the two empty mugs and carried them to the bar. Only one man was talking to the bartender. The other man had left with a woman who came in after him. When Karl returned, he sat in the booth and pushed a beer toward John. "Anyone that knows you isn't going to believe you killed someone for money."

John thanked Karl for the beer and kind words, and then stared at him. "This may be our last drink together, old friend."

Karl pursed his lips and tilted his head to the side. "I hope not, but if it is—it's been nice knowing ya. I wish you and Kate the best a luck." The wiggling flame of the candle between them caused shadows to jump on their faces. "Do you need help getting out of town?"

"No, but please do what I asked, and tell Kate what happened. She'll be at Doyle's by eight o'clock. I'm sure Tyler will be spending his leisure time in our part of town where he can find a card game. Sooner or later, our paths would cross. Besides, if he hears my name from someone tonight, he'll probably be looking for me straight away. And if he didn't come after me personally, he'd contact the sheriff and get the law after me."

"How are ya leaving town?" Karl asked. "There ain't no train until tomorrow. By then, someone may be waiting at the station looking for you."

John leaned back in the booth. "I'll go to the stables and buy a horse and riding gear. They always have horses and saddles for sale. I'll ride as far north as I can this evening, then get a train tomorrow. Don't say anything about this to anyone, except Kate."

Karl drained his glass again with two large gulps. "You have my word that I'll be at Doyle's tonight."

"I'd better get moving." John drank some beer and left the mug a third full. "I have to get my money out of the bank, then go to my apartment and pack some clothes. Thanks for your help and the beers."

Karl blew out the candle, as they left the booth. When they got outside, they shook hands and walked in different directions.

An hour later, John patted the bulge inside his dark blue jacket assuring himself his money was still there. He was nervous, and knew he would remain so until he was riding out of Alton.

He figured it was almost five o'clock because the sun was slipping below the western horizon. He turned north into a dirt alley behind stores along Union Avenue, taking long, quick strides past boxes and garbage cans lining the alley. Black steel bars were over many of the rear doors and windows. A gray cat jumped onto a wooden crate and watched him walk by. He continued north, counting the number of streets he passed, calculating his nearness to Whalen's Stables. A few blocks ahead, he could see the open field and corral that separated Alton's rich from the poor.

When he walked out of the alley into the field, he looked back, relieved no one was following. He angled toward a weathered log house that served as the stable office. A pulsing lantern shone through its windows. The stable and barn were just a few yards from the office.

As John stepped into the office, a man sitting behind the desk spat a stream of brown tobacco juice into a brass cuspidor. He wiped his mouth with both of his sleeves and removed his booted feet from the top of the desk. The nameplate on his desk read, James Demoot.

Pictures of horses and riders hung on the walls. A display cabinet across from the entrance door exhibited blue, white and red ribbons among tall, shiny trophies.

Mr. Demoot, who didn't appear all that ambitious, looked up at John. "Kin I help ya?"

John smiled at the laid-back character. "I'm interested in buying a horse."

"At this hour?" James asked. He rested his forearms on the desk and waited for an answer.

"What's wrong with this hour? You do sell horses, don't you?"

"Yep. Just seems like a late hour to be buying a horse, that's all. Got a couple of good horses, too." Mr. Damoot removed a gray ledger from the center drawer of his desk and flipped through the pages until he found what he wanted. His index finger slid down the page until he got to the name *Tully*. His finger slid past another name with a pencil line through it, then stopped at the name, *Shoby*. "I got two mares that are full of fire. You couldn't go wrong buying either one and they're the same price."

John leaned over the desk and looked at the ledger. "You say both are good horses?"

"I'd stake my reputation on them."

John was curious as to what that reputation would be. "I like the name 'Tully', so I'll take her. What's her price?"

"Says here in the book, seventy-five dollars, including the saddle, blanket and bridle." Mr. Damoot leaned back in his chair and reached for a bag of Bull Durham Tobacco from his shirt pocket.

Knowing he had to buy a horse, John had put a little more than a hundred dollars in his wallet, so he wouldn't need to take money from inside his coat. "Got it even," John said, laying his money on the desk.

"What's your name?" James asked, pulling a receipt book from his desk drawer.

"John Moore. That's M-O-O-R-E."

"I knew a guy named Moore," James said, with a slow drawl.

John rolled his eyes and ignored what Mr. Damoot was prattling about.

With great difficulty, James scratched with a pen until he filled in the blanks on the receipt. Without looking at it, John took the receipt from him and stuffed it in his jacket pocket. Mr. Damoot lit a black railroad lantern and led John out the door into the darkness and toward the stable. James stopped at the third stall and hung the lantern on a spike driven into a post.

"This is Tully," James said, pointing to a brown and white mare. "Might as well get acquainted. Like I said, she's a good one."

John was surprised. Tully was much better than what he expected. It was going to be difficult for him to give her up after a few hours. "I plan to ride her for about an hour. I'll turn out the lantern when I leave."

"Do ya plan on boarding her here?"

John lied. "Sure. I'll be in tomorrow to make the arrangements."

"This is her bridle," he said, pointing to the post. "Her saddle and blanket are in the tack room. Her name's hanging over 'em. Have a good ride and I'll see ya later." He turned away from John and strolled back to the office.

John lifted the bridle and reins from the other side of the post where the lantern hung. He entered the stall and patted her rump, while talking softly to her. She jerked her head twice and watched him, wide-eyed and nervous. "Easy girl. I'm your friend," he whispered, while gently stroking her neck. Her feet shuffled on the straw bedding until she calmed. He slipped the bit into her mouth and buckled the brown leather bridle, then walked her outside to saddle her under the moonlight. He tied her to a fence-post and went back to the tack room for her saddle and blanket.

John examined the fatigued riding equipment and decided it was good enough for his purposes. After saddling her, he went inside the stable to turn off the lantern. When he returned, he faced his mare and stroked her neck again. "We're getting as close to Baltimore as we can tonight," he said. "I'll try and find you a good home before I get on a train."

At the mill, Kate was in high spirits as she locked the office door. She held the handrail and descended the stairs thinking of John and his long stay in Alton, well past Christmas. She accidentally rubbed her coat against the dirty wall, causing flakes of paint to stick to her coat sleeve. She entered the dark prairie, brushing them off.

Being Monday, most shops on Union Avenue were closed at this hour, making the avenue darker and less active. The sound of jingling bells and a creaking sleigh got louder, as it slowly approached her from behind. Kate entered Doyle's, and was enveloped by a thin haze of tobacco smoke. She saw Meg getting drinks at the bar and a pinch on her bottom by a passing patron. The green leaves and red berries of holly spiraled around the wooden columns at each end of the bar. *Merry Christmas* was painted on the mirrored wall behind it.

Kate sat at a table by the window to watch for John and be entertained by the passing pedestrians. She wore a brown winter-weight skirt and a beige cotton blouse, with lace trimming on the collar to please John. He liked those colors with her brown hair. A black knit shawl covered her back and shoulders. She pinched her cheeks to give them color, then waited.

Emil Kurst was at a table with his wife and Bob Grast, of Grast and Son Funeral Parlor. Tom Nauz was playing cards in the corner of the room, with his attorney friend, Donald Wagoner, and two other men she didn't know. It was a popular table for cards. It was under a gas lamp, away from much of the floor traffic.

Meg delivered drinks to a table near the front door and walked through a fresh cloud of cigar smoke. She fanned her face with the serving tray, making her way to Kate. "Evening, my dear," Meg greeted. "Order now, or wait for John?"

"I need something to warm me, so I'll order now. Make it tea, with rum on the side. Might as well bring two boiled eggs and a shaker, too."

"Got it," Meg said, walking away.

Kate gazed beyond the window to the other side of the street where Frankie and his brother, Eli, were walking toward home, toting a paper or two. She scrutinized the boys in their tattered clothes. *Rags,* she thought. *Everything on them is raggedy. I don't want children like this. John is right. A farm out West would be better.*

Kate wondered if Frankie had his corncob pipe in his pocket, then looked at Eli's left hand, a mitten covering what she knew was only a thumb. Four of his fingers were cut off by a metal stamping machine when he was eleven-years-old. The company didn't need him anymore.

She searched the street for John, wondering why he was late.

"Here ya go," Meg said, returning to the table. "Hot tea, sip a rum, two chickens and a shaker."

"Thanks! Hot tea should warm me up in no time. It works better than the rum."

"Look's like your man's late?" Meg remarked. "Not like him to be late." She turned and headed for the card game.

Kate's first sip of tea generated a rush of heat through her body. She closed her eyes and concentrated on its warming effect, then cracked an egg on the table and began peeling it. Her thoughts returned to leaving Alton and removing herself from abused children and that pig, Frank Dragus.

As the door opened, she looked up. It was Mrs. Gretsch and her husband Rupert, a tall, slender man with a little box mustache. Mrs. Gretsch nodded to Kate and she nodded in return. She watched them select a table in the center of the room where it was warmest. Kate assumed it must have been a special occasion since they rarely mixed socially.

It was well after eight o'clock when Meg returned. "Want something else?" she asked, concerned.

"Tea and rum the same way. If he isn't here soon, I'll go home."

"Don't know of any trouble at the docks," Meg assured her. "If there was, I'd a heard about it here."

Kate agreed. "Perhaps there was a problem with the ship. Lord knows, there's always something to fix on those freighters."

Even though it turned cold, Kate finished her tea. She looked around the room, hoping to find someone who might know of John's whereabouts. Emil and Ida Kurst waved to her from a table near the bar. When she raised her hand to respond, someone entered the pub. It was Karl Polen. Karl was as wide as a redwood and strong as an ox. His coat collar was turned up behind his thick neck. From under a brown leather cap, he intensely stared at Kate, walking toward her without acknowledging anyone else. He pulled a chair from the table and slammed himself down.

"You seem to have come with a purpose," Kate remarked. "Is there a problem? Is John hurt?"

Meg returned with Kate's tea and rum. "Anything for you, Karl?" Meg sensed that Karl was bringing news about John.

"Naw," Karl mumbled in his raspy voice. "Just stopped to see Kate a minute."

Meg gave Kate a puzzled look before walking away.

"He ain't hurt that I know of," Karl answered, "But there is a problem."

Kate peered into his hazel eyes. "Such as?" She watched him turn down his coat collar and unbuttoned his coat. "Tell me!" Kate insisted. "John was to be here at eight o'clock, but never showed."

"Sure, I'll tell you. Better down that rum first. It might help." He pushed his cap back on his head and gritted his teeth.

Kate was getting nervous. She drank the rum and sat back in her chair, her hands clasped together on her lap, waiting for Karl to explain.

Karl leaned closer to her before beginning his tale. In a hushed voice, he revealed what John wanted her to know.

Kate rocked gently to and fro, her eyes expressionless. She looked past Karl and out onto the street. She believed what Karl had just told her, but didn't want to believe John was gone.

"He'll be back for you," Karl assured her, trying to lift her spirits.

"He'll be back when?" she questioned. "A month? A year?"

Karl felt sorry for Kate. He knew she missed John when he was at sea for weeks at a time. Now, it was even worse. "Want me to walk you home?"

"No, thanks. I'll be fine." She thanked Karl for coming to her, as he left. Kate began to feel uneasy, as questions mounted. She decided to go home and think things through.

She sipped the last of her tea and stood to put her coat on, lingering until Meg looked in her direction. Meg was standing with her arms resting on the bar while the bartender placed drinks on her tray. Kate signaled Meg that she had left money on the table and walked out.

After receiving such shocking news, the cold night air was stimulating. She thought of the possibility of never seeing John again. *Will he come back? Am I alone again?* She was dumbfounded by the sudden turn of events, anxious to get home to ponder her future.

It was almost ten o'clock when she climbed the dimly lit stairs to her one room apartment. The small gas lamp down the hall provided barely enough light to see the keyhole. She pushed the door forward and stepped on a piece of folded white paper. She bent over and grabbed it quickly, then closed herself in total darkness. She was sure it was a note from John.

She reached out, groping for a kerosene lamp on a small table next to the door. After finding the lamp, she slid her hand across the table for a box of stick matches. Kate removed the glass stack to light the wick and held the paper at a slight angle to the flame. Her anxiety faded as she read, *I haven't done anything wrong. I'll be back for you. I love you, John.*

Kate carried the lamp and note to the kitchen table and dropped into a chair, relieved to have heard from John. Nevertheless, the same question began to nag her. *He'll be back when?* She read the note again, and held it over the lantern's flame. She carried the burning paper to the kitchen sink, trailing the flames behind her hand, so she wouldn't get burnt. She turned on the tap and washed the ashes down the drain. There were three knocks on her door. Kate moved quietly, wondering if it was John. She placed her ear near the door, listening for a familiar sound. The three knocks were repeated. "Who's there?"

"Wade Widner!" was the response. "John's foreman at Crossroads Shipping. Sorry to bother you at this hour, but I need to talk to you, *now.*"

Kate had met Wade twice when she was with John, once at Wade's birthday party in Juul's Scandia restaurant, and again last year at a Christmas party. She remembered him being soft-spoken and polite, someone she could trust. She considered him one of John's better acquaintances.

"One moment," Kate replied. She turned the key to unlock the door, then stepped back so he could enter.

Wade was a tall, husky man, filling every inch of his long black overcoat. His graying hair and red cheeks gave him a distinguished demeanor. He was two or three years older than John, so she guessed him to be about forty.

"Good evening, Kate," he greeted, entering the apartment. "Wish I was here under more favorable circumstances."

"Evening," she replied. "Have a seat at the table, while I start a fire in the stove. I'd have one going, but I just got home."

"I know. I followed you." Crossing the room, he examined the one room apartment. He was impressed with the cleanliness of an apartment in such a rundown building. The table was draped with a faded, white oilcloth that needed replacing. He noticed small corners of flowered wallpaper curling away from the wall near the window. He pulled a chair from the table and watched Kate bend over to gather bits of wood from a large tin box. "I was waiting for John near Doyle's, though I was sure he wouldn't show."

Clutching scraps of wood, Kate stood upright and turned toward him. She waited nervously, as he lowered himself onto the fragile kitchen chair, afraid it would collapse under his weight. "I was there from seven-thirty until you saw me leave. I didn't know what to think."

"Do you know the story about John and the Sharpe brothers?" Wade asked, watching Kate's every move. He had been interested in her since the first night they'd met.

"Yes," she replied. "I learned about it tonight. He's innocent."

"This evening, Tyler Sharpe saw John's name on a ship's roster. He got real excited and assigned three of us to look for him. I was sent to find you, and get what information I could. When I saw you sitting at a table waiting for him, I assumed you didn't know where he is."

"John was to meet me at eight o'clock, but he never showed," Kate said, putting bits of wood and paper in the stove. She ignited a stick-match against the side of the matchbox and lit the crumpled paper mixed with wood. "I can't tell you anything 'cause this is news to me." She turned to face Wade. "I don't know when, or whether, I'll ever see him again."

Wade turned up the wick in the oil lamp, so he could get a better look at Kate.

His eyes revealed his interest in her, but she was confident he wouldn't make advances. She had recognized Wade's feelings for her in the past, but he had always remained a gentleman.

"I've always liked John and I was very disturbed when I learned of the accusations. I don't believe John would kill anyone."

"I know, you two had a good relationship," Kate said, placing the stove lid over the fire. She walked to the table and sat across from him. "In all honesty, I don't know where he is."

"He won't be able to return to Alton without being seen," Wade warned. "The company will be watching for him, as well as keeping an eye on you."

Kate slid the lamp toward the end of the table. "Would you care for some tea?"

"No, thanks," he replied and stood to leave. "I've been keeping you up as it is. I just stopped by to let you know the company is looking for John."

When they reached the door, Kate looked up at him. "I'm sure ya understand I won't be squealing, if John does return."

"I only came to tell you the company's thinking on the matter." Wade nodded and smiled, then stepped into the dark hallway.

CHAPTER TEN

The noisy machines and thirty-eight stairs to the second floor weren't bothering Hillary today. It was Christmas Eve, and all was well in her world. With a combination of quick steps, skipping and smiling at everyone, Hillary made her way toward the row of knitting machines along the outer wall. It was still dark beyond the windows and she could see her reflection get larger and larger, as she neared the wall. She walked down the aisle between windows and knitters, wishing everyone a Merry Christmas. Mary Claire and Rosemary were laughing so hard over a funny story about Mrs. Gretsch, they returned Hillary's greeting with only a quick wave of the hand.

Next to them was Ellie Tuzik. She was standing in front of her machine with her arms crossed over her chest, as though warming her upper body. Dark skin surrounded her sunken brown eyes, and her tiny teeth leaned in different directions. Hillary wondered how many body bruises caused by her father were hidden under her clothing. She gave Ellie a Christmas greeting and a hug as she passed. Ellie's robust smile showed how thrilled she was that someone had acknowledged her with affection.

Hillary pressed the red button to start her machine, reminding herself to keep her mind off Christmas and be careful where she put her hands. She knew that machine couldn't do great harm, but swinging metal parts could give her hands a painful whack.

At eleven o'clock, Hillary glanced between the oily machines for Vera, but couldn't find her. They had planned to eat lunch near Mr. Dragus's office, while exchanging Christmas presents. Her search for Vera was interrupted by the sound of someone wailing.

Ellie was standing on her wooden box, bending backwards in front of the knitter. She jumped from the box and dropped to her knees to reduce the severe cramping in her back. Ellie had reached her limit of endurance and began sobbing from intense pain.

Mrs. Gretsch came and massaged her back, then with little effort, lifted Ellie into her arms and carried her past the machines into another room. Heads turned left and right, as girls nearby paused to look at each other, their eyes expressing mutual sympathy for Ellie, who lived a life more wretched than theirs.

At twelve o'clock, the powerful red horn mounted high on the brick wall began blaring the signal for lunch. Girls began chatting immediately, making up for their long silence. Most were discussing Ellie as they filed past rows of abandoned knitters, recalling other occasions when she had to leave her work because she wasn't strong enough to maintain the pace. They knew that one day soon, she would be fired and her father would punish her severely.

Hillary saw Vera sitting on the bench, unwrapping her lunch. They had selected that bench, hoping to catch Kate leaving the office, so they could invite her to eat with them. Vera spread her newspaper on the bench and displayed her food for bartering. Hillary spread open the drawstring of her lunch bag and dumped the contents onto the newspaper.

"I saw Mrs. Gretsch carrying Ellie down the aisle this morning," Vera said. "She's near skinny as a rail."

"I know. I was working near her when she fell to the floor, crying. Her back was cramping so bad she had to quit working. I think she'll lose her job, if she hasn't already."

"I don't think she's strong enough to work," Vera remarked. "I wish she could leave her father and live with someone who would be kind to her."

The girls turned their heads, as the door to Mr. Dragus's office opened. It was Frank. As he walked past the girls, Hillary called to him, a bold move she normally wouldn't make. "Excuse me, Mr. Dragus, is Miss Moran in the office?"

He stopped and looked at the girls, focusing mainly on Hillary. "No. She won't be back until three o'clock." He started to leave, then returned and squatted before them. He placed his hand on Hillary's thigh and wished them a Merry Christmas.

Vera took a loud bite from her apple and began chewing. Hillary gave her a chastising glance, but its meaning wasn't absorbed.

"Mrs. Gretsch tells me you girls do excellent work," Frank said, dwelling on Hillary's pretty face. "Hard work builds good character and a healthy body."

"We're extra careful," Hillary replied, ignoring the cigar smell that surrounded him. "If a person works hard, time seems to go faster."

"I think so, too," Vera said, swinging her legs.

Frank agreed with them, prolonging the small talk so he could continue to feel Hillary's soft, shapely thigh. He began creating mental images of her youthful body, as he spoke to the girls. She excited him, but he didn't want other employees to see him overly attentive to a girl so young. "I'd better leave, so you girls can finish your lunch," he said abruptly, then returned to his office.

Frank sat at his desk, staring at the center drawer before opening it. He removed a small white envelope from under a brown ledger and retrieved an old picture of a young girl hanging laundry in his back yard. "Merry Christmas, Megan, wherever you are," he muttered.

He closed his eyes, recalling the day Megan arrived at his house to assist Mrs. Oakley with the housekeeping chores. She was a fifteen-year-old orphan from Ireland, arriving with just the clothes on her back. A small storage room in the basement was converted into a bedroom for her.

Frank's parents worked Megan and Mrs. Oakley every day and often into the night for room and board, and a small stipend. His parents often referred to Megan as the bastard, and ordered Frank to refrain from being friendly to her, lest she think she could become an equal. Frank liked Megan and thought it a cruel name for her, especially since his parents didn't really know her background.

With his thumb, Frank gently stroked Megan's image on the picture, thinking of that special day four months after she arrived. They were alone in the house and he needed a button sewn onto his shirt cuff. When he arrived at Megan's bedroom with the shirt flung over his shoulder, she was standing nude at her dresser, brushing her hair.

Frank stopped and stared.

Megan smiled at him through the mirror and continued brushing her hair.

His seventeen-year-old body responded to the most exciting vision of his young life.

The love affair that followed overshadowed the abuse they both received from his oppressive parents. They had a secret, a daring life they kept to themselves, loving whenever they could. Together, they were "somebody." Frank could still remember the smell of her hair and the feel of her young, frail arms and thighs caressing him as they made love. He never wanted it to end. Yet, after one year in their house, and without any explanation, his parents sent Megan to a home in Ohio. Frank turned slowly in his chair and glared up at his parents' picture hanging on the wall. "I never forgave you for taking her from me," he said bitterly.

CHAPTER ELEVEN

It was a tradition at St. Paul's to celebrate Christmas Mass after sunset, when the lanterns and candles shined most brightly. Laura and Hillary arrived early, so they could sit near the front. As they walked up the center aisle, Laura looked for a pew with space for three people. *Habits are hard to break*, she thought, realizing her mistake. *Even after five years, I still think there are three of us.* Hillary followed her into a pew where there was space for two. They watched Mr. Crowley and Mr. Storch light candles along the outer walls, as the organist practiced Christmas music. A steady flow of people moved quietly up the aisles and sidestepped into a pew. Hillary looked around the church and was pleased with the decorations.

A white cloth was draped over the arms of the large wooden cross, and three red poinsettia plants stood at each end of the altar. Children in the small choir began singing, "Silent Night." The scent of burning candles spread through the church, their shadows dancing on the walls behind them. When the choir faded, Father Adams came out of the sacristy, blessed the assembly and proceeded with mass.

Hillary searched again for Pina, hoping she was there to enjoy her first Christmas Mass at St. Paul's. Kate was sitting in a pew on the other side of the main aisle. She saw Vera with her parents, four rows behind Kate. Many of her classmates were there with their parents.

After mass, Laura and Hillary remained outside of the church talking to friends they rarely saw.

Kate talked with them for a few minutes, then walked east on Howard Street toward Doyle's Pub. What remained from the previous week's snow was piled along the curbs and had turned to ice. Despite Laura's assurance that her friends would show loyalty to John, she was nervous about returning to Doyle's.

The number of people around Kate diminished, as she distanced herself from St. Paul's. When approaching Union Avenue, a voice from behind called her name. Kate turned to find a stranger coming toward her. He was lean and blond, with broad shoulders, about six feet tall. Kate figured him to be in his mid-thirties. His wide smile gave him a handsome, yet somewhat devilish appeal. She knew by his clothes that he was from somewhere out west. His animal hide coat reached to just below his waist and his turned up collar exposed a fleece lining. He wore tailored black pants and black western style boots.

"Are you Kate Moran?" he asked, deliberately giving her full name.

"Yes, I am." The street lamp above her illuminated the vapor coming from her mouth, as she spoke. She was somewhat embarrassed by it.

"The name's Biff. I'm a friend of John Hanley's. He asked me to contact you."

Not wanting to draw attention to themselves, they moved from under the street lamp and continued walking. Kate was cautious, wondering if he had been sent by some authority to obtain information about John. Since there was nothing she could reveal, she felt secure in continuing the conversation. "How do I know you're who you say you are?" she asked, intending to scrutinize his every word.

Biff slid his hand out of his coat pocket and extended his open palm to her, presenting a pocketknife with a picture of a schooner. "I was told you won this in a Chinese laundry," he said, giving her a curious glance. "John wants you to keep this for him until he sends for you."

Kate smiled, examining the knife before putting it in her coat pocket. She relaxed and accepted this stranger as a friend. "Where is he now?" Kate asked.

"Can't say. That'll come later. If you don't know, you won't have the responsibility of protecting that information. It will be easier this way."

"How did you know who I was?"

"John gave me your address and told me what you looked like. He also said you would probably go to St. Paul's for Christmas Mass. As people came out of church, I approached two of them and gave your name. They pointed to you."

"Where are you from?"

"Nice try," Biff replied, smiling. "That will come later, too. Periodically, I will be bringing you messages from John, but I can't be seen going to your apartment. So, the first thing we must do is to find a third person for me to contact. I must stay anonymous, so I'm not followed. We need someone you can trust."

Kate believed he was telling the truth, so she cooperated. "There's my friend, Meg. She'd be easy for you to contact. Meg's a waitress at Doyle's Pub, and I can certainly trust her."

When they arrived at Union Avenue, Biff suggested they remain on a darker street. He took Kate's arm to cross the street and guided her straight ahead. "She won't do. It would look suspicious, a stranger going in and out of the pub just to talk to a waitress. We need someone who leads a quieter life."

The answer came immediately. "Laura!" she blurted. "How obvious. I should have thought of her immediately. She'd be perfect."

Biff released her arm. "Who's Laura?"

Kate described the woman and young girl she had been talking to in front of church, but Biff hadn't noticed them.

"What about her husband?"

"She's a widow. It's just the two of them. She should be home from church now. We could ask her tonight."

"Does she go to Doyle's?" he asked.

"Not at all. Laura's very much a home girl. She'd be easy to contact and no one would suspect her of being involved in John's affairs."

"Then she's the person we want." Realizing they shouldn't be seen together, they devised a plan to separate and meet at Laura's apartment. Kate gave him Laura's address and apartment number before crossing Union Avenue again.

Biff lagged far behind her on the opposite side of the street. If Laura agreed to help, Kate was to stand in front of the window for a moment, then walk away. If not, Kate would return to him in minutes.

Biff moved slowly, pretending to look at merchandise in store windows, while keeping an eye on Laura's second floor window.

Twelve minutes passed before Kate stood in the window. She waited a few seconds and walked away.

Biff crossed the slush-covered street toward the building's entrance. As he climbed the creaking stairs, he noticed the poor condition of the building. The hallway was dimly lit and empty, except for a decrepit wooden chair at the top of the stairs. Biff walked to the north end of the hall to find the apartment. The number 5 was missing from the door, but its outline was still visible. He knocked and unbuttoned his coat. The sound of a crying baby came from an apartment at the other end of the hall.

Kate opened the door quickly and stepped aside, so he could enter. Laura was standing next to Kate, anxious to meet this messenger from somewhere. Kate introduced him to Laura, as Hillary crossed the room from a chair by the window, smiling at his curious clothing.

Biff interpreted her smile as a friendly greeting.

"This is my daughter, Hillary," Laura said, proudly. "She was reading a Christmas story to me when Kate arrived. It's a tradition of ours."

"Nice to meet you," Biff said, as Kate took his coat. "That's a fine tradition." He looked down at Hillary. "I'm sure your mother enjoys it very much."

"I enjoy it, too," Hillary admitted. "Would you like some hot tea?"

"I certainly would. It's very cold outside." He gave Laura a wink, signifying he liked Hillary.

"You two sit at the table," Laura suggested. "Hillary and I will get the tea."

Kate and Biff sat opposite each other, resting their arms on a blue tablecloth. A kerosene lamp of clear glass stood flickering at the center of the table, with the coiled wick bathing in a pale yellow fluid.

"It's kind of you to help," Biff said, watching Laura at the stove. "It will be easier and safer for us to make contact this way."

"I don't mind. Kate's a good friend." Hillary came to the table, carrying four cups and a white sugar bowl with a spoon protruding from it. Laura followed with a white teapot and four spoons.

"Fortunately, I had water heating before you arrived," Laura said, placing cups around the table.

Walking back to the stove, Laura asked Kate to pour the tea.

"Do you use sugar?" Kate asked, while pouring.

"I usually do, but I'll go without, now that I see what Laura is bringing."

Laura was carrying napkins and a plate of cookies to the table. "Hillary and I made these for Christmas and I know men enjoy cookies as much as children."

Biff smiled, reaching for a butter cookie sprinkled with sugar crystals.

"First time we're with a stranger on Christmas," Hillary remarked. "It's kind of nice, like one of the wise men following our star."

"Yes, it is a pleasant surprise," Laura said, looking down at her tea.

Kate looked at Laura, then at Biff. She sensed he was studying Laura with great interest. Kate turned to Laura again. She was still looking into her cup, as she raised it to her mouth, avoiding eye contact with Biff. "Another cookie, Biff?" Kate asked.

Kate glanced at Biff's ring finger. It was bare. *That's why he's roaming on Christmas,* she thought. *He's probably without a family.*

"I'll take my tea and cookies to the window, so you three can talk," Hillary said.

"Good girl," Laura replied. "We do need to talk."

While enjoying their snack, they decided that in the future, Biff would contact Laura in person or by leaving a note, announcing when he would return to the apartment. Then Laura would inform Kate when to be there. Each visit, Biff would bring a letter from John and take one from Kate.

"Simple enough," Laura remarked. "I don't think anyone will be watching my place."

Kate leaned forward slightly to rest her arms on the table. "How long are you going to be in town?"

"I leave tomorrow." He sat back and folded his arms. "I've been here two days already and it will be another two days on the train. Fortunately, I enjoy riding trains."

"When will you be back?" Kate asked.

"It depends on John," Biff replied, with a faint frown. "Probably five or six weeks. Be patient. John would have you come now, but he's on the move searching for his perfect piece of land. By the way, I've got John's letter in my coat." Biff took a fast bite of his cookie and went to his coat hanging on the back of the door.

Laura brought a pencil, paper and an envelope to Kate. "Here, write your letter. We won't peek," she joked.

Biff handed John's letter to Kate, which she read immediately. Smiles appeared and faded, as her eyes moved back and forth across the paper. When Kate finished reading the letter, she began writing.

Without being obvious, Biff inspected the one-room apartment. Although it was only one room, he was impressed with its size. It was scrubbed clean, but needed painting. The only closet stood next to the bed, meaning Laura and Hillary had limited clothing. The bed and kitchen set were old and showed a great deal of wear. He knew they were poor because of where they lived, but Laura's manner was that of an educated person. He hoped to eventually learn her circumstances.

Kate finished her letter and placed it in the envelope. She handed it to Biff, thanking him for his help.

"I enjoyed spending some of my Christmas with you," he said. He looked over at Hillary sitting by the window. "Next time, I want to spend more time with you, young lady."

Hillary smiled. "Merry Christmas. And next time, stay longer."

"I'm leaving, too," Kate said. "You two can get back to your Christmas story. I believe I had a nice Christmas after all."

Laura closed the door behind them and walked toward Hillary. "He's nice looking," Hillary remarked.

"I suppose some people might think so. He's built like your father."

In the stairwell, Kate stopped Biff before stepping outside. "You go first. I'll wait a couple minutes before leaving."

Biff paused while opening the door. "Laura is a fine lady, isn't she?"

"She's a beautiful person. Good-bye, and thanks for your help." She watched Biff through the glass panel in the door, as he crossed the street. Biff looked up at Laura's window.

CHAPTER TWELVE

It didn't snow the two weeks following Christmas, but almost ten inches had accumulated by the end of the third, and the girls intended to use it. Hillary and Vera were meeting Iris on the corner by her apartment before going to the pond. She lived near Thilmony Brothers Packing Company, where they could find material in the garbage to use as sleds. They planned an afternoon of making snow figures and sledding down the riverbank onto the Clarion River.

When they arrived at the corner, Iris wasn't in sight. They waited. After a few seconds, Vera was hit in the back with a snowball. Then one flew past Hillary. "Kill the devils!" Iris shouted, charging from a doorway nearby. Her left arm cradled numerous snowballs, which she threw rapidly while circling around them.

"Kill the devil killer!" Vera shouted back. Hillary and Vera scooped snow as fast as they could, retaliating wildly. The three ran erratically, dodging and throwing, screaming and giggling, until they tired, which didn't take long. Their coats were peppered with blotches of snow where they had been hit by snowballs.

"When we get to the river, you'll be making angels in the snow … face down," Vera shouted to Iris.

"Ah, your mother wears an oat bag!" Iris yelled back.

"And your mother chews tobacco!" Vera replied.

"Your father wears horseshoes!" Hillary screamed.

Iris and Vera stopped and stared at Hillary, giving her a dubious look.

"Not funny?" Hillary asked.

"You do nicey-nicey. We'll do the jokes," Vera suggested.

"We're wasting time," Iris hollered. "Let's head for Thilmony's."

They plodded across the street, with their boot heels kicking up snow behind them. They could see Thilmony's yellow and black sign two blocks ahead, hanging vertically over the snow-covered sidewalk.

When they arrived, the girls entered the alley cautiously, hoping no one was behind Thilmony's building. They were in luck. The trio wasn't sure if taking from the garbage was stealing, so they would only pick when no one was around. They quickly searched through the piles of junk strewn along the brick wall, hoping to find pasteboard, thin pieces of wood, heavy packing paper, or anything they could use as a sled.

Two pasteboard boxes, partially covered with snow, were wedged between two broken barrels. Vera slid them out and beat the snow off with her gloved hand. "Look at these," she called. "I've got two sleds already."

"Watch out for rats!" Iris yelled, picking through the trash. "If you get bit, you could die."

"If I see one, I'm getting out of here quick," Hillary replied.

"I see a pasteboard box under this crate," Iris hollered. "Come over and lift the crate, so I can pull it out."

Hillary and Vera walked over and put their gloved hands between the slats of the crate, lifting it with great effort.

"Hold it there," Iris directed, wiggling the folded box back and forth. Suddenly, the box broke free, sending Iris backward into the snow. "Success!" she screamed, lying on her back.

Hillary and Vera extended a hand to help her from the ground. When she was halfway to her feet, they jerked their hands away, letting her fall onto her back. They stood over her, laughing.

"Thanks, friends. I'll remember this. You'd better watch your backs today." She rolled onto her knees to get on her feet.

Each girl carried a folded box under her arm, marching for the pond. They walked west on Gail Street to Union Avenue, then turned south toward Mill Prairie. Frankie was walking toward them, hawking newspapers and smoking his pipe.

"He acts like he's the biggest frog on the pond," Vera remarked.

Hillary moved left of the girls to speak to Frankie. "I haven't seen you since my birthday. I wanted to thank you for the incense."

Before Frankie could say anything, Vera leaned toward him and yelled, "Thanks for nothing on my birthday, you smoked turkey!"

"You look silly with that pipe in your face," Iris declared.

"You're gunna stunt your growth," Vera said, waving her finger at him.

Vera pretended she was holding a cigar between her fingers and began blowing warm vapor at him. "Look! I smoke, too, you knuckle-head."

"Your teeth are gunna turn brown and fall out," Iris declared, as they passed him.

While they wisecracked, Frankie's eyes rolled from one girl to the other.

"Stick it in your britches. It'll keep you warm," Vera yelled.

"Don't burn your nose off," Iris whined, looking back at him.

Frankie removed the pipe from his mouth and hollered after them, "It sure was nice seeing you girls."

When they arrived at the pond, about fifty people were spread along the riverbank, taking turns sliding down the hill or just watching. Two children were gliding across the ice in their shoes, pretending they were wearing skates.

A boy was sliding down the riverbank on a round barrel top, turning as he went, while other boys threw snowballs as he passed. Each had to take a turn being the target under the threat of having their face washed in the snow.

With rosy cheeks and red noses, the girls dropped their simulated sleds on the snow and looked down at the river. Iris was eating little balls of snow stuck to her blue, wool mittens.

"Let's race," Vera suggested. "We'll see who can go the fastest and the farthest."

"Great idea," Hillary said, adjusting her scarf around her neck. "The one who wins will be queen of the Wildflowers today."

"Sounds good to me," Iris agreed. "When I count to three, we push off."

With hands poised to push, they lay on their flattened boxes at the crest of the riverbank. When Iris counted to three, they shoved their bodies forward into an uncontrolled slide over bumpy snow. Halfway down, the front of Iris's box folded under her, reducing her speed. Hillary was slightly ahead at the bottom of the hill, but when they slid onto the ice, Hillary drifted sideways, while Vera continued on a straight course to take the lead.

"I win!" Vera shouted. "You shall call me 'Her Majesty,' or off with your heads."

"Enjoy it while you can," Hillary said. "Tomorrow, Mrs. Gretsch will be queen."

"God, what a thought!" Vera moaned. "A queen that looks like her?"

Iris turned to Hillary, while beating snow from her coat. "Let's race to see who's princess," she said, hoping to win a title.

"Since I'm queen," Vera said, "I'll give the signal for you to start."

Hillary and Iris returned to the top of the riverbank, while Vera waited at the bottom. The girls got on their knees and dropped across the boxes with hands ready. Vera raised her hand to give the signal, waiting longer than necessary just to tease them. When she dropped her arm, they slid down the hill at equal speed until Iris's box began to tear apart, turning her sideways. Hillary went on to win.

"No fair!" Iris shouted. "My sled is junk."

"Then you can be a junky peasant," Vera said, grinning.

"This snow is too wet to give a good slide," Hillary groaned. "Let's go to the top of the hill and make angels."

Vera agreed with Hillary. "Leave the boxes here, so some boys can use them."

Cautiously, the girls sidestepped up the embankment, trying not to fall. When they got to the top, a red sleigh pulled by two gray horses stopped a few yards past them.

"Do you girls want to go for a ride?" the driver yelled. He was heavily covered in winter clothes.

Hillary stared at the man in the driver's seat, wondering who he was.

"It's Mr. Shert, the blacksmith," Iris hollered, with excitement.

"Yes!" they screamed at once, running toward the sleigh. He smiled at their enthusiasm. One by one, the girls stepped on the running board, then into the sleigh.

Mr. Shert turned to look at the girls. "There's an old blanket back there. Wrap yourselves in it."

"This is very nice of you," Hillary said, pulling the dirty quilt over her lap.

"Yes, thank you," the other two chimed in.

"Where would you girls like to go?" he asked, reins in hand.

"New York City," Vera shouted.

"I'd like to," he said, smiling, "but we'd be starting too late in the day. I think we'll go to the woods, circle around the mill, then I'll let you off at Union Avenue."

"That will do just fine," Iris said, looking over her shoulder toward the woods.

Mr. Shert flipped his reins and yelled, "Ee'aah!" prompting the horses to trot forward. He turned the sleigh around and headed for the woods at a moderate pace, so the ride would last a decent amount of time.

The girls tugged the quilt high around their waists, then sat back and relaxed. Vera turned to Iris. "Brush the snow off my shoulder, peasant. Ee'aah!"

"Ee'aah, yourself," Iris retorted, elbowing Vera.

Hillary leaned forward toward Mr. Shert. "I didn't know you had a sleigh?"

"I don't. I repaired it for a man in Black River Falls. Now, I'm taking it for a test ride, so I know it's fixed proper."

The girls watched people playing along the river, leaving them behind as they made new tracks in the prairie snow.

"I hope the horses don't lift their tails," Vera whispered.

Iris looked surprised. "While they're trotting?"

"Sure," Vera said, softly. "They don't have to stop like we do."

"They might do something else," Hillary snickered, pinching her nostrils together.

"There's a fox at the edge of the woods," Mr. Shert hollered, pointing ahead.

"I see it," Hillary squealed. "He's running away from us."

"I see it, too," Vera cried out, looking over Hillary's head.

"I don't see it," Iris moaned. She flipped the quilt from her lap and knelt on the seat for a better view.

Hillary pointed at the fox. "By those two fallen trees," Hillary said. "He's going toward the river."

"Oh, yeah!" Iris screamed, watching it intensely. "He sure does want to get away from us. Look how he leaps through the snow."

"He's going back into the woods," Hillary said. "Sit down, Iris. Maybe we'll see something else."

Iris snuggled under the quilt and the girls searched the woods. The trees seemed to loom higher and higher, as the sleigh moved closer. Mr. Shert was enjoying the girls, as much as they were enjoying the ride. He drove the sleigh close to the woods without leaving level ground, pointing to rabbits and a stray hog he suspected to have escaped through a farmer's fence.

After a half hour ride, Mr. Shert directed the sleigh toward the mill, then on to Union Avenue. The girls were disappointed the ride had ended, but were thrilled with the experience.

One after the other they climbed out of the sleigh and thanked him again. Mr. Shert waved to the girls, flipped the reins and yelled, "Ee'aah!"

All at once the girls hollered, "Ee'aah!" as the sled pulled away.

The following morning, Hillary and Vera arrived at Mill Prairie at the same time. They saw each other through the crowd of workers and maneuvered themselves, so they could walk together. Vera pulled Hillary by the arm, steering her behind two large men for shelter from the wind.

"Good morning, your majesty," Hillary joked.

"What do you have for lunch, Princess?" Vera asked. "I forgot mine, again."

"Nothing fitting enough for a queen," Hillary replied. "Maybe Lady Gretsch will have something for you?"

"Can't imagine wanting anything *she'd* eat," Vera said, making a sour face.

They walked out of the dark prairie into the lighted stairwell, comforted by the sound of the hissing radiator that would begin warming their cold bodies, nearing the top of the stairs, Mrs. Gretsch signaled them to hurry and follow her. She led them to rows of spinning machines, pointed to one and pushed Vera in that direction. Hillary was taken to a machine two aisles further, where she would work between Rosemary and Clara, two Dutch girls she liked. They spoke decent English and told funny stories that amused her. Their blond hair was braided in a different style each day. Hillary was amazed at the number of ways hair could be braided.

At eleven o'clock, Hillary was replacing spools on the machine when she sensed someone watching her. She looked to her right, just in time to see Mr. Dragus turn away. He began inspecting spools and scanning areas of a machine next to him, not something he normally did. Hillary assumed Mrs. Gretsch reported a problem that needed his attention.

During lunch, Hillary and Vera sat on a bench near Mr. Dragus's office eating Hillary's lunch. Vera forgot her food two or three times a month, but Hillary didn't mind sharing. They talked about the fun they'd had the previous day at the Clarion River, and how mean Iris and Vera had been to Frankie.

Hillary was talking about his pipe smoking when, in mid-sentence, she stared in silence.

Vera turned to see what Hillary was looking at, but didn't see anything unusual. "What's wrong?" Vera asked.

"Did you see that girl?"

"I didn't see anyone."

"A girl was carrying cleaning supplies into the ladies washroom, but it wasn't Pina." Hillary placed her lunch on the bench and ran over to Mrs. Gretsch sitting at her desk nearby.

"Who's that girl cleaning the women's washroom?" she asked, anxiously.

Mrs. Gretsch sensed Hillary's deep concern about Pina, so she had to tell her that Pina no longer worked at the mill. "Marie," Mrs. Gretsch answered. "New girl."

"New girl? What do you mean? Where is Pina?"

Mrs. Gretsch hesitated before answering. "Pina gone. Sometime December. Go New York."

Hillary was bewildered. *Pina gone?* The question repeated in her mind. She returned to Vera who was nibbling the last of her cheese.

Vera could see Hillary was upset. "What's wrong?"

"Pina moved to New York. That's why I haven't seen her here, or at church all these weeks. She didn't say anything to me about moving."

That evening, Laura watched Hillary mope around their apartment. "You have been quiet tonight. Losing a friend isn't easy, but you must accept the fact that Pina moved to New York. They probably found better work there, or have joined relatives."

"I accept it," Hillary replied. "I just don't like it. No! That isn't true, either. I haven't accepted it. Mrs. Gretsch told me about Pina like she was making it up, like she was hiding something."

"Nonsense," Laura responded. "Why would she do that? I'm certain what she said is true." Laura gave Hillary a kiss on the top of her head. "Enough about Pina. It's time for bed."

Hillary rolled to her side of the bed and wormed herself under the covers. Laura lied down and covered herself with the blanket. She reached to turn off the kerosene lamp and gave out a yelp, jolted by a sharp abdominal pain.

Hillary opened her eyes and looked at her mother. "That pain again? It's the fourth time this week. I think you should see a doctor."

CHAPTER THIRTEEN

It was six weeks before Biff returned to Alton. He stepped from the train into a cold February wind that slapped his coat collar against his face. At the other end of the passenger car, a porter was unloading luggage from the train onto a flatbed wagon, while a little girl watched. She had long blond curls and wore a matching maroon coat and hat. The doll she was holding was dressed nicer than most children in Alton.

Biff walked toward the end of the station, hoping to find a wagon and driver waiting for a fare. Looking through the waiting room window, he saw people sitting on benches that had been moved close to the potbelly stove. A large calendar with a picture of a steam engine hung on a paneled wall near the ticket window. At the end of the station, he found only one wagon available. The driver was sitting on a bench seat, with the reins draped over his legs. Pulling back on the lapel of his coat, the driver returned a bottle of whiskey to his inside pocket.

"That'll keep you from freezing," Biff said, approaching the wagon.

"Nothing better, except a good woman," the driver grinned.

"Are you for hire?"

"Sure am," he replied, wiping his mouth with his coat sleeve.

Biff threw his brown leather bag into the back of the wagon and climbed up next to the driver. The gray mare was nodding and discharging clouds of vapor from her nostrils. Biff knew this would be a cold, miserable ride, but it was faster than walking.

"My name's Buff," the driver announced. "Where ya headed?"

"And I'm Biff," he replied, with a smile. They laughed at the similarity of names. "Do you know Widow Schmidt's rooming house by the wharf?"

"Sure do," Buff assured him. "Got a good reputation." Buff flipped the reins, stirring the mare into action. The wagon jerked and bounced, as it navigated deep ruts in the frozen mud.

The coldness of the hard wooden seat penetrated Biff's denim pants, but there was nothing protective to sit on. Biff was relieved when they rolled onto a brick paved street that would give them a gentler ride. During the fifteen-minute ride, Biff thought of the whiskey bottle in Buff's coat, but never asked, unwilling to share a bottle with a stranger.

When Laura entered her apartment that evening, she found a folded piece of paper on the floor. She assumed it was from Biff. Laura lit the lamp on the kitchen table and unfolded the note. *See you at eight o'clock tonight, Biff.* Laura was pleased he had returned, but felt guilty for feeling so—being that she still loved her deceased husband, Jeremiah.

She waited until Hillary came home from work, then set out after Kate. She walked toward Lakeview Street, hoping Kate would be at her apartment and not Doyle's Pub. When she was about to turn the corner, she saw Kate coming toward her, looking into the store windows. She sidestepped a few people to meet Kate head on.

"Good news. Biff arrived today. He left a note saying he would be at my place at eight o'clock."

"Good news for me, or for you?" Kate asked, teasing Laura.

Laura reversed her direction to walk alongside Kate. "What do you mean?"

"I mean, I think both of you were smitten the night you met. It was subtle, but it was there."

"Don't be silly. I don't have my mind on any man."

"Maybe your mind ain't," Kate replied, with a smile, "But the rest of you should be. You're well overdue."

"Please stop," Laura insisted. "I'm fine with my life the way it is. There's no room for a man in our lives."

"If you say so," Kate answered, with a smirk. "I'll be at your place before eight. Have the kettle on."

That night, Laura and Kate were sitting at the kitchen table when Biff arrived, his face red from the cold night air. As he entered, Hillary gave him a hearty greeting from her chair by the window and Kate took his coat.

Laura went to the stove. "Take a seat at the table," Laura said. "Tea is ready."

Biff warmed his hands by rubbing them together before removing an envelope from his shirt pocket. "Here's a letter from John," he said, with a chuckle. "He's quite anxious for you to join him, but he knows he's not ready."

Kate slid her letter for John across the table to Biff. "Feel like a pony express rider?" she joked.

Laura came to the table carrying four cups of tea. She placed three on the table and took the fourth to Hillary sitting by the window. On her return, she stopped at a cabinet next to the stove for a plate of raisin bread.

Biff's eyes followed Laura around the room. He smiled, as she placed the offering on the table. "You just served one of my favorite foods. We ate raisin bread as kids, but I haven't had it in years. This is a special treat for me."

"What a nice surprise," Kate remarked, glaring at Laura. "When did you bake this?"

"Yesterday," Laura answered, glaring back at Kate. "Hillary asked me to make it. It's one of her favorites, too."

"Just in time for company," Kate said, with a smile. "How fortunate. It's amazing how raisins can stay warm for such a long time."

"Are you still being questioned about John?" Biff asked.

"Occasionally," Kate answered. "They can watch me all they want, but they're wasting their time."

When Biff finished his slice of raisin bread, Laura pushed the plate closer to him. "We have plenty. Take all you want."

"You may be sorry you said that," Biff said, smiling. "I have a large appetite."

They snacked and talked about Alton, John and farming for almost two hours.

Kate watched Laura and Biff closely, believing that something was developing between them. It was subtle, but she believed her instincts.

"It's starting to snow," Hillary announced from the window. "Everything will be nice and white again."

Biff looked at his watch. "It's ten o'clock. I'm wearing out my welcome."

"I don't think you have to worry about that," Kate said, cleverly.

Laura retrieved their coats from the door and stood next to Kate. She began feeling the sensation that always preceded the abdominal pains. She prayed they wouldn't begin until Biff and Kate were gone.

As Biff looked inside his coat to put Kate's letter in his pocket, Kate whispered to Laura, "Should I take Hillary home with me?"

Laura jabbed her elbow against Kate's side.

"John will probably buy land before my next visit," Biff predicted. "He's constantly looking, but being selective. I'm sure he'll find a place you'll be proud of." Biff looked at Hillary to say "good-bye".

She smiled and waved, then continued to watch the falling snow.

Biff faced Laura, thanking her for her help and hospitality.

Kate knew her presence wasn't needed, so she returned to the table to clear the dishes.

Seeing Laura again increased Biff's desire to be alone with her. He decided to say something quickly. "I would like to extend my next visit a day or two, so I can repay your kindness," he said, with a gentle smile. He knew she understood his intent, so he refrained from saying more.

Their eyes met and she returned his smile without responding.

After mass the following Sunday, Father Adams joined the parishioners in front of the church, giving inspiration where needed. Laura saw it as an opportunity to recruit Father Adams's help in finding a doctor about her abdominal pains. He finished talking to an elderly couple and turned to Laura and Hillary, as they approached him.

"Ah! Two of my loyal customers," he said, smiling. "I haven't talked to you since Christmas. I want to thank you again for decorating the church. You are always there when help is needed."

"I think we get more out of it, than we put in," Laura replied. "It gives us a chance to socialize with people we seldom see."

"I suppose that's true," he agreed. "With the hours people put into their jobs, there isn't much time for social life." Father Adams looked down at Hillary and placed his hand on her shoulder. "I see you are doing excellent work in school, young lady. Undoubtedly, your mother is proud of you."

"Thank you. I'm proud of my mother, too."

"And so you should be. She's a fine lady."

"You had better get moving, or you will be late for school," Laura said. "Mrs. McLeen is going to Black River Falls today, so you'll only have two hours of classes."

They watched Hillary run off to school, chatting with classmates. "A beautiful child," Father Adams remarked. "You two seem to have a fine relationship. All families should be as dedicated to one another."

"I rue the day she leaves me. I will be very lonely, especially if she moves to another part of the country."

"Life is filled with adjustments," he replied, nodding at a passing family. "We must deal with them as they come."

"If I may," Laura asked, "Could I ask a favor of you?"

"Of course. Let's go into the vestibule and get out of this cold wind." He continued to nod and smile at parishioners, as they made their way into church. Once inside, he faced Laura, waiting for her to speak.

"A few weeks ago, I developed severe abdominal pains and now they're more frequent. I don't have a doctor because we've always had good health. My other concern is the expense of a doctor. My savings are meager."

"Most people in Alton have the same financial problem," he explained. "I'll talk to Dr. Merges. I'm sure he will see you. I'll tell him you will be contacting him soon."

"Thank you, Father. I'll talk to Dr. Merges at the end of the week."

After school, Hillary spent little time talking to classmates and set out to meet Iris and Vera in front of Thompson's. When she arrived, they were throwing snowballs at a lamppost. "Who's winning?" Hillary asked. "Or should I ask, who's losing the least?"

"It's a tie," Vera answered. "We both hit it twice in fifteen tries."

"We're very proud," Iris joked. "But I think we should try something else."

"I got an idea when I was in school," Hillary announced. "With all this snow, we can make snow sculptures by the train tracks. It'll be something for people to look at as they go by."

"Good idea," Vera agreed. "Let's make a dragon's body with a pig's head. That should confuse 'em."

"I have a better idea," Iris shouted. "Let's make a dragon with a rag hanging out of its mouth, like it just ate somebody."

"Dragon sounds good to me," Hillary replied. "We can think about it, as we walk to the tracks."

"What about Mr. Thompson?" Vera asked, jerking her thumb toward the store.

"Not this time," Iris suggested. "Let's not take advantage."

The girls marched down the avenue under a cloudless sky, dragging their shadows behind them. "I squished you," Vera yelled, jumping on Iris's shadow.

"I broke your legs," Hillary yelled to Vera, kicking through the snow.

"Here's a kick in the bottom," Iris screamed to Hillary.

"Hold it, girls!" Vera yelled. "Look who I see across the street."

Frankie was walking down the avenue, puffing on his pipe, trailing a cloud of smoke. He noticed the girls, but pretended not to. At the corner, he turned toward the bay, leaving the trio behind.

"That steam engine doesn't want to run into us again," Vera declared. "He's probably afraid we'll take his newspaper money."

"I don't blame him," Hillary said. "You weren't very kind last time."

"Let's keep moving," Iris insisted. "We're almost to the prairie."

Numerous paths had been cut through the snow in Mill Prairie, most leading to the pond. The girls walked straight south, creating a new path directly to the tracks. They stopped about thirty-five feet short of the rail bed, estimating that would be a proper distance for passengers to see their sculpture.

"They should be able to see it good from here," Vera said, clearing an area of snow with her feet.

"Let's start rolling big snowballs, then line them in a row," Iris suggested.

"Not in a straight line," Hillary said, making waves with her hand. "It should have curves like a snake."

"Yeah. It wouldn't look real in a straight line," Vera agreed.

Iris put her gloved hands on her hips. "I don't think anyone will believe a white dragon is real. We just want to show off our artistic talents—whatever they are."

"It'll be beautiful," Hillary shouted. "Us Wildflowers can do anything, no matter how difficult."

The girls went in different directions to gather snow and rolled it to a central location. The largest ball formed the head, the others diminished in size toward the tail. After working nearly an hour, they began to tire.

"This is taking longer than I thought," Hillary declared. "We'll never finish before dark."

"You're right," Iris agreed, sitting on a large snowball. "We'll have to finish next Sunday. But if it snows during the week, we will have to start over again."

"Quiet!" Vera shouted. "Listen. I think I hear a train."

The girls stood motionless, with their heads cocked in the same direction. "I hear it, too," Hillary agreed. "It's a train, alright."

"Let's get closer to the tracks," Vera suggested. "When it passes, it'll throw snow on us."

"We haven't seen an orphan train since before Christmas," Iris commented. "I'll bet the orphans didn't have a merry Christmas."

They watched in silence, as the train approached. The light at the center of the engine was barely visible. Snow flew wildly from its wheels, concealing everything behind it. The girls raised their coat collars to protect themselves from the snow about to fall on them.

Vera backed up a few yards in an attempt to get a better look at the train.

"Is it an orphan train?" Hillary called to Vera.

"Can't tell. Too much snow flying." She backed up a few more feet and waited. A line of gold glittery lights began to appear at the end of the train. "It is!" Vera hollered. "Two passenger cars on the end."

Vera ran back as quickly as she could, raising her feet high to avoid getting her boots stuck in the snow. She got back to the tracks, as they were getting sprayed with snow and enveloped by a thick cloud of black smoke. With their gloved hands, they shielded their eyes from the flying snow. After a few freight cars passed, enough snow had been cleared from the tracks, so they could see clearly again.

They stared at the passenger car windows, as the train pulled forward, each sharing similar feelings of curiosity, compassion, and pity. They waved, smiled and threw kisses at the orphans, as they rolled by.

Hillary reasoned that the children who returned smiles and waves expected a life better than what they had, while the sad children had lost a life they had wanted to keep.

Near the center of the last car, a girl stood at a window gazing at them. Hillary was drawn to her by something familiar. A red scarf covered the girl's head; black hair draped her forehead. She held the scarf in place by gripping it under her chin. Hillary took a few steps forward, staring at the girl's face until she recognized her. Blood seemed to flush through her body with one forceful swoop, making it difficult for her to breath. Hillary gasped, trying to restore air to her lungs. She began running with the train, her eyes fixed on the girl, while wiping away tears. Hillary stared at her, trying to freeze in place, an image of someone she would never see again. She wanted to touch her, kiss her, and rip her from that train to oblivion. Their eyes held each other in desperation, helpless to do anything as the train moved on. With the hand holding her scarf, the girl flashed four fingers, while drifting out of Hillary's life. "Pina!" Hillary screamed. She dropped to her knees, sobbing.

That evening, Hillary stood at the kitchen sink washing her hands without saying a word. There was tension about her and her silence was as alarming as a scream. Normally, she returned home bubbling about her afternoon activities and the fun she'd had, but not today. Laura turned to her. "You've been crying," she said. "Is there a problem?" Laura continued looking at her, waiting for an answer.

"I saw Pina today."

"So, why are you crying? You should be excited."

"She was on an orphan train," Hillary mumbled, while rinsing soap from her hands. "She was pitiful as she waved to me, like she was so helpless and afraid."

Laura went to Hillary and put her arms around her. "I guess you were right about Mrs. Gretsch's story. She probably said what she did to protect your feelings. You must forgive her for that."

"Why does God make orphans?" Hillary sobbed. "He could keep families healthy, so they stay together."

"Supposedly, He knows best and we are not to question Him," Laura replied, tightening her arms around Hillary. "Life can be difficult in many ways. Nothing is perfect."

"It isn't right," Hillary cried. She rolled her head against her mother's blouse to wipe away her tears.

Laura kissed the top of her head. "All we can do is pray that Pina gets a good home."

"If I knew where Pina was going, I would write her," Hillary murmured.

"I'm sure we'll never know." Laura brushed her fingers through Hillary's hair. "All you can do is keep memories of her."

Hillary felt comfortable and secure in the warmth of her mother's arms, hearing her gentle voice and the beating of her heart. She believed they would always be together.

Chapter Fourteen

Hillary entered her apartment, as Laura was putting supper on the table. "Wash for dinner," Laura said. "It's Tuesday, and I have an appointment with Dr. Merges. It wouldn't be polite to arrive late."

"Where is his office?"

"He has an office at the hospital and one in his home. We're going to his home office."

"Doesn't the doctor go to the patient's home?" Hillary asked, walking to the kitchen sink.

"At times," Laura said. "There are people who are bedridden and can't go to the doctor. And when it's an emergency, he has to go to them."

Hillary raised her dress sleeves to wash her hands. "What's for dinner?"

"Carrots, fried potatoes and sausage. I guess we'll eat the last of the oatmeal bread, too."

Hillary walked to the table and dropped onto a chair. "Biff sure liked your raisin bread. He had four slices, then kept looking at what was on the serving plate."

"It's not polite to count," Laura reminded her. She turned to Hillary and nearly laughed, seeing her slumped in the chair like a rag doll. "Why would you think of that now? That was two weeks ago."

"I think he likes you," Hillary declared. "He watches you all the time when he's here."

"You, too?" Laura retorted. She wished she hadn't said that. She knew Hillary would question her remark.

"What do you mean, me, too?" She sat erect in her chair, glaring at her mother, waiting for an answer.

Laura began scraping potatoes from the frying pan onto Hillary's plate, deliberately avoiding eye contact. "Kate said the same thing," Laura confessed. "I think both of you are daft. You seem to have very busy eyes and ears for a young girl." Laura took the fry pan to the stove and returned with the oatmeal bread, changing the subject. "Wear your boots tonight. When we get there, we can take them off, so we don't mess their floor. I'll carry extra shoes in a bag, and make sure you don't have holes in your stockings."

It was dark and Laura had difficulty reading the house numbers to find the doctor's house. Some numbers were in full view, while others couldn't be found anywhere. Fortunately, the number they were looking for was displayed clearly under a porch light. They stood in the dark, admiring the two-story brick house surrounded by a large snow-covered yard and black wrought-iron fence. Beyond the lace curtains, lighted rooms displayed warmth and comfort.

"I'm glad I came with you," Hillary remarked. "I'm going to enjoy seeing the inside of this house."

Neither uttered a word, as they ascended the stairs to a spacious porch extending around both corners of the house. On either side of the varnished door were vertical columns of beveled glass, backed by white, sheer curtains. Inside, they could see a stately wood staircase with green carpeting down its center.

Laura twisted a brass butterfly knob mounted at the center of the door. She could feel the vibrations of the clapper banging the bell. Laura was nervous, whereas Hillary was anxious for the show to begin.

A slim woman with graying hair came to the door. She was wearing a blue cotton dress, with a white knitted shawl across her shoulders. The woman opened the door and leaned forward a bit, waiting for Laura to identify herself.

"I'm Mrs. Cook. I have an appointment with Dr. Merges."

"Of course, my dear, come in." She stepped back, allowing them to enter.

"This is my daughter, Hillary," Laura said, closing the door.

"Nice to meet both of you. I'm Mary Strawl, the doctor's assistant. I'm also his sister," she added, proudly. "Come, let's go into the sitting room."

"We'll take our boots off," Laura said. "We brought shoes, so we wouldn't mess."

Mary drew her shawl tighter across her shoulders and nodded to Laura. "That was considerate of you. Not everyone thinks of those things, or else they just don't care. You can hang your coats on the tree next to you."

After changing shoes, they followed Mary through a hallway, carefully examining the house without being obvious. Hillary and Laura gave each other an approving look, as they passed the dining room with a huge crystal chandelier, large gold-framed paintings and beautiful porcelain figurines.

The sitting room extended approximately twenty feet with an arched entrance at the other end. Lace curtains covering the windows were framed by heavy green drapes, tied back by gold tasseled cords. "Make yourselves comfortable," Mary said, sweeping her hand toward the pale green settee'. "I'll let the doctor know you're here."

"I'm glad I came," Hillary said. "It's like being in a palace." She laughed to herself, recalling Iris's lesson on how to marry a rich man.

Dr. Merges entered under the arch, approaching them in a casual manner, smiling all the way. His gray suit complimented his thinning white hair. "Mrs. Cook, a pleasure to meet you," he said, genuinely. "Father Adams speaks very highly of you and your daughter."

"Thank you," Laura replied. "We've been admiring your home."

"I have to thank my banking father for all this," he confessed. "I don't do nearly as well doctoring."

Laura and Hillary liked him immediately, because of his friendly, sincere manner.

Mary returned to ask Hillary if she wanted something to drink, while Laura was with the doctor.

"No, thank you, but I would like a walk through the house."

"Hillary!" Laura snapped, turning to her quickly. "You don't make such a request. I can't believe you asked that."

Mary and the doctor smiled at Hillary's enthusiasm. "Your mother is right," Mary said. "But if she agrees, I would be willing to give you a tour."

Laura looked down at Hillary.

"Yes'm," Hillary replied, solemnly. She was somewhat ashamed, but still glad she asked.

"Now that, that is settled, we can go to my office," Dr. Merges said, leading Laura to another room. "First visits usually don't take long." He had Laura sit in a leather chair in front of his desk. "Let's start with your symptoms. What has been bothering you?"

"Just before Christmas, I began having abdominal pains. They have become more frequent and more intense. Sometimes they subside quickly, while other times they're prolonged."

"Any other symptoms, such as dizziness, or vomiting?"

"Well, I feel more tired than usual, even weak at times. Then there are times when I feel nauseous, but never enough to vomit."

As she talked, Dr. Merges wrote everything she said on a printed form. "Have you noticed if your bowel movements are black?"

"No," Laura replied, and straightened up in the chair. "Can't say I've looked carefully, either."

The doctor asked Laura to go behind the oriental screen to partially undress for a physical examination. She felt uncomfortable doing so, but knew it was necessary. After checking her heart, lungs and cranial orifices, he examined her torso as best he could, but admitted he couldn't make a diagnosis.

"Then there is nothing to worry about?" Laura asked, while dressing.

"I didn't say that. If you have pain, there is a reason. Whatever it is, I'll find the cause." He looked at his notes a few moments before continuing their discussion. "It's possible you may have an ulcer, but that is only a guess." He pulled his chair closer to the desk. "I suggest you drink milk for a while and less tea. If you have an ulcer, the milk will coat it, giving the ulcer a chance to heal. Other than that, I suggest you come back in two weeks and tell me of any changes."

When Laura and Dr. Merges returned to the sitting room, Mary and Hillary were sitting on the settee' studying a geography book.

"I've toured the house. Now I'm touring Asia," Hillary declared. "We're drinking tea from Ceylon, a beautiful island country that smells of tea and spices. It sounds like a country I would love to see." Hillary looked to the doctor. "How is my mother?" she asked, casually.

"I think she will improve. As soon as I discover the problem, she'll be fine again.

The following evening, Frank Dragus was standing at his desk gathering papers for the large black safe behind him. Kate was arranging the table and chairs for Frank's evening of poker. A few feet away stood the black leather sofa where Frank entertained himself with young girls. Kate wouldn't sit on it or touch it because of what it represented. It had become a symbol of her disgust for him.

"Hillary Cook told Mrs. Gretsch that her mother was ill," Frank commented. "Has she been to a doctor yet?"

"Yes. The doctor said she might have an ulcer."

Frank placed a stack of papers and a ledger in the safe and removed a small stack of money from a hidden compartment. "Is her daughter worried?" Frank asked, casually.

"Not really. Hillary assumes the doctor will cure Laura's problem. Besides, nothing traumatic has happened to make her feel it's serious." Kate walked behind Frank's desk to hand him additional documents for the safe.

"I'd better double-lock the safe," he said, slamming the safe door shut. "You never know, killer John may have returned to Alton."

"Idiot!" Kate snapped. She removed her coat and purse from the tree, as Paul Martane and George Strattin entered the office. The cold air they just came out of was still clinging to their clothes.

"Leaving so soon?" George asked.

"Not soon enough," replied Kate. She didn't think much of Frank's friends and was eager to leave when they arrived. They were all businessmen, but none were considered exemplary citizens.

"Going to Doyle's to meet John?" Paul asked, smiling at the other men.

Kate ignored the remark and continued out the door. It was cold and dark, as she walked through the prairie with her hands in her pockets. She wore a red scarf and her coat was buttoned at the neck. People on Union Avenue were walking at a quick pace to get to their destination and out of the cold. She arrived at the pub just as Karl Polen was leaving, his wide body filling the doorway.

"Hi, Kate!" he said with his raspy voice. "Heard from John yet?"

"Nothing," she replied, waiting for him to leave the doorway.

Karl closed the top button of his coat and turned up his collar. "Don't give up. I'm sure you will. When ya do, say 'hello' for me." Karl continued down the avenue and joined a small gathering of men standing under a street lamp.

No matter who asked, Kate wasn't about to say, "yes" to that question. She felt she could trust Karl, but a $200.00 reward could loosen many tongues.

Again, Kate sat at a table by the window to watch the pedestrians on Union Avenue.

Meg came over and gave her a questioning look.

"Not a word," Kate said. "Any specials tonight?"

"Absolutely," Meg answered, eagerly. "We've got chicken and boiled potatoes, chicken with rice, or chicken with fried potatoes." Meg sat at the table to wait for Kate's order.

"Stunning," Kate remarked. "I feel sorry for the chickens around here. But then, the pigs feel safer."

"We still have the usual," Meg added. "Chicken in the shell, sandwiches, and soup."

"Chicken and rice sounds interesting," Kate decided. "I can't remember rice ever being offered before. Do you have a new cook?"

"Right again. Doing a good job, too."

"Really? I'm anxious to try the chicken and rice. Include hot tea and rum on the side." Kate grabbed Meg's arm before she could leave. "Don't bring chopsticks."

"Nice ta know ya still have a sense of humor," Meg said, walking away.

Kate gazed at the window, observing the reflection of the room behind her. Three-quarters of the tables were occupied and a few men stood at the bar. She knew friends would come to her to inquire about John, people who sincerely cared about him, hoping to hear good news. She looked out to the dark street and row of lighted shops. An occasional snowflake drifted lazily to the ground. Frankie and Eli were walking on the other side of the street, as they had the night John disappeared. It was the night she had planned to say, "Yes."

"I love you, wherever you are," Kate whispered. "How long before I join you?" Biff had told her it would be soon. All she had to do was wait.

Meg brought Kate's tea and shot of rum with a copy of the *Alton Reporter*. "Someone left this newspaper on a table," Meg said. "I thought you might want to read it, while waiting for your food."

"Thanks. I haven't read a newspaper for a couple days. I'll check to see if I came into any money from a rich relative."

Meg took silverware and a napkin from her apron pocket and laid them on the table before returning to the bar.

Kate sipped the tea with her eyes closed, concentrating on its warming effect, then sipped again. She added half the rum to her tea and stirred the mixture.

Kate saw Ellie Tuzik walk past the window, her blue knit hat pulled down over her ears and forehead. Her frail body was lost in a bountiful coat that almost reached the ground, hiding her skinny legs. She was staring straight ahead, with lowered eyebrows, talking to herself. Kate could see that she was upset. She assumed Ellie was going to her father's hangout, The Anwood, one of Alton's two bars that would accommodate Philo Tuzik, a town drunk. Kate wondered if Philo was expecting his daughter. If he wasn't, Ellie might get another bruise or two.

As they were leaving, Mr. and Mrs. Perry, a couple who owned a shoe store on Market Street, stopped at Kate's table. They inquired about John, and said they missed seeing him at Doyle's. Mrs. Perry changed the subject quickly and invited Kate for a Sunday dinner at their home.

Kate was surprised by the unexpected invitation and promised to stop at their store and give them a date for dinner.

Mrs. Perry leaned forward and said, "If John doesn't return …"

Mr. Perry said, "goodnight," and guided his wife away from the table before she could say more.

Kate heard Mrs. Perry mention the name, "Wade" as they approached the door. She chuckled to herself. There was only one Wade in Alton that she knew of. Now she understood the invitation for Sunday dinner. She had to admit to herself, though, if she didn't have John she might be interested in Wade.

Meg brought Kate's chicken dinner, with another hot tea and shot of rum. "This rum is on the house. I did a little finagling for you."

"Thanks," Kate said, stirring the tea. "Has Wade Widner been in here lately?"

"Yeah," Meg replied, looking down at Kate. "Last night and two nights before. Both nights, he mulled over a drink for about half an hour, then left. Not that he's ever been a big drinker. He's been coming in more often than usual, though. Could be he doesn't like the new bartender at The Crow's Nest."

Kate smiled. "That's possible." She watched Meg place the empty shot glass and teacup onto her tray, returning to the bar. Kate was delighted with her chicken and rice dinner, which now became her first choice on the menu. As she ate, she noticed a number of people walking hurriedly past the pub, then two men running down the center of the street. She looked outside and saw a crowd gathering in front of The Anwood. A man at the table next to her got to his feet, as a white ambulance rolled by. The crowd in front of The Anwood stepped back quickly, avoiding the oncoming ambulance pulled by two brawny horses. The driver and assistant, both in white uniforms, jumped to the ground and retrieved a stretcher from the back of the wagon. When they entered the pub, the crowd outside closed ranks again, blocking Kate's view of the tavern.

No one at Doyle's knew what was happening, so Donald Wagoner and Emil Kurst went to the Anwood to learn what they could. Different theories were shouted throughout Doyle's, as though there were a prize for the correct prediction.

"Somebody probably got the shit beat out of 'em," Aean Batrin yelled, leaning toward the window.

"Could be another knifing," a heavy woman bellowed from a table near the front door.

"Anybody see someone's wife go in with a fry pan?" the bartender shouted.

Kate continued eating her meal, while it was still warm. She was enjoying it too much to let it to get cold.

"Sure is a little guy," Meg yelled, as the stretcher was lifted into the ambulance. "If it weren't for the street light, I wouldn't know anyone was on the stretcher."

"He's covered with a blanket," Hank Mertes said. "Must be dead."

Donald Wagoner and Emil Kurst came out of The Anwood talking to Jim Tisen, the bartender. They left Jim at the entrance, slipped through the crowd of onlookers and returned to Doyle's.

"What did you find out?" someone shouted.

Don Wagoner stood on the support rung of a bar stool, elevating himself above the crowd. The noise in the room ceased, as though it had been shut off with a spigot. "I'm afraid it's worse than we expected. I don't know how many of you knew her, but little Ellie Tuzik just killed herself. I was told she went to the bar where her father was standing, then yelled, 'See, I can drink, too.'" She pulled a small brown bottle from her coat pocket and uncorked it. One drink and it was over."

Kate pushed her plate of food to the other side of the table.

The next morning, Hillary and Vera were walking together on the gravel path to the mill, when they overheard two men talking next to them. They were discussing Ellie Tuzik's suicide. The girls looked at each other in bewilderment and joined hands. At the mill entrance, the girls heard two men and two women standing beyond the iron doors, talking about Ellie. As they climbed the stairs, Hillary and Vera heard other conversations about Ellie. When they got to the second floor, Kate was standing at Mrs. Gretsch's desk.

Kate saw the girls enter the room and immediately walked over to them. She knew by their solemn faces that they had heard about Ellie. She put her arms around the girls and walked them to a bench against the wall. Kate looked directly into Hillary's eyes, grasping for words of comfort to offer the young girls.

"When did you hear about Ellie?" Kate finally asked.

"While we were walking here," Vera replied, looking stunned.

"I didn't believe it at first," Hillary said. "But when we heard more people talking about her, we knew it was true."

"Ellie's suffering is over," Kate said. "She had a very difficult life and now she's at peace in heaven."

"I don't know why I'm not crying," Hillary said. "I feel relief instead of sorrow. Is that wrong?"

"Not at all. You witnessed Elli's pain for a long time and you were released from her misery as she was. Ellie understood her life would be very difficult, so she ended it."

Two young doffers in bare feet walked past them, laughing and talking loudly. One boy pointed a finger to his head and said to his friend, "Old man Tuzik put it to his head and, POW, blew his brains out." The boys continued laughing, as they walked on.

"I didn't hear about that," Kate said. She clasped her hands together, suggesting they say a prayer for Ellie and her father.

CHAPTER FIFTEEN

Biff returned the second week of April, more interest in seeing Laura, than in delivering messages. He planned to stay five days, hoping to share a generous portion of that time with her. He arrived on a Thursday, allowing time to make plans for the weekend.

When Biff arrived at the boarding house, he saw Mrs. Schmidt standing on the front porch, talking to a cat sitting on her steps. It was his third stay at her boarding house and their relationship was becoming a friendship. He followed her inside to her desk, in what was once a butler's pantry, next to the dining room. He signed a guest sheet and she gave him a key to room number six and a set of towels.

When Biff got upstairs, he unpacked and bathed immediately. He returned to his room feeling refreshed, with time to relax before dinner. He took both white pillows and leaned them against the brass headboard. Still in his black robe, he turned back the patch quilt, leaned against the pillows and yanked the quilt over himself. The oval mirror above the dresser reflected past the multi-paned window across the room, exposing an endless blue sky. Biff interpreted the image as clean and infinite; a good omen.

His thoughts centered on Laura and how he would approach her about dining with him. His preference would be Sunday, around noon, giving them a good portion of the day together. He wanted to be alone with Laura, but would invite Hillary, leaving that decision to Laura. Either way, he would be pleased. He liked Hillary and would enjoy time with her, too. He also realized that Laura might say no.

To avoid a myriad of boarding house questions and remain anonymous, Biff arranged to eat before the other guests. He entered the dining room, as Mrs. Schmidt placed a white covered bowl next to his plate. Little pink roses with green leaves and stems were painted under the glazed surface. The aroma was inviting.

Mrs. Schmidt raised the lid on the bowl. "Hot beef stew," she announced, proudly. "That'll hold you for the rest of the day."

"Smells good and looks good," Biff said, with a relishing grin. "Can't wait to dig into those potatoes."

"You Irish?"

"I'm sure there's a piece of Ireland in me somewhere," he replied. "Lord knows I'm a Scottish variety."

She laughed and started for the kitchen. "My friends call me Glo. You can do the same." Glo was a heavy woman, with a pleasant disposition. She had unusually pink skin and numerous freckles on her arms. Her graying brown hair was pulled to the top of her head and pinned into a knot.

While eating, Biff decided he would go to Laura's about eight o'clock. He assumed they would be finished eating and he could see her without Kate being there. He devoured two helpings of stew, then sat back in his chair.

"Can't quit now," Glo said, returning to the room. "Got something for your sweet tooth."

"My sweet tooth will be grateful."

The smell of warm apples and cinnamon filled his nostrils, as she presented a large piece of pie. "It was a favorite of my husband's."

"Is that his picture on the wall?" Biff asked.

"It is. Paul was big, but gentle. I was never crazy about his short, white beard, though. He had a small fishing boat with a crew of six. Three years ago, a storm struck sudden-like. Haven't seen him, the crew, or a piece of the boat since. Was like they went off the edge."

"Sorry," Biff responded. "Then you manage this place by yourself?"

"I do," she replied, wiping her hands on her apron. "My brother lives close by, so when I need fixing around here he gives me a hand. Other than that, it's been long hours and a bunch of work. I don't mind, though. It's mine."

Glo returned to the kitchen and Biff enjoyed his pie. He never saw more than five boarders at one time, including himself. *Is she having difficulty making the business pay,* he wondered? *Does she have more boarders when he wasn't there? But then, Alton isn't a town people rush to for a good time.* Before leaving, he stuck his head into the kitchen to compliment Glo on her cooking.

"Glad you liked it," she shouted back.

As he made his way to Laura's apartment, Biff was nervous, wondering whether she was interested enough to accept his offer. In his heart, he believed she was. Even if he had misinterpreted her feelings, it was worth a try. He crossed Union Avenue looking up at Laura's apartment. Hillary was sitting in the window, with her back to the street. It appeared that she was reading. He climbed to the second floor and paused at her door. He stopped to polish the tips of his boots against the back of his pant legs. He knocked three times.

"Who's there?" Laura asked from behind the door.

"Biff," he replied. Quickly, he brushed the front of his shirt with his hands in case there were pie crumbs hanging on.

Laura was about to adjust her clothes and hair, but refrained, knowing Hillary would be watching her. She opened the door and stepped aside.

Hillary walked over from her chair by the window as Biff entered.

"This is a surprise," Laura said, wiping her hands on her apron.

"I imagine it is. I didn't have time to leave a note earlier, so I took a chance you would be here. I hope my timing isn't inconvenient?"

"Not at all." Suddenly, Laura remembered the blouses and bloomers drying on the line stretched over the stove. She pulled out a chair at the end of the table, so Biff would have his back to the stove. She signaled Hillary to remove the clothesline.

Hillary responded immediately, rolling the line and clothes together just as they were, put them in a wicker basket, then covered them with a towel. "Is Kate coming?" Hillary asked, on her way to the table.

"No," Laura answered. "She doesn't know Biff is here. I'll tell her tomorrow."

"I'll be here for five days," Biff announced. "Tell Kate, we can meet anytime that's convenient."

Laura remembered his comment when he had departed weeks earlier, stating that he might stay longer when he returned. His spice-scented pomade didn't go unnoticed, either. His intentions were quite clear. "I'm sorry," Laura said. "I didn't take your coat."

"I'll take it," Hillary insisted.

Biff removed his coat and handed it to Hillary. "I still plan to spend time with you, pretty lady."

"Fine," Hillary replied, walking to the door with his coat. "You can take me to Ceylon for tea someday."

Biff sat down and watched Hillary stand on her toes to reach the coat hook. "Sounds good to me," he replied with a broad smile. "It should only take about six weeks."

"I have time," Hillary answered, returning to the table.

Laura placed her hands on her hips, looking at Hillary. "I've never had an offer like that, and you're only twelve."

"I'm special," Hillary replied, with her nose in the air.

"That's for certain," Biff remarked.

Hillary looked across the table at Biff. "Where do you live?" she asked.

"Near the Mississippi River. Do you know where that is?"

"Sure do. It's west of Ohio and runs through our country, top to bottom. That doesn't tell me where you live, though."

Biff leaned toward Hillary. "Where I live must remain a secret for now. Your mother understands why I can't tell you."

Laura took pleasure in watching them interact. They truly seemed to enjoy each other. It reminded her of Hillary playing with her father.

Biff suggested a meeting with Kate the following evening at 8 p.m., hoping to keep Saturday night or Sunday free for him and Laura. She agreed and assured him Kate would be there.

"Would you care for something to eat?" Laura inquired.

"No, thanks. I had a large dinner at the boarding house. Besides, I shouldn't stay. You and Hillary have to rise early for work tomorrow. I just wanted you to know I'm in town."

Hillary remained seated, as Laura walked Biff to the door. He removed his coat from the hook and faced Laura. He was nervous and his heart began to beat faster. If he intended to ask her to dinner, now was the moment. "When I come to Alton, I'm always dining alone." He looked directly into Laura's eyes. "I would enjoy my meals more, if you were at my table. Possibly Sunday, at one of your favorite restaurants?"

He meant to include Hillary and Saturday night as options, but amid his anxiety, it didn't come out that way. Biff tried altering his proposal. "Of course, Hillary is invited, too."

Laura understood exactly what he meant. "I would like that. I'll discuss it with Hillary."

"Then you will let me know tomorrow, if you'll join me Sunday?"

"No," Laura answered, with a friendly smile. "Tomorrow, I will let you know if Hillary is joining us."

"Eight o'clock tomorrow," Biff said, backing out of the apartment.

Laura faced the room, pushing the door closed with her back. Hillary had moved to her chair by the window to watch her mother and Biff. Laura knew exactly what Hillary was thinking.

The following day, Kate arrived early at Laura's apartment, so they could talk before Biff arrived. As usual, Hillary was reading by the window, so she could look outside. Laura told Kate about the dinner invitation for herself and Hillary, and how he came to her smelling like spices.

Kate snickered. "That's sweet. So, who's going to dinner Sunday?"

"I left the decision to Hillary. She said she would like to join us, but she chose to be with her friends."

"Good answer," Kate whispered.

Laura felt uneasy about the next topic and began fidgeting with the blue tablecloth. "Hillary asked me if I like Biff." Laura paused. "I said yes, as a friend."

"Stop here," Kate said, and grabbed Laura's wrist. "You mean temporarily as a friend, more to come later?"

"As a friend," Laura insisted. "I explained to her that he doesn't know anyone in town and wanted someone to talk to—nothing more."

"Did she believe you?"

"Not totally. She had been talking to me in a guarded way and I knew what was bothering her. Finally, she asked if I was forgetting her father. I assured her that I would never forget him and that I will always love him."

Kate put her elbows on the table and rested her chin on clasped hands. "And if something develops?"

"I don't know," Laura replied, leaning back in her chair. "I'll deal with that, if it happens." Laura looked over at Hillary to see whether she was listening to their conversation. Hillary was either reading a book, or pretending to. Laura flapped her hand at Kate, suggesting they keep their voices down. "It's a good thing this is a big room."

A knock on the door interrupted their conversation. As usual, Biff was on time. Hillary ran to the door to let him in. "Hi, friend!" she said, attempting to label his relationship with them.

Laura and Kate looked at each other. They clearly understood the word "friend."

Laura could see a need to be cautious with Hillary, if her relationship with Biff flourished.

"Hi, friend, yourself," he replied, hanging his coat on the door. Biff removed a small paper bag from his coat pocket. "This is for you," he said, handing it to Hillary. "Mr. Thompson told me what you like."

"Then it's peppermint, or butterscotch," Hillary said, opening the top of the bag.

"I guess he knows his business," Biff replied, walking to the table.

Hillary thanked him and returned to her chair by the window, positioning herself so she could observe them. She intended to keep her eyes and ears open.

Biff sat down, as Laura reached across the table to raise the wick in the lamp. He was anxious to tell his news, so he began immediately. "John has made progress since my last visit. He bought a parcel of land four weeks ago. It borders on a river and has a clear stream running through it. There is plenty of level land for planting and cattle grazing."

Laura looked at Kate and smiled. "You must be excited—a new start for you and John, away from Alton. I'm thrilled for you."

"I'm thrilled, too, but where's he getting the money for all this?" she asked, looking at Biff.

"John saved a good amount of money from working all these years. He's put money in the bank and when his parents died, they left him a modest sum, which my father and I invested for him. That grew to a reasonable amount, too. All in all, he had more money than he imagined."

"Praise the Lord!" Kate whispered, looking up at the heavens.

"By the way, your farm isn't isolated, either. You'll be near a fair-size town with plenty of social life. John knew you wouldn't want to be stuck in the middle of nowhere, living the life of a hermit."

Kate leaned toward Biff. "Tell him he can spoil me as much as he likes. When do we leave?"

"Sorry, Kate, not for a while. The house, barn and sheds are being built now, but then he will have to buy livestock and machinery. It may be six or seven weeks before he's ready. Then, you're home."

Seeing the disappointment on Kate's face, Laura reached across the table to hold her hand. "You're getting out. Another two months is nothing. Alton will be out of your life forever."

"When the time comes, you will have to leave immediately," Biff insisted. "No one should know, except for Laura and Hillary. Take most of your money from the bank, but leave some so nobody becomes suspicious."

Kate and Laura realized their friendship was in jeopardy, but they never discussed the inevitable. Their separation was going to be difficult.

"How hard is it for a woman to find respectable work out there?" Kate asked, desperate for a favorable answer.

"You won't need to look for work. You will have plenty to do on the farm."

"I'm not talking about me," Kate replied, tilting her head toward Laura. "Could Laura get proper work?"

Laura was surprised by the proposal. "Me?" she questioned loudly. It was obvious she had never considered herself in Kate's migration. Laura and Biff looked into each other's eyes, searching for a mutual commitment.

Any doubts Kate might have had about those two were immediately dispelled. Laura and Biff were completely unaware of how obvious they were about their feelings for each other.

"It never entered my mind," Laura gasped. "I've only been thinking about you and John, and what your life would be."

"Well, it occurred to you now," Kate said, leaning toward Laura. "This is a dead end town. There's no reason you shouldn't start a new life, too."

Laura did think of a reason, but didn't want to discuss it in front of Biff. "It is certainly worth considering," she said, as though already trying to decide.

"Consider?" Kate cried out, banging her fist on the table. "Consider it done!"

"What's going on over there?" Hillary shouted from her chair by the window.

"Nothing," Laura replied. "Kate got a little excited."

Kate looked at Biff. "Since we don't know where this paradise is, we don't know the opportunities for Laura."

"What kind of work are you doing now?" Biff asked, Laura.

"I do bookkeeping for some of the smaller businesses in town."

"I really don't think there would be a problem. I'm sure you can find a variety of work." Biff knew he could give her a job at the bank he and his father owned, but he didn't want to divulge his personal wealth at this time.

"I still have to think about it," Laura insisted. "Hillary's friends are here, and well, I have other obligations to consider."

"Let's talk about it later," Kate suggested, leaning back in her chair.

Biff removed John's letter from his shirt pocket and handed it to Kate. "He's anxious for you to get there."

"No more anxious than me." Kate pulled out a letter from her dress sleeve, placing it in front of Biff. "We're like two magicians," she joked.

Kate unfolded the three-page letter and began reading.

Biff turned to Laura to seize the moment. "Have you and Hillary decided about Sunday?"

"Yes. Hillary likes the idea of dining with us, but since she has so little time with her friends, she decided to be with them. She said you two would have plenty of time together when you go to Ceylon."

Biff laughed, then looked at Hillary reading in the glow of her lantern. He quickly returned his attention to Laura. "Would one o'clock be a good time?"

"That would be fine."

"You select the restaurant," Biff suggested, as he stood to leave. "As you know, I'm new in town." He slid his chair against the table. "Good night, Kate. Think happy." He turned to Hillary, as she nodded in and out of sleep in her chair. He didn't want to startle her, so he turned to leave. Laura walked him to the door. "See you at one o'clock," Biff repeated.

Laura returned to the table, knowing Kate would pressure her to leave Alton.

Kate looked at her as she sat down. "Why would you hesitate leaving Alton? Is it Jeremiah?"

"Definitely," Laura answered. "If we left Alton, I know we would never return. I would feel like we were abandoning him. I know it's not rational thinking, but it's difficult to do. We would have left Alton before, if he wasn't buried here."

"You have to change your thinking," Kate insisted. "There are better opportunities for you elsewhere. You can talk or pray to Jeremiah from anywhere. You don't need to be at his grave."

Laura lowered the lamp wick to where it had been before Biff arrived. "I assumed I would be buried next to him."

"What happens during life is more important than after," Kate whispered. She glanced at Hillary sleeping. "The best thing you could do for Hillary, is get her out of Alton."

"I've thought of it many times," Laura admitted. "But when we go to his grave, I commit myself to staying with him, believing he is listening and finding comfort in my promise."

"But now there's Biff. Do you think you're going to get an opportunity like this again? If things are good between you two, go with him. I'm sure Jeremiah would prefer you and Hillary have a better life with Biff, than stay here and rot." Kate lifted her letter from the table. "It's been an exciting evening," she said, rising from her chair. "I'm going home to think about the future."

"You'll be lucky if you can sleep," Laura said, walking to the door.

"You think about your future, too," Kate suggested. "Good luck Sunday. May it be the most successful dinner of your life."

Chapter Sixteen

At exactly one o'clock, Sunday afternoon, Laura opened the door for Biff. She guessed right that his clothing was limited. Except for his shirt, he was dressed as before. She was relieved, worried over her own limited wardrobe. Laura was wearing a beige cotton dress with tiny yellow flowers. It had mutton leg sleeves that gave her a perky look. Her hair was combed up in the back, exposing her slim neck, which she thought was one of her better features.

Biff watched Laura step out of the apartment and lock the door, presenting her with a broad smile of approval. His eyes were intense for a moment, taking pleasure in the face she turned up to his. "You look lovelier each time I see you."

Laura dropped the key into her purse and gave him a coquettish smile. "That's quite a bold statement for a first courting ... but you can continue."

When they stepped out of the building, Biff extended his arm to Laura, just as Jeremiah would have done. She recognized the gesture immediately.

"I'd be proud to walk with you on my arm," he said. "To the right, or left?"

"Left to the corner, then right across Union Avenue, straight to Delaware Bay." Laura took his arm and looked to the sky. *Forgive me Jeremiah.*

"And the name of this dining establishment?" Biff asked, as they began walking.

"The Crab House. It's one of the older, established restaurants in town. They serve a variety of meals, but seafood is their specialty." She gripped Biff's arm a little tighter, as they hurried across Union Avenue, avoiding horse-drawn wagons and buggies moving in both directions.

"I'm looking forward to dinner," Biff declared. "The only fish I eat comes from the Mississippi River, and I don't have it that often."

"The restaurant serves a variety dinner. That way you can get a wide sampling of our seafood."

"Good suggestion. That might be what a land-locked guy like me needs."

Laura greeted neighbors they passed on the street. Some, knowing she was a widow, gave her a long discerning stare, wondering who that man was with her. She enjoyed the interest she created by walking with Biff.

Laura and Biff were comfortable together, each enjoying the physical contact of walking arm-in-arm. The weather was cooperating, too, with a clear, sunny sky and an unseasonably warm temperature. The ocean breeze and smell of saltwater became more intense, as they approached the bay. Sea gulls appeared, gliding on strong air currents, constantly searching for food.

"We are almost there," Laura announced. "The restaurant is across the street from the last house on the left."

It was a tired old frame building, with its back to Delaware Bay. Streaks of black and brown permeated the wood siding from years of exposure to harsh weather and salty air. White lace curtains filled the second floor windows in stark contrast to the building's dark exterior. In front of the building, a weathered wooden sign with black and gold letters stood near the door. It read, *CRAB HOUSE, Good Food and Libations, Robert Ryan, Proprietor.*

They walked into a nautical atmosphere that Biff had imagined he would find in a seaside restaurant. At their left, beyond a drapery of fish netting with floats, stood a varnished wood bar. Two men leaning against the bar gave Laura a thorough look-over. One of the men spit a saturated chaw of tobacco onto the wooden floor, missing the brass cuspidor. Biff could see they weren't a threat. They were so drunk they could barely stand. Beyond them, two more men, each wearing a black derby, played darts in the corner of the room. Biff guided Laura in the opposite direction into a dining room dominated by a huge stone fireplace and a row of large windows facing the bay. Most tables were occupied, but two were available at the windows. Laura noticed them and led Biff for a view of the bay.

On their way to the table, Biff glanced at food-filled plates to observe the quality of the meals. He was pleased with what he saw, while enjoying the smell of garlic and lemon.

Arriving at a table, Laura said, "I win," teasing Biff that she had won a race to the table.

"You certainly did," Biff agreed, with a chuckle. "I guess I owe you dinner."

"Good," Laura replied, as she sat in the chair. "I'd hate to feel indebted."

Laura scanned the room to see who was there. She saw Tom and Marian Mullins, owners of a dry-goods business in Thompson's building where she lived. They were sitting a few tables away, nodding and smiling to her in a way that was difficult for Laura to decipher. She wasn't sure if they were smiling because they finally saw her with a man, or because they were approving of the man she was with. Laura smiled in return, without Biff being aware.

"The seafood looks good," Biff remarked. "It's certainly different from what I get back home."

"And where is that?" Laura asked, hoping for an honest answer.

Biff smiled. "The same place I said before—out west. I don't mean to be difficult, but I think I should wait a little longer before answering that question." He looked directly into Laura's eyes before continuing. "When that time comes, I'll have a great deal to tell you."

Laura understood his meaning. It made her feel uncomfortable, yet at the same time, she was pleased. "Do you have family out west?"

Biff leaned forward with his elbows on the table and his hands clasped together. "My parents live on a farm about fifteen miles from me. I have one sister and she lives in a town about thirty miles away, where she and her husband own a general store. They have a seven-year-old daughter and a five-year-old boy." Biff leaned back in his chair again and smiled. "They named the boy after me."

"Having your family close together, sounds cozy," she said, with a smile. "What is your sister's name?"

"Nora. She was named after our grandmother."

"Do you have a first name other than Biff?"

"Robert. When my father was a kid, he had a friend named Biff. Dad said I looked like him, so he started calling me Biff and it stuck."

"I like it. It's a fine, masculine name. Were you ever married?" Laura tried to appear casual, while asking questions. "Do you have any children?"

"No family of my own, and no great love stories to tell. I spend most of my time running my business. If I had met someone I cared about, I would have married, but it never happened."

A waitress with a slight limp came from a table nearby. She rubbed her nose with the back of her hand and produced two handwritten paper menus from under her arm. "Hi. I'm Della. Do ya want something ta drink?"

Laura and Biff were startled by Della's abrupt manner.

"I'll have a glass of white wine," Laura said. She pretended to read the menu, while listening to Biff's drink order. She thought it might possibly give her a clue as to where Biff was from, or something about his character.

"I'd like a Brandy Sour," he said, eagerly.

Laura and Biff could tell by the blank look on Della's face, neither she nor the bartender would know what that was.

"Some people call it a Civil War Sour. It was created in the '60s." Biff could see she was baffled by his request. "Let me change that order," he suggested, trying to save her embarrassment. "I'd rather have an Apple Brandy."

The expression on Della's face was steadfast. "My father owns this joint and I doubt he heard of those drinks, either."

Biff guessed that his choice of drinks weren't popular in this part of the country. "Better yet," he continued, "Bring me a Dooley's Ale, please."

Della smiled, and wrote it down on her order pad, then walked away.

"Don't be concerned about the food because of her. The food comes highly recommended. I don't know anything about the service," Laura said.

"I'm not concerned. I'm enjoying the view," he replied, without taking his eyes off Laura.

She smiled and studied the menu. "Is my wine included with the dinner I won?" Laura asked, peeking over the menu.

"Certainly," Biff answered. "Dessert, too."

"This *is* my lucky day!" she responded with a big smile.

It wasn't long before Della returned with their drinks, dropping napkins and silverware on the table in front of them. With pad and pencil in hand, she stood silently looking at Laura.

"I've decided to have the filet of white fish," Laura said "I assume it's fresh?"

"They caught it early this morning," Della replied, writing on the pad. She looked to Biff for his order.

"I'll have the mix of shrimp, clams and filet of white fish," he said, handing her his menu.

"A popular choice," Della said, taking Biff's menu. "It won't take long 'cause it's cookin' already." She placed the two menus under her arm and walked into the other room.

Laura and Biff were looking out at the bay when he broke the silence. "What have Hillary and her friends planned for today?"

Laura turned from the window to face him. "What they plan to do, and what they actually do, are not always the same. First, they were going to the pond to see if the wild flowers were blooming. I think not. Then, they were going to the cemetery to read headstones."

Biff broke into a hearty laugh, causing people at nearby tables to look in his direction. "Read headstones?" he questioned, lowering his voice. "Is this something they do often?"

Laura pretended not to notice the glances directed at them. She sipped her wine before responding. "Go to the pond, yes. To the cemetery, not often."

"They sound like three adventuresome young ladies," Biff remarked.

"Haven't you ever read headstones?"

"Can't say I have. The only time I go to cemeteries is when I need to. When the formalities are over, I leave."

"You can find interesting verses on headstones," Laura assured him. "Some are humorous, some sad, and others can be enlightening."

"Alright," Biff said. "One day, I'll read headstones with you and Hillary. I'm always willing to learn. But first, I would like you to do me a favor."

"It depends," Laura answered, waiting with her head cocked slightly to the side.

"This afternoon, I would like you to take me to the pond that's so popular with everyone."

"Good idea. We have a perfect day for it. But let me clarify that the pond is not actually a pond, but a deep spot in the river. Most of the swimming is done there. We can go after our meal, which I see coming now."

They dined watching gulls soar over the bay and boats with full sail cut through the waves. Without being obvious, they each hurried their meal, both preferring to be outside walking arm-in-arm. When they finished, Della returned to ask if they wanted dessert. Both declined. Biff pushed back on his chair and paid the bill.

When they stepped out into the warm air, Biff raised his arm, which Laura took readily. They walked south along the bay to Pontiac Street and the railroad tracks, then turned west, leaving the bay behind.

They were in the oldest part of Alton, with rickety frame houses and crumbling picket fences surrounding grassless yards scattered with junk. Pontiac Street was paved with gravel, separating the houses from the railroad tracks. People stood waiting at the station with luggage and boxes at their feet, while bored children meandered about the platform looking for something to amuse them.

They entered Mill Prairie on a direct course for the pond. Biff asked Laura the name of the river.

"Clarion," she answered, with enthusiasm. "It's a vital part of Alton. Without it, there would be little recreation for the people."

"They can go to the cemetery," Biff responded, giving her a side-glance. "I understand the reading is excellent there."

Laura frowned at him. "Very funny. What I said about the river is true. Our best memories as a family are at the pond. Hillary considers the pond 'our' place because we went so often. Picnics and swimming in the summer, sledding and skating in winter. Everybody likes it here. It's relaxing."

They stopped to watch a father help his small son send a kite aloft. After three nose-dives, it soared upward, wiggling as it climbed. The little boy squealed with excitement, as he held the line, his father yanking it occasionally when it began to falter.

"Kate and I were wondering how you know John Hanley?" Laura asked, suddenly.

"He's my cousin. When he left Alton, he came directly to me. It's been good having him back home."

They were approaching the trees by the pond when a slender boy about ten years old walked over to them. He was wearing a battered gray and black tweed cap and an oversized black coat that hung to his ankles. Old dirt covered him.

"Shoe shine, Mister?" he asked. "Shoelaces, cigars, gum, cigarettes, candy, matches—flowers for the lady?"

Biff was amused by the industrious figure before him. "You seem to have many things for sale, but I don't see any merchandise."

"I got it, alright," the boy insisted. He whipped his coat open and stood like a bat with its wings spread.

Biff estimated there were twenty pockets, crudely sewn into the lining of the boy's coat, each containing items for sale. He was a walking variety store. "That's a clever coat you have," Biff snickered.

"I sewed them pockets on meself," he declared, proudly. The boy removed his cap and turned it upside down to show two more pockets. "I keeps me matches an' shoelaces in here. People call me 'The Pocket Merchant' because of me coat and hat."

"Well, Mr. Pocket Merchant, where are those flowers for me lady?"

"Right here," he answered, reaching into his top left pocket. He retrieved three paper flowers with wire stems wrapped in green paper. "One red, one white, an' one yeller," he announced. "I don't say I got something I ain't. Variety is what people want, so I'm versadle. More sales that way."

Biff and Laura were totally entertained by the "Pocket Merchant," and his wardrobe. "What else do you have to offer?" Biff asked.

"Do ya chew?"

Laura took interest in that question and stepped closer to make sure she heard the answer. Biff smiled at the boy. "No, I don't chew, do you?"

"Sometimes. Not often."

"How much do you want for the flowers?" Biff asked.

"All three?" he questioned, twirling them between his fingers.

"Yes, the whole bouquet," Biff replied, searching for change in his pocket. Biff prepared himself for the haggling that was about to begin.

"Well, let's see," the boy mumbled. "I guess I'd let 'em go for five cents."

"I didn't hear you," Biff replied, turning his ear toward the boy.

"Four cents would be okay, I guess," he whined.

"I still didn't hear you," Biff replied.

The lad paused for a few moments before responding. "She looks like a nice lady. You can have 'em fer three cents. Bottom price, though."

"Sold!" Biff said, handing him the coins.

"Anything else?" the boy asked, extending the flowers to Biff.

"No, that's it. Thanks for the flowers."

"Been nice doing business with ya," the youngster replied, running off into the prairie.

"That was fun," Laura commented, while reclaiming Biff's arm. "I felt like taking him home and giving him a bath."

Biff twisted the three flower stems together and handed them to Laura. "Bouquet for me lady," he said. "One red, one white and one yeller."

"Thank you," Laura chuckled. "I was wondering if you were keeping them for yourself." She spun them between her fingers. "I think I like the yeller one best. Imagine, dinner and flowers in one day? You're making my head spin."

Biff liked Laura's sense of humor and everything thing else about her. "I have a question," he asked, with a slight frown. "You're an educated woman. How did you end up in Alton?"

"I'll give you a brief summary," Laura said, as they continued walking. "Girl from comfortable family falls in love with poor boy. Girl's parents refuse union of girl to boy. Girl and boy run away to Alton and marry. Girl's parents return to England and are never heard from again. Boy and girl have baby. Boy dies, leaving girl with baby."

"Sad summary," Biff responded. "How did the boy die?"

"He was a carpenter," Laura continued. "One day, a brick wall collapsed on Jeremiah and two other men. All three were killed. The company they worked for gave each of the wives twenty-five dollars and their sympathies, in exchange for their husbands. Amen."

"Sorry," Biff replied. "I'm sure you've had a difficult time."

Laura looked back at the father and son flying the kite. "I have, but we had no choice but to go on."

"Where did you meet Jeremiah?"

"We attended the same church in New York City. He lived about five streets from me." She paused and looked up at Biff. "On the other side of the tracks. We saw each other frequently, but didn't talk except for a passing, 'Hello.' I was twenty-one years old when he began working at the house next door to ours, repairing a wooden fence and building cabinets for their kitchen. I was in the yard hanging laundry one day and we began talking over the fence. The fire was lit and we continued talking until he died."

"How many years were you married?"

"Nine years. Nine-good years. We didn't have much, but we were happy."

"Would you consider leaving Alton?"

"Difficult," Laura said. "I would feel I was abandoning Jeremiah."

"Could there ever be a reason for you to leave Alton?" Biff asked, looking for a crack in her armor.

"Yes, if it was good for Hillary. Even better, if it is good for Hillary and me."

Biff was satisfied with her answer. They continued walking arm-in-arm toward the trees. "Any brothers or sisters?"

"No brothers or sisters," Laura answered. "As for my parents, they saw to it that I had enough education to be a proper wife for a man of means. They wanted me to marry money, so it would help them socially. So, when I married Jeremiah, they went back to England. I haven't heard from them since, and I don't even know what part of England they went to, or if they're still alive."

Biff looked at Laura, digesting her cruel story. He could see hurt in her face, as she peered off into the distance. "Maybe the best part of your life is coming?"

"I have Hillary. She makes up for most of what's missing in my life. We don't have much, but we're relatively happy."

They stopped by the river, three oak trees, and soon to be blooming wildflowers.

"So, this is the pond?" Biff remarked. "A nice setting. I imagine it is quite attractive in full bloom. Shall we sit and watch the river roll by?"

"I can't think of anything I'd rather do today," she replied.

Laura waited while Biff leaned against a tree, with one leg stretched out and the other folded back with his knee raised. Laura sat directly in front of him facing the river, watching families walk along the riverbank. She could see white clouds and birds in flight reflecting on the passing water. Laura looked over her shoulder at Biff and sniffed her small, three flower bouquet. "Heavenly," she sighed.

Biff concentrated on Laura, watching the river. Delicate curls at her temples lifted and dropped in the gentle breeze, increasing his desire to hold her and feel her warm body against his. He reached for one of the curls, as if catching a butterfly, then carefully held it between his fingers. Laura leaned back against his raised knee.

Chapter Seventeen

It was just before seven o'clock when Hillary entered her apartment. Laura was standing at the sink with the water running. Hillary went directly to her chair at the window to watch Mr. Brummer load furniture onto his wagon. The back of the wagon was facing the street lamp so he could see inside. Darby was being petted and talked to by a thin old woman wearing a small straw hat with a single red flower on the side. Hillary believed she was "tet'ched in the haid."

"Did you see any wildflowers blooming at the cemetery?" Laura asked.

"Just us girls," Hillary joked, looking down on the avenue.

"We didn't notice any, either. It will probably take another three or four weeks."

Hillary looked down at a green and gold beer wagon pulled by four large brown horses. It was dusk, but light enough to see that the driver had a mustache almost the width of his face. "You and Biff went to the pond?" Hillary asked, studying the man and his mustache.

"It was a beautiful day and Biff wanted to see it." Laura paused before continuing. "Do you know the boy who calls himself, Pocket Merchant?"

"Everyone knows him. He doesn't get close to soap and water too often, but he's a good hawker. Says he'll be president of our country someday. Can you imagine?"

"I wouldn't be surprised if he is," Laura responded. "Heaven knows we have enough dirty politicians already."

Hillary turned when she realized her mother's voice sounded strained and she hadn't moved a step. Laura was standing rigid, gripping the edge of the sink. "Are you going to vomit again?"

"I think so," Laura answered, with difficulty. "Is the hall bathroom empty?"

Hillary rushed out of her apartment and saw the bathroom door partially open. She returned waving her hand, signaling her mother to hurry before someone came. Laura raced past her, hoping to get there in time. Hillary heard the door close, then the upheaval. She sat on the bed, waiting for her mother.

When Laura returned, she lay on the bed next to Hillary. "I'm glad I didn't do that earlier. It would have been quite embarrassing for me, and Biff."

"You should see Dr. Merges again," Hillary insisted. "I don't like you doing that. It happens too often for it to be just an upset stomach."

Laura placed her hand against Hillary's back and gave it a few pats. "I have an appointment with him Tuesday evening. Do you want to go with me?"

Hillary glared at her mother. "Of course! He's got to fix what's wrong with you."

Laura closed her eyes, her hand still resting against Hillary's back.

"Did you have milk with your dinner?" Hillary asked.

Laura smiled at her naïve question. "No, I had wine with my dinner."

"Well, that didn't help." Hillary rolled onto her stomach to face her mother. "Do you feel well enough to go for a walk?"

"Sorry, my dear. I would like to, but I'm very tired. I'll just lie here and read." Laura opened her eyes and looked at Hillary. "Do you have schoolwork?"

"Yes. I'll do it next to you."

Hillary was glad when Tuesday evening finally arrived. She believed the doctor would figure out her mother's illness, and put an end to it.

It was as warm as Sunday had been, and Hillary enjoyed her walk to the doctor's office. For Laura, the walk was taxing; she had been tired even before they left home. When they arrived at the doctor's home, she let Hillary turn the butterfly knob that rang the bell. Mary greeted them warmly and led them into the sitting room.

Dr. Merges entered the room, gave them both a friendly smile and motioned for Laura to follow him. "We might as well go directly into my office." The doctor then suggested that Mary entertain Hillary again, which she was delighted to do.

Laura followed Dr. Merges to his office and stopped in front of his desk. "I see you lost some weight," he said immediately.

"I guess I have. I've had a difficult time keeping food down."

"Vomiting?" "When did this begin?"

"About a week after my last visit."

Dr. Merges brought a chair for Laura and went behind his desk. "What about your bowel movements? Any blood?"

"No, I haven't noticed any. But I do feel tired and weak. I assume it's a lack of nourishment, since I can't keep food down."

"Blood in the vomit?"

"No."

He examined Laura again, hoping to find a symptom that would explain her malady. After some probing, he examined her nose and throat, discovering her mucous membranes had changed from a normal pink to tan. Next, he discovered patches of tan pigmentation on her hands and arms. He recalled reading of such symptoms, but couldn't remember the condition that caused them. "Can you return

Sunday at two o'clock? I would like to confer with another doctor on my findings."

Laura nodded. "Should I be concerned?" she asked, nervously.

Dr. Merges paused before answering. "It isn't a common illness, so a second opinion is always best. We'll know more by Sunday."

When they returned to the sitting room, Hillary was sitting on the settee' holding a stereoscope, studying three-dimensional pictures. "It's like magic," Hillary commented, still holding the viewer to her eyes. "I feel I'm there with the people, like I could reach out and touch them. We're standing on a cliff, looking down into the Grand Canyon. What will they invent next?"

"I know you could sit there for hours looking at pictures, but we have to get home."

Dr. Merges promised Hillary the stereoscope would be available whenever she was there.

Hillary stood and faced the doctor. "Do you know what's wrong with my mother?"

"I believe the next time your mother comes to me, I'll have an answer. Be patient just a little longer," the doctor said, confidently.

Mary walked them to the front door. On the carpeted stairs, leading to the second floor, was a small white box with pink ribbon tied around it. Mary picked up the box and handed it to Hillary. "I baked some cookies for you. There's a mix of sugar, peanut butter and ginger cookies."

"That's a good mixture. Thank you very much." Hillary looked at her mother. "Shall we go home and have tea and cookies?"

"I couldn't say no to that eager little face," Laura responded. They thanked Mary again and stepped outside. Laura was disappointed because the doctor still couldn't identify her illness. As they proceeded down the street, a sharp pain darted through Laura's abdomen, almost causing her legs to give out. Laura fought the pain, so Hillary wouldn't be alarmed. She began to seriously worry about what her illness might be.

Dr. Robert Merges prepared a letter to be delivered by messenger that evening. He had grown fond of Laura and Hillary, and Laura's condition weighed heavily on his mind. He requested a Friday evening meeting with Dr. Lawrence Mackin, a renowned physician and professor at the Delaware Institute of Medicine. He believed Dr. Mackin was the only person around Alton who would have knowledge of Laura's condition.

Friday came with intermittent clouds and light rain that seemed to be turned on and off by a divine hand. Hixton, where Lawrence Mackin lived, was also the location of the Institute. Alton to Hixton was a half-hour coach ride, through some of Delaware's most scenic countryside. Robert sat back in his coach and enjoyed the ride.

It was drizzling when he arrived, and he was anxious to learn of Lawrence's findings. Stepping out of his coach, he opened his umbrella, while hurrying to the porch of the doctor's house. Arda Mackin, the doctor's wife, was waiting in the open doorway. She put his umbrella into an umbrella stand and led him down a hall to her husband's library beyond the parlor. The library walls were lined from floor to ceiling with rich mahogany bookcases. Robert approached Lawrence, standing behind his desk. Lawrence was in his fifties, six feet tall and slender.

"Thank you for agreeing to a consultation," Robert said. "I was sure your expertise would be helpful."

"My pleasure. I enjoy a challenge. It's like putting a puzzle together. Please be seated."

Robert pulled a black leather chair closer to the desk, while Lawrence placed an open book in front of him. "From your description, I assumed it was a glandular problem, so I researched in that direction. Of course, I'll be more certain after I see the patient Sunday."

"I gather this book is the reference?" Robert asked.

"Yes. What I read here matches perfectly with your patient's symptoms. Years back, I saw two such cases in New York. When I see Mrs.

Cook, I should be able to determine if she has Addison's disease. The key characteristic here is hyper-pigmentation of the skin and mucous membranes. It is usually a definite sign."

"I read about it years ago, but have had no experience with it," Robert admitted.

Lawrence pulled his chair closer to the desk and leaned forward. "To describe it simply, when the adrenal gland fails, many body activities malfunction, causing a breakdown of the body's performance. The text doesn't explain what causes the condition, so I can't help you there. The condition was identified in England by Dr. Thomas Addison around 1850."

"What is the treatment?" Dr. Merges asked, lifting the book from the desk.

"Sadly, there is none. We usually give them sugar pills. It gives them hope for a period of time. Soon, she will weaken to a point where she won't be able to work. Then, she'll deteriorate quickly."

Dr. Merges glared across the desk at him. "She is a widow with a twelve-year-old daughter. Are you positive there isn't anything—something new?"

"I'm sorry," Lawrence replied. "Being that she is at this stage of the illness, I'd say she has about six to eight weeks to live."

CHAPTER EIGHTEEN

Biff Arley and his father, Benjamin, were prominent men in North-western Illinois. Their family had settled in the Galena Territory in 1820, becoming a driving force in its development. Lead mining brought their family wealth, until its decline in 1850. The family then went into banking. By 1875, they owned a bank, and large tracts of land they turned into productive farms and cattle ranches.

Biff lived alone on one of his farms in a large frame house on 800 acres. He welcomed the sudden appearance of his cousin after his long absence. As boys, they had been good friends, spending most of their free time together. During the past four months, Biff helped John resettle in the Galena area.

Biff was sitting at the kitchen table, repairing a bridle when he heard John ride into the yard on Shandy, a black mare with a white patch on her forehead. Biff took Kate's letter from the table and headed for the yard. His boot heels banged against the wooden porch until he leaped over four stairs to the ground. He approached John removing his saddle and blanket from Shandy.

"Got mail for me?" John asked, confidently.

"Think I went to Alton for nothing?"

"No, I think you go there to see Laura." He stepped up to Biff until they were almost nose-to-nose. "Did you get to spend time with her liked you hoped?" he asked, playfully.

Biff smiled, broadly. "Yeah, I did. We had a great day together. Got along just fine."

"Sounds like you're getting hooked," John said, as they walked toward the stable. "I take that back—I think you are hooked. Each visit seems to get you more excited."

Biff continued to smile, as he accompanied John to the tack room to store his saddle.

"You haven't stopped grinning since I mentioned Laura's name," John said. "I guess that's a sign?"

Biff held Kate's letter in his outstretched arm. "Must have cramps in my cheeks? I'll have to get them fixed."

"Only one way to fix that," John said, grinning at Biff. He walked over and placed his hand on Biff's shoulder. "I've known Laura for a long time. She's a fine woman, and if you feel that way, you couldn't do better."

They discussed business and local news, while walking Shandy around the corral before bedding her. When she cooled down, John took the horse to her stall.

Biff climbed onto the corral fence and waited. A cardinal landed on a fence post not more than fifteen feet away. Biff knew it was a male because of its bright red color. The bird tilted its head from side-to-side, as if evaluating Biff. After looking at each other a few moments, the bird flew off.

When John returned, Biff dropped from the fence, kicking up dust as he landed on dry ground. On their way to the house, Biff gave John a strong shove without warning, knocking him sideways. Biff pointed toward the ground. "Didn't want you to step in that before going into the house," he declared.

John slumped into a kitchen chair, one leg crossing the other, reading Kate's letter.

Biff was at the sink, pumping water into a dented green and white speckled coffee pot. "Cup of coffee, Greenhorn?" Biff asked.

"Thanks, shit-kicker," John responded, continuing to read his letter.

Biff raised a round metal lid on the stove to add wood to the fire and stepped back to survey its overall condition. Small repairs had been made with non-conforming parts through the years, and porcelain on the face of the oven door was chipped in several places. He decided Laura should have a new stove, if they got married.

"This letter says Kate's trying to get Laura and Hillary to come here," John said, rocking back on the chair. "Do you know anything about that? Sounds like Laura must have her eye on you, too, or Kate's trying to be a matchmaker."

"Kate mentioned it when the three of us were together. Laura seemed to like the idea. I know I did." Biff turned and looked squarely at John. "You're right about what you said earlier. I am hooked, and I wish she were here now. I'm going to do whatever I can to make it happen."

John left the room to wash road dust from himself and his boots, while Biff prepared supper. By the time he returned, clouds rolling in from the west darkened the kitchen. John lit the lamps on the kitchen table and stove, while Biff carried two bountiful plates to the table. They devoured a dinner of fried steak, fried potatoes and a whole jar of stewed tomatoes. After the table was cleared, Biff pulled the lamp closer, so he could continue repairing the bridle he had worked on that afternoon.

John put two additional pieces of wood into the stove to heat a kettle of water for washing dishes. "Want to go to Galena Saturday night?" John asked. "I heard they're having the annual spring dance at Town Hall."

"Sure. It's always a fun night, and I get to talk to people I seldom see through the year. It'll be a late night, though, so we should stay at the De Soto Hotel and ride back in the morning."

"Should be some young ladies looking for a partner," John said.

"Looking for a permanent partner," Biff added, cutting at the leather strap. "One reason for the dance is so parents can display sons and daughters prime for marriage."

John looked over his shoulder at Biff. "I hear Alissa Newman will be there. Or, I should say, Widow Coakley?"

With the bridle spread across his lap, Biff looked up at John, his eyes following him across the room, until he sat at the other side of the table. "Widow?" Biff questioned, waiting for further explanation.

John reached for the Galena newspaper lying on a chair next to him. He held it in his outstretched arms, shaking kinks from the pages, so it would fold properly. He shook it more than necessary to tease Biff's patience before answering.

Biff began tapping his toe against the floor, glaring at John, aware of the waiting game he was playing.

John removed a handkerchief from his back pocket and wiped his nose a few times, until he decided he had stalled long enough. "She returned from Chicago about two weeks ago, with an eight year-old daughter and six year-old son. She's been a widow five months. I was told her husband died of pneumonia." John glanced across the table at Biff, searching his eyes for his true feelings for Alissa. "I understand you were sweet on her at one time. Is that true?"

There was a pause before Biff answered. "That was more than ten years ago," he said, thrusting the bridle on the table. "Where did you hear about her?"

John rolled the newspaper into a tube and began turning it in his hand. "I stopped at Lengstrom's General Store and got to jawing with Arvid. There was a sign on the wall telling about the dance, so I asked him about it. He said you might be interested in knowing Alissa will be there. Care to explain?"

Biff rested his forearms on the table and smiled. "He caught us smooching behind a display of stove pipes one afternoon. Her face turned strawberry red when he caught us. I see he hasn't forgotten, either."

John flipped the rolled newspaper on the table. "Hell, I've been caught doing worse than that."

"That doesn't surprise me," Biff responded. "But a widow of only five months, going to a dance? That surprises me."

"She volunteered to work the refreshment tables. She's not going there to dance, unless someone …"

Biff stared at John sitting on the other side of the flickering lamp. "Unless what?"

"Unless you two decide you're still interested in smooching behind stove pipes."

"Can't say I'm not curious," Biff said, casually. He got up from his chair and walked to the window to examine the grounds before there was total darkness. "All gates closed and no animals running free." Biff turned to face John. "Alissa couldn't replace Laura, but a polite encounter wouldn't hurt."

"Seeing her could be a good test of your feelings. You'd be miserable if you brought Laura here, then discovered you had stronger feelings elsewhere."

"Not a chance," Biff said. He returned to the chair at the table and began removing his boots.

"Why did she marry this Coakley guy?" John rocked back on the legs of the chair, waiting for an answer.

"The marriage was arranged by the parents," Biff said, carrying his boots to the back door. With his toe, he unfurled a brown knit rug and dropped his boots on it. "They were close friends, and they pushed their kids together from the time they were school age. I heard he was a nice guy, but I don't think she loved him."

John lowered the front legs of his chair onto the floor and folded his arms. "You weren't interested enough to steal her away?"

Biff returned to the table in his stocking feet, rolling up his shirtsleeves. "Interested? Yes. But we never had an opportunity to explore our feelings fully, because her parents made her unavailable to suitors other than Coakley."

"I guess it wasn't in the cards," John said. "Say, that's not a bad idea. Want to play poker tonight?"

"Might as well. Nothing else going on."

Saturday night, Biff stood before the dresser mirror, pushing silver buttons through the buttonholes of his black shirt. A brief spring rain had just ended and turbulent gray clouds moved on. In the mirror's reflection, he could see the sun, a round orange blaze setting beyond the barn. Birds hopped along tree branches singing a day ending song. Biff lit the oil lamp sitting on the dresser, as the last of daylight ebbed away. A branch of the tree next to the house tapped against the siding, as the evening wind rose and fell.

Biff was thinking about the Sunday afternoon he had shared with Laura, and of seeing her again, when John stepped into the room carrying an oil lamp, singing, "Oh! Susanna." Biff was bent over, pulling the bottoms of his tan pants over his black boots. "I hear you singing that quite often. You turning into a rebel?"

"Nay, Yankee cousin! I like the song. That doesn't make me a turncoat." John stepped in front of the mirror to admire himself in his green shirt, tan pants and dark brown boots. "Do I look dapper, or do I?"

Biff stood next to John, looking at him in the mirror. "If I catch you grinning at yourself in the mirror, I'll tell everybody how conceited you are."

Biff went to the window to inspect the weather for their ride to Galena. Two raindrops slid down the wet glass, leaving parallel lines. "Full moon and hardly a cloud," he said. "We're in luck, just enough rain so the roads won't be dusty." Biff walked over to the bed and lifted his leather jacket from the bedpost. "We'll register at the De Soto Hotel first to get rid of our bags. Then we'll take the horses to the stable. After that, the fun will begin."

Biff extinguished the lamp on the dresser, expecting to be in total darkness. Instead, soft blue moonlight filled the room. A chill spread through his body, leaving him with a dreadful intuition. *What direction is this coming from?* Biff wondered.

John led them down the stairs, carrying what Biff called his floating lamp, the one he carried through the house and placed by the back door when he went out for an evening. The kitchen was still warm from hot embers smoldering in the stove. John got their leather overnight bags from a row of coat hooks next to the back door and went outside.

Biff extinguished the kerosene lamp and placed it on the small table by the back door, then stepped outside and locked the door.

John was waiting behind him, watching rainwater drip from the porch overhang and splash on the stairs. As they crossed the yard, a bat flew erratically above them in the moonlight. John was ready to swing his bag, if it got too close.

They backed their horses from the stalls and tied them to a railing next to the tack room. Both animals waited patiently to be saddled, as though eager for an evening run.

They rode out of the stable and stopped in the shadow of the corral fence spread across the ground. As he inspected the sky, Biff patted his horse, Creo, on the neck. "Still hardly a cloud. We should have good light all the way." He noticed John twisting a long piece of straw between his teeth. "I hope nothing dropped or splashed on that straw," Biff chuckled.

John spit the straw from his mouth and kicked his heels into Shandy. Biff followed him out to the road.

A half-mile later, they saw widow O'Connor and her dog standing in the glow of a fire behind her house. She was burning trash that had been stacked in her yard since autumn. Her dog turned and barked at their black silhouettes riding by. Without looking she waved her hand over her head, confident it was Biff. She watched the smoke and sparks soar and drift far over the dirt field.

They rode at a controlled pace for thirty minutes, pulling up on a ridge overlooking Galena. The prairie before them sloped down to the Galena River flowing along the edge of town. They lowered their reins and gazed at the town lights glimmering under a star-filled sky. Moonlight winked at them a thousand times on the surface of the river, and the sound of crickets soothed their consciousness.

"Kate will love it here," John said, with pride. "A couple more weeks and you can bring her home. With luck, Laura and Hillary will come with her."

"I was thinking the same thing. They certainly deserve more than what they have." Creo became restless and bolted ahead of Shandy. Biff leaned back and reined her in again, pointing to a red brick house 150 yards away. It had a small wrap-around porch and white window frames. "At one time, that house was the home of President Ulysses Grant." It was difficult to see in the moonlight, but one could tell it was a modest home for such a prominent person. Lantern lights flickered in three of the rooms.

"Is that so?" John said in a condescending manner. He wasn't interested in President Grant's home at the moment. He was thinking about his future with Kate. "I'd like to thank you for all you've done for me and Kate. I don't know where I'd be now, if I didn't have your help."

Biff shifted in his saddle to look back at John. "I live here, so it didn't take much effort on my part. Buy me a beer and we'll call it even."

"Good idea," John said, bolting past Biff. They raced down a trail curving through prairie grass, then onto the bridge. Horseshoes hitting wooden planks echoed across the water. At the edge of town, it became apparent that the rainfall had been greater around Galena because depressions in the ground made by wagon wheels and horses still held water. They proceeded up Main Street toward the De Soto Hotel, passing shops and offices vital to a thriving town. The street in the town center was paved with plump brown bricks, still wet from the evening rain. Tall gas lamps illuminated the avenue and the people passing under them.

The De Soto Hotel was alive with lights and active patrons, entering and leaving the lobby through handsome varnished doors with polished brass hardware. Biff and John dismounted and tied their horses to a hitching post next to a water trough. They removed their overnight bags from behind the saddles and entered the glowing lobby, with its plush forest green carpet and opulent crystal lanterns. Rich brown woodwork throughout, accentuated the hotel's elegance. The top of the reception desk was beige marble, with streaks of golden brown flakes of metal.

At the desk, Biff placed his bag on the floor next to John. "You check us in. I'm going to inspect the new dining room." Biff passed through a curtain of brown and green beads, then stood against the wall. Every table was occupied, except one next to him at the entrance. The round tables stood on a thick red carpet, covered with green cloths and gold napkins. Polished brass lamps with red glass shades hung over each table. Next to the bar, a corpulent lady in a flowered dress was playing, "A Hot Time in the Old Town" on the piano. Her hair was combed to the top of her head and held in place with a curved pearl comb.

Biff watched people eat steak and greens, sip wine from delicate crystal glasses. He imagined how nice it would be to share this with Laura and Hillary; an evening or weekend of indulging in fine living before returning to the farm house, stable, and muddy yard.

John interrupted Biff's concentration with a tap on the shoulder, telling him the bags were in the room. As they passed through the lobby, John gave Biff a second key to the room in case one got lost.

Their hips rocked forward and back on the saddle, as they rode slowly down Main Street. They passed the dance hall that was surrounded by braying horses and rattling wagons filled with families intent on having fun. Light spilled onto the street through two open doors, unveiling dancers spinning and dipping to the rhythm of fiddles.

John inspected the crowd milling outside and those going in.

Biff reminded him that Kate would be arriving soon and shouldn't "auter" hear gossip she wouldn't like.

John grinned, rolled his eyes, and swayed his body to the sound of music and feet pounding on the dance floor.

Will Monagan, a slight man with gray hair and thin, white mustache, stood in front of the stable puffing his corncob pipe, as they rode in. Biff's family had done business with Will for three decades and treated him like a relative. During the Civil War, he had sold horses to the Union Cavalry and still liked to talk about it.

"Yer getting a late start," Will said, in a scratchy voice. "Good thing the hall is just down the street. Give me those horses and go have fun."

Biff thanked him and handed him the reins. "Should be back about mid-morning," he said, walking away.

The crowd on the street thinned, as men and women moved into the hall. Mrs. Bitzel, owner of a popular bakery in town, sat at a table by the door selling tickets. "One dollar for five dollars worth of fun," she said in a loud voice. "Good to see ya, Biff. It's been a while."

"Yes, it has." He placed his hand on John's shoulder. "This is my cousin, John. He's been living with me the last few months and I've told him about your pies."

John laid two silver dollars on the table. "Biff says your pies are the best in the land. Is that true?"

"He likes to exaggerate, but never about my pies," she boasted.

Before she could continue, the music started again. The five musicians were dressed in bib overalls, colorful cotton shirts and raggedy straw hats. The plucking of a fiddle mixed with short and long strokes of a bow sliding across the strings filled the air. There was foot stomping and howling, making the night an early success.

Mrs. Bitzel raised her voice so she could be heard above the music. "You stop by my place and I'll let you try my new lemon tart."

"It's a deal," John yelled. The men smiled and moved in with the crowd. It was a large hall with bare essentials. Windows were spaced along the plastered walls, with wood paneling covering the lower three-and-a-half feet. Three wagon wheel chandeliers hung from the ceiling and there were lanterns mounted on the walls between the windows.

Meris Noolin, a spirited, redheaded schoolteacher, walked toward them twisting her torso so her skirt would flare. "Hi, Biff. I was wondering if you would show tonight."

"I knew you'd be here, so I had to come."

"I didn't realize I was such an influence," she replied, with a side-glance. "You'll dance with me before the night is over?"

"Wouldn't have it any other way," Biff said, with a big, friendly smile.

"Who's the good looking fella next to you? I haven't seen him before. If I had, I would have remembered."

John stepped forward, eager to introduce himself. "I'm Biff's cousin. The name is John. When Biff told me about you, I moved to Galena straight away."

"You certainly are related," Meris said, trying to be heard above the music. "You guys can toss more manure in two minutes than any two people I know." Before parting, Meris stepped closer to Biff. "I suggest you stop by the refreshment tables. You may find the treats more interesting this year."

"I'll make sure I do," Biff said, fully aware she was referring to Alissa.

They moved further into the hall, with the intent of getting a beer. Chairs were lined against the walls to allow room for dancing and people to mill about. Biff displayed two fingers to the bartender, as he and John stepped up to the bar. Two glass mugs dripping with foam were in front of them in record time. Biff threw a large coin on the bar and raised his mug to John, who responded in kind. They leaned back against the bar, as fiddlers began to play. Couples rushed to the dance floor and soon the room was in motion. Those who weren't dancing watched and tapped their toes to the music.

Biff saw Meris Noolin slipping through the crowd toward the dancing. She grabbed the arm of George Broadbend, a local lumber dealer, and pulled him onto the floor. Biff thought they danced well together, as though they had shared many hours on a dance floor.

John finished his beer, watching Meris and George dance. When the music stopped, they talked briefly, then left in different directions. John quickly moved toward Meris.

Biff looked through the crowd toward the refreshment tables at the other end of the room. He drank the last of his beer and ambled across the hall, nodding and talking to friends and business associates. He passed women wearing shawls to shield themselves from the cool April air sweeping through the room. Three teenage boys were scurrying around the perimeter of the hall, closing windows and doors. Biff arrived at a row of windows leading to the refreshment tables in the corner of the hall. He gripped the handles to close a window when he heard voices outside. He stuck his head out the window and saw two men urinating against the side of the building. Biff backed up and pulled the window down, glancing toward the refreshment tables. For a moment, he saw Alissa through the crowd, smiling and passing a plate of pastries to an elderly couple with pure white hair.

Biff scanned the hall for John unsuccessfully, then made his way to the corner of the room. Four women from the Unity Church were managing the refreshment tables when Biff arrived. Expecting Alissa to return, he stalled for time, examining a mixture of colorful fruit and beverages in glass bowls, and pastries on white paper napkins. The paper tablecloth was white with small pictures of the American flag.

"I wondered how long it would take you to get to the refreshment tables?" came a voice from behind. Biff composed himself for his encounter with Alissa. Calmly, he turned and stood face-to-face with Meris.

"If you hadn't spent so much time talking with those pompous stuffed shirts, you wouldn't have missed her."

"Missed who?" Biff asked, pretending not to know.

Meris chuckled. "Let's not play that game. Alissa's father came for her a moment ago. Her daughter has a fever, so he took her home."

"Oh! *That* who," he said, brandishing a wide smile. "I'm sure there will be other opportunities."

Whoops and hollers began to fill the hall, as wild fiddles and banjos ignited the crowd into action. "Have you danced yet?" Meris asked.

"Not a step. Let's go."

At the dance floor, Biff saw John hooked arm-in-arm with Marlene Zinnoff, twirling and stomping to the delight of the crowd. Her long dark hair swung parallel to her flaring skirt when she leaned back in full motion. The crowd showed their appreciation by clapping in rhythm and stamping their feet. She was the center of attention. It was a thrilling time for an eleven-year-old girl.

Chapter Nineteen

Hillary ran from school to meet Iris and Vera at Thompson's store. She was excited. Today, she and her friends were going to the blacksmith's to feed and pet the horses. Hillary loved horses and dreamed of having her own to ride down any road, into the woods, or along a beach, with nobody to tell her when to come home.

Mr. Thompson was outside talking to Iris and Vera when Hillary arrived, his white apron flapping in the breeze. He smiled at Hillary, as she approached, panting from her long run from school. "I understand you girls are going to the blacksmith's," he said. "If you intend to feed the horses, I'll give you a treat for them." Avery waved his hand, signaling them to follow him into the store and proceeded to the produce section against the back wall. He returned with six carrots, dropping three into each of Hillary's deep apron pockets. "They fit perfectly. Two for each of you."

When the girls started for the door, Mr. Thompson grabbed Hillary's arm and turned her toward him. "How's your mother?"

"No better. She's with two doctors now. They're trying to decide what's wrong with her."

"They will," he assured her. "Give her all the help she needs until she gets better." He stood at the door and watched Hillary join her friends, carrots bouncing against her thighs with each step.

Along the way, Hillary and Iris teased Vera. Even though she denied it, they knew she liked the blacksmith's son, Russ. Her face would get red and she would mispronounce and slur words when she was taunted. She even tried to change the subject to make them stop teasing.

Soon, they heard the sound of metal hammering metal in the distance, confirming that Mr. Shert was working and they could get into the stable. The shop was a dilapidated frame structure, with a slight lean toward Delaware Bay. Sunlight seeped between gaps in the boards and small openings in the roof. The girls stood outside peeking in at Mr. Shert, waiting to be discovered. He was bent over his anvil, hammering a piece of metal into a weather vane, as smoke from hot coals drifted toward the roof. Hillary and Iris watched him work, while Vera's eyes roamed for Russ.

Mr. Shert straightened up and leaned his large body backward to ease his aching back. Sweat dripped from his short brown beard and thick eyebrows. His sleeves were rolled up to the elbow and a wild spray of chest hair flared from the top of his shirt. He was surprised when he saw the girls standing in the bright sunlight, peering into his dingy shop.

Iris raised a hand and wiggled "hello" with her fingers.

Mr. Shert couldn't help but smile and wiggle his thick, dirty fingers in return. "Haven't seen you girls for a while."

"That's the truth," Hillary replied. "Not since you gave us a sleigh ride last winter. Know why we're here today?"

"Gotta idée. I don't think ya come to sweep my floors with them carrot greens sticking out your apron pockets." He pulled a red and white handkerchief from his rear pocket to wipe his brow. "Go ahead," he said, nodding toward the stalls. "Be kind to them and they'll be kind to you."

"Is Russ working today?" Iris asked.

"Yep. He's off to the Wildcat Saloon in Neillsville, returning two horses. Won't be back for a couple hours."

Hillary and Iris turned to Vera, teasing her with sad, pouting faces.

Vera rolled her eyes in disgust, then burst between them, stomping her way to the horses.

The small stable had five stalls on each side and only three were occupied. A thin layer of straw covered the twisted, splintered floorboards, and straw dust glowed in the sunlight streaking through the walls.

Hillary handed two carrots to each of her friends, which they broke into smaller pieces. Mr. Shert's rhythmic hammering on metal continued, as they fed and petted the horses. They learned from experience that the safest way to feed a horse was with an open palm so their fingers wouldn't get bitten. After the horses had eaten the carrots, the girls attempted to create new names they thought appropriate for each horse. They giggled at funny names and swooned over ones they deemed perfect.

With all the hammering noise and their attention centered on the horses, the girls were unaware a train was approaching. As soon as they heard the train pulling into the station, they hurried out to the street. Hillary saw a girl with short black hair sitting in one of the coaches. She began thinking of Pina, wondering where she was and what kind of life she was having. Then, she thought of Pina's mother, who had seemed healthy but died suddenly. She knew of other people who had died the same way—not many, but enough for Hillary to realize that death could come without warning. She put her hand inside her apron pocket, held the medal of the Blessed Virgin and prayed her mother would recover from her illness.

"I wish we could ride the three horses into the woods," Iris said, glancing back into the stable.

"Me, too," Vera said, looking at Hillary, who was obviously disconnected from the conversation. Vera tapped Hillary's arm. "We were saying how we would like to ride the horses into the woods."

"Then let's walk to the woods," Hillary responded, taking her hand from her apron pocket. "I'd like to go into the woods, too."

"It's a mile away at the other end of the prairie," Vera stated, her arm pointing west.

"We've walked ten miles on a Sunday," Hillary responded. "Besides, we can stop in the Italian neighborhood along Mill Prairie and see what it's like."

"I'm willing," Iris said, "but we should thank Mr. Shert before we leave." She led the girls through the stable and into the workshop.

Mr. Shert lowered his hammer and listened to their words of appreciation.

Hillary and Vera waved and Iris wiggled her fingers, again.

Mr. Shert smiled and nodded.

The trio followed a path through the prairie, kicking small stones and ripping off the tops of weeds. They stopped to examine a Monarch butterfly clinging to a weed that teetered in the gentle breeze. "Look how slowly she moves her wings," Hillary said, observing it closely. "I guess she does that to keep her balance."

"How do you know it's a she?" Vera asked. "Did you look?"

"I wouldn't know where to look," Hillary replied. "I'm just guessing it's a she."

"Who cares?" Iris said. "Let's move on." Iris began walking up the path and the others followed. The path got wider and curved gradually toward the mill. When they were halfway through the bend, they came upon a black and white cat lying on the path. It watched the girls, allowing only thirty feet of distance between them, then got up and walked ahead, occasionally looking back to see that they didn't close the gap.

The girls left the path angling between the mill and Alton. Vera faced the mill, and again saluted it with her tongue. Once past the mill, they walked directly toward the Italian ghetto. The streets were busy with vendors selling from carts and horse drawn wagons. As if it were an artistic endeavor, men flaunted ornate mustaches that were curled, twisted and waxed. Hillary vacillated as to whether she liked the mustaches or not. Iris liked them, but Vera thought they looked like black butterflies on the men's lips.

The girls stopped where a portion of the street was roped off for repairs. Italian stone workers with steel pry bars separated bricks from the street and stacked them along the edge of the sidewalk. The girls were surprised at how fast the street could be dismantled. It seemed so permanent. The men were sweaty and dirty, but their mustaches remained undisturbed.

"Let's go in this store," Vera said, peering through the doorway.

"Not inside," Hillary squealed. "If they talk to us, we won't know what they're saying. Then what?" The girls moved to the store window where a large variety of pasta was displayed in glass jars. Behind the jars, tall wicker baskets held long loaves of bread. There were cans and boxes of food the girls couldn't identify.

"We don't know what these foods are," Vera said. "I think we should just head for the woods and stop looking at things we're not familiar with."

Iris positioned herself alongside Hillary. "You told me Pina lived here, in the Italian ghetto. Do you know what building she lived in?"

"I never found out. Pina's mother made her work every Sunday making paper flowers in their apartment, so I was never invited."

The girls looked into the shops and listened to people speaking Italian. Their vigorous use of hands when they talked amused them. Except for an occasional skirt, shawl or hat, they didn't see an abundance of traditional Italian clothing they'd hoped to see. Hillary wished she'd been able to walk the streets with Pina and learn the customs and what people were saying.

Iris placed her hand over her mouth and giggled.

"What's funny?" Vera asked.

Iris pointed across the street at a large woman wearing a burgundy dress and white lace collar. Her one hand balanced a basket of laundry on her head, while the other gripped a rope tied to a brown and white goat following close behind.

"Do you think she did her laundry in goat's milk?" Hillary asked.

"With the size of her breasts, I'd say she's got enough milk of her own," Vera laughed.

The girls entered a field of tall grass that expanded to the woods. "It looks dark in there," Iris said, staring ahead into the trees.

"It's so thick with trees, not much sunlight gets in," Hillary said. "It will be cool in there, so button your coat."

They stopped at the edge of the woods, their shoes covered with dirt and pollen dust. Tall pine, birch and oak trees shadowed the forest floor. Rotting trees streaked with green moss lay on the ground, blending with a variety of creeping ground cover, ferns, leaves and pine needles.

"Look, trees leaning against other trees," Vera said, pointing to the woods. "We better be careful where we walk."

"I don't want to go in too far and get lost," Iris said, entering the woods. Twigs snapped with each step as they moved forward, scaring birds into flight.

"You can hear the wind blowing through the leaves," Vera said, scanning the treetops. "We should sit on a log and listen to all the sounds."

Iris was first to find a log lying across the ground. She spread her dress and sat where there wasn't any moss.

Vera went to a clear spot at the end of the log to sit. The rotten fibers of the wood held her for a few seconds and collapsed. A squealing Vera sat on the remains of the log, with her legs spread out before her.

Hillary and Iris laughed. "Toilet time?" Iris asked.

"Very funny!" Vera snapped. "Help me up."

Hillary and Iris each took a hand and pulled her to her feet. Vera began beating dirt and small pieces of rotten wood from the back of her dress. "Let's find a rock to sit on."

The girls moved forward between the trees, scouting for boulders. They ducked under branches and stepped over decaying timber and depressions in the ground. "Eeewww," Vera wailed. "Look at this. What is it?"

"It's a mushroom," Hillary answered, looking at what seemed to be an ivory dinner plate protruding from a log. "Don't touch it. It could be poisonous."

Vera stepped forward and kicked it with the toe of her shoe. A large piece fell to the ground, exposing a pure white interior. "It looks harmless."

"People die from eating harmless-looking mushrooms," Hillary said. "You have to know what you're doing if you want to pick them. We can find a variety of mushrooms here, but we don't know which are good ones."

"I wouldn't touch one," Iris said. "They're ugly and scary looking."

"Quiet!" Vera said. "Someone or *something* is walking around here." The girls dropped to their knees behind a bush.

"I hope it's not a bear," Hillary said, peeking over the bush.

"A bear?" Iris whispered in fear. "Poison mushrooms, bears, dangerous logs—why are we here?"

Vera pointed ahead to the left. "Listen! The sound is coming from over there."

The girls' hearts beat a little faster, as the sound of snapping twigs grew closer. They peeked over the bush, exposing as little of themselves as possible, their eyes searching between the trees for the intruder.

"There!" Vera whispered, pointing to the left. "Where two trees lean against other trees. It's a deer!"

"I see her," Hillary murmured. "She's beautiful."

The deer stepped into a ray of soft evening light streaking through the tall trees, cautiously inspecting her surroundings. "I see her now," Iris said. "What a pretty color. It's like a rusty-brown."

The doe moved on and a fawn stepped into view. "Look!" all three girls moaned, simultaneously.

"A baby. Don't you want to hug it?" Hillary asked.

Vera tapped Hillary's shoulder with her fingers. "Look behind it. Another fawn." As if on cue, they all sighed again.

"The babies have white spots on their sides," Iris said, pushing down on the bush.

The fawns stayed twelve feet behind the doe, learning from the mother's actions. She took a few steps to her right, then paused to look and listen. The fawns seemed to understand their mother's lessons.

As daylight faded, the girls continued to watch. When the deer disappeared among the trees, the girls returned to their feet and listened for new guests. Nothing.

"That was worth the walk here," Hillary said, brushing dirt from her knees. "We should come here more often."

"As long as we see deer and not bear," Iris replied.

"The sun is going down," Vera said. "I think we should leave for town."

The girls stepped out of the woods and into the field of knee-high grass, walking directly toward town. As it got darker, they could see lights going on in Alton.

Hillary wanted to be home when her mother returned from the doctor's office. She believed her mother's illness wouldn't be serious, because she had always been in good health. Even though there was a possibility, God certainly wouldn't take both her parents.

CHAPTER TWENTY

Laura showed no emotion after listening to her prognosis. She thought of Hillary at the blacksmith's, visiting the horses and laughing with her friends. What was Hillary's future? *God, I don't want to leave her. Help me!* She silently prayed.

Dr. Merges handed her a small glass of brandy that she sipped once and placed on his desk. She scanned a row of bookcases against the wall behind Dr. Merges' desk. There must be a hundred volumes filled with medical knowledge, but nothing that would help her. Dr. Mackin tried comforting her with remote possibilities of recovery, but his presentation wasn't convincing. It was an awkward time for the three of them, so Laura thanked the doctors for their help and prepared to leave.

Dr. Merges said he would call on Laura in the future, since it would become increasingly difficult for her to travel. Realizing she was tired, he offered his carriage and driver for her return home. Laura accepted his offer with a slight nod and an appreciative smile. As he walked Laura to the front door, she took a long look around her, realizing this was the last time she would be in such a home. Dr. Merges helped her down the porch stairs to the side drive where the carriage waited. He assisted her into his carriage, giving additional words of encouragement that were a combination of sympathy and kindness—nothing more.

Mary came out to the porch, as the carriage was pulling away. She made no gestures or utterances, just stood in place dabbing her cheeks with a white handkerchief, watching Laura ride away.

Laura settled into the shaded corner of the carriage and watched people stroll under the afternoon sun. They were healthy, vibrant, ready for what tomorrow would bring. Why wasn't that true for her? Why should she die now, so prematurely and with a daughter so young? "Help us, God!" She began to cry, not for herself, but for Hillary, sensitive and unprepared to face a future without parents. An *orphan.* The word made Laura cringe.

Wiping her tears, she decided to see Kate. Laura opened the portal between herself and the driver, gave him Kate's address and sat quietly swaying with the carriage. She looked at the fine shops she and Kate always admired when they strolled north of Perry Street. Laura smiled, passing the photography shop where they had laughed at many of the pictures. Even now, she felt a bit guilty for having done so. She'd had fun with Kate. Their relationship made life a little easier for them both. Laura loved her like a sister and knew Kate felt the same. She rode past the small vegetable and fruit market on the corner of Perry Street and entered *her* part of town.

The driver turned the carriage onto Lakeview Street, slowing the horses as they passed through a group of boys playing stickball on the street. Standing like pillars with only their heads turning, the boys tried looking into the carriage to see what wealthy person was inside. "Wish I had your life," one boy yelled. Laura pondered the blindness of the boy's statement. When she arrived at Kate's building, she asked the driver to thank Dr. Merges again for the use of the carriage.

Laura held the handrail, as she climbed the dirty staircase, then paused when two boys ran past her to get down to the ball game. The smell of boiled cabbage was stifling, almost making her dizzy. The climb was tiresome for Laura, leaving her breathless at the landing. She compared her endurance with two weeks earlier when she could climb stairs easily, causing her to wonder what her condition would be after another two weeks. She became more conscious of her fragile existence, defining how precious her last weeks of life would be.

Laura knocked on the door, hoping Kate would be home. She heard Kate's footsteps come toward her, then the turning of the key.

"Come in," Kate said, obviously surprised by the visit. "I was going to your apartment tonight to find out what the doctor said."

"That's why I'm here. I need to talk to you."

Kate sensed urgency in Laura's voice, but had no inkling of what was to come. Closing the door, she followed Laura to the kitchen table. Giggles and screams from little girls floated up from the alley. Kate removed an empty laundry basket from the table and closed the window. Laura pulled a chair from the table and lowered herself, slowly.

"I really don't know where to begin," Laura admitted. Her voice softened unintentionally, as she revealed the details of her illness and its inevitable conclusion.

Kate listened without uttering a word, then walked to Laura and stood next to her. It took all her willpower to refrain from screaming, or throwing something, or cursing God. Instead, she kissed Laura on the cheek and held her.

"It's obvious I won't be going west with you," Laura stammered. She buried her face in a handkerchief, as the tears flowed, her courage dissolved by the comfort of her friend.

Kate stood behind Laura with her arms around her, resting her head against Laura's. Suddenly, Simon's words returned to her. *Take care of yo friend*, he said, staring into her eyes and gripping her hand. *How did Simon know?* She wondered. Again, she decided not to mention it to Laura. There was no good reason to.

"I decided to join you and John once you were settled," Laura revealed, wiping her eyes with a handkerchief. "I don't even know if I'll last until Biff returns."

Hearing the desperation in Laura's voice, Kate didn't offer any meaningless statements of comfort. There weren't any comforting words. Laura was going to die and Kate was going to be there for her until the end.

"How are you going to tell Hillary?" Kate asked, with tear-filled eyes.

Laura placed her hands on the arms that were holding her and pressed them against her chest. "I'm not," Laura answered. "If I don't tell her, she can have hope. I want her to have that as long as possible." A tear fell from above onto Laura's hand, as Kate held her tighter.

"I'll walk you home," Kate said. "I could use some air to filter that boiled cabbage smell from my nostrils."

Kate was startled by the physical change in Laura, as she watched her descend the stairs, then walk with difficulty to her apartment. It had been only a few days since they were together, and Laura hadn't shown any signs of weakness then. Kate, agonizing inside herself, pretended not to notice.

It was dark when Kate left Laura with Hillary and walked to Doyle's Pub. She recalled the fun-filled days she shared with Laura, strolling to the pond, or window-shopping on the north side of town. She remembered the ferry rides to Hatfield, and picnics and parties with Hillary. Kate was too depressed to stay alone in her dingy apartment. She needed rum and diversion to help her cope with the dreadful news.

The brick paved streets were still wet from a brief April shower, reflecting ghostly yellow images from tall streetlights. People around her walked briskly, afraid it would rain again before they reached their destination.

Kate crossed the street towards Doyle's. She saw Wade Widner leave two men standing under the street lamp then make his way for the pub. She calculated they would arrive at the entrance simultaneously, but not accidentally. His timing was perfect.

Wade held the door for Kate to enter. "Evening, Kate," he greeted.

She responded in kind, wondering if his presence was for interrogation, or self-promotion. She assumed the latter.

"Care to join me for dinner? It will give us a chance to talk."

"Why not? Maybe both of us can learn something about John, the local bad boy." Kate made her way to a table by the window and removed her coat.

Wade carried their coats to a row of brass hooks mounted on the brick wall between two windows. On his way back to the table, he signaled Meg for service.

"What do you know about John?" she asked, as Wade sat down. His shoulders were the width of the table and the back of his chair was completely hidden from her.

Wade chuckled. "Seems like that's a question I should be asking. I guess your question is making a statement."

"Right from the start," Kate responded. "I would like to learn what you know about John. I'm still in the dark, waiting for who knows what."

"We haven't learned anything, but the company hasn't given up. My gut feeling is he'll never come near Alton. He can't contact you by mail or telegraph without exposing his location, so his only option is sending someone to you."

Kate was startled by Wade's comment, afraid he knew about Biff. She raised her hand to her mouth to cover a fake cough, attempting to hide any facial expression that might indicate he was right. "Another option is, I may never see him again. I have no guarantees."

"I doubt he would abandon you," Wade assured her. "I'm sure he will contact you in some manner."

"Well, if he does, I hope it's soon, so I can plan my future." Kate looked toward the bar to see if Meg was coming for their order. She saw her thirty feet away, walking directly at them.

"Well, ain't this interesting," Meg remarked, flipping her order pad against her chest. "Both sides of the coin at the same table. If ya want mixed drinks, may I suggest a Man-O-War to stimulate your evening?"

"There isn't going to be a war," Wade said. "We're having a friendly discussion about current events."

"I can think of only one current event you two would be talking about." She readied her pad and pencil. "What'll it be?"

"I'd like to order my meal now," Kate said. "Please bring me the cod dinner and tea. I'll also have that Man-O-War you suggested."

Meg rolled her eyes toward Wade. "Ya sure about a friendly meeting?"

"I'm sure," Wade repeated, smiling. "I'll have a Dooley's Ale and the chicken and rice."

"Chicken and rice is one of her favorites," Meg said, nodding toward Kate. She wrote their food orders on the order pad and looked around the room for customers wanting service. "Drinks will be here in a minute."

Wade leaned back in his chair with his hands folded on the table. "Hardly anyone I know believes John killed Jessie Sharp. But now that Tyler is a part owner of the shipping company, and he thinks John is guilty, he wants John brought in to be punished. As I said earlier, I don't think John will come to Alton again. Do you?"

Kate wondered if he was asking out of his own curiosity, or for the benefit of Crossroads Shipping. "I really don't know. All I can do is wait a period of time, then decide he isn't." Kate was enjoying her charade, knowing she, too, would disappear from Alton in the near future.

"You sound as though your patience is wearing thin," Wade said, hoping her dedication to John was waning. "The uncertainty must be worrisome for you." He looked for signs of fatigue in her waiting for John. If so, he was ready to take a more aggressive role in courting her.

"I don't like not knowing where I stand. I need to get on with my life. I'm not getting any younger." She folded her hands on the table and looked into his eyes. "Have you ever been married?" She knew that question would appear she had some interest in him, but she had to make conversation.

"No. When I was in my twenties and early thirties, I was in the U.S. Army as an artillery officer. That kept me from an active social life. Afterwards, I never got involved with anyone. I'd like to have a family, though, so I haven't given up."

Meg sidestepped between two tables, while balancing their drinks and a bowl of peanuts on a tray. "Here, chew on these for a while. Dinner will be comin' soon. Try that Man-O-War now and let me know what ya think."

Kate took a slow sip of her drink. "This is good. Will it put me in a fighting mood?"

"A few of those will probably do the opposite," Meg grinned.

"Keep them coming," Wade said. "I'm anxious to see what happens."

"You're the enemy, remember?" Kate quipped. "I don't think there will be any peace treaties tonight."

"Gotta go take another order," Meg said, sliding the tray under her arm.

"You don't seem to be putting much effort into catching John," Kate said, reaching for a peanut.

"Just enough to appear I'm trying. Sitting here with you now, has certain people thinking I'm attempting to get information."

"Is that why you asked me to dine with you?" Kate asked, with a curious glance.

"Partly. My true desire was to have dinner with you, but if someone wants to interpret our being together as something else, that's fine with me. It will be a feather in my cap at Crossroads Shipping."

Kate shelled another peanut. "Which side are you on? John's, or the company's?"

"Like I said before," Wade explained. "I like John, and I don't believe he killed anyone, but I doubt he's coming back to Alton. I don't think they will ever find him. If the company wants to pay me extra to spy on you, I'm more than willing to go through the motions."

"Sounds like easy money," Kate snickered. "How long do you think you can fool them? I can make up lies to keep them interested."

"I don't think that will be necessary. They'll tire of the search after a while." He leaned over the table toward her. "By that time, you may have given up, too."

Kate was amused by his new attitude toward her. As if proposing a toast, she raised her glass. "Let's see what tomorrow brings."

Kate looked around the room to see which of her friends were there. She smiled and waved to Emil Kurst and his wife sitting next to the card game. Karl Polen was leaning against the bar talking to Tom Knauz, peeling a boiled egg.

"I've noticed a new face coming to town," Wade said. "He stays a couple days, disappears for a few weeks and returns for a couple days. It appears he's visiting someone up the street. Nice looking fella, about six-feet tall, wearing cowboy boots."

Kate tensed, assuming he was referring to Biff. Again, she had to refrain from looking alarmed. She waved and smiled at the wall far behind Wade, pretending to acknowledge someone.

"Why would that interest you?" she asked.

"I know where he's been visiting." He paused a few moments before continuing. "He seems to have an interest in Laura Cook. I believe she's a friend of yours?"

"Oh, him," Kate replied casually. "That would be Laura's cousin. He comes to visit occasionally." She reached for another peanut to keep her hands busy and hide any signs of nervousness.

"Cousin?" he questioned. "Or messenger?"

"Have you mentioned him to anyone?" she inquired.

"Not yet. Why do you ask?"

Kate frowned and threw her empty peanut shell into the bowl with force. "Cousin!" she insisted, staring into his eyes. "Sit back in your chair and I'll tell you more about Laura Cook." Kate continued to glare at Wade, holding his undivided attention.

He was surprised by her spirited reaction. Wade sat back in his chair and waited for her story to unfold.

"Since you're keeping an eye on me and others going into her apartment, you must have seen a little girl with her. Am I right?" she asked, firmly.

"Yes, a pretty little blond girl. I assume she's her daughter?"

"Correct. Her father died five years ago and Laura will die within a few weeks. If you don't believe me, watch her again. She doesn't walk like a healthy person. Do it soon because she won't be able to walk much longer." Tears filled Kate's eyes, as she continued her story. "I spent two hours with her before coming here." Kate paused momentarily, unable to talk. She used the table napkin to wipe tears from her eyes. "The next time that man comes will be his final visit—for her funeral. Please! Don't pester her these remaining days. I'd never forgive you for that."

Wade sat back in his chair and sighed. "If what you say is true, I certainly wouldn't want to cause them more pain. I can wait."

CHAPTER
TWENTY-ONE

Kate walked into the office and hung her coat and purse on the coat tree next to the door. Frank was sitting at his desk, filling in blanks on an order form. She stepped to the window overlooking the west half of Mill Prairie and saw two small birds attacking a crow that was diving and weaving to avoid them. Kate wondered if they were protecting their nest, or punishing the crow for destroying it.

To the south, Kate could see the cluster of oak trees and the pond, realizing that Laura had been there for the last time. It was early May, Laura's favorite time of year, when plants were beginning to bloom and warm weather was setting in. She gazed at the sky, praying that Biff would return, as though a spiritual messenger would carry her plea. She began to cry for Laura.

"What are you whimpering about?" Frank asked, impatiently from his desk.

Kate continued looking out the window. "Hillary Cook's mother is confined to her bed. She's too weak to walk, or even sit for any length of time." Kate crossed the office to her desk, gathering papers to take to the file cabinet.

"Does Hillary know her mother is dying?"

"She hasn't been told that, but I'm sure she's thought of it. She's a scared girl."

Frank bit his lower lip, deep in thought. "How will they pay their food and rent?"

"I don't know," Kate answered, returning to her desk. "Their only close friends are, me and Mr. and Mrs. Thompson, their landlord and grocer. I'll have to see what I can arrange with them."

Frank paused, tapping his silver letter opener on the desk. "I have papers in the leather pouch. I want you to take them to the bank. Wait until Mr. Kerner signs them and bring them back. The best time to leave would be eleven o'clock." Frank sat, smiling to himself.

At 11:15 a.m., Frank went to Mrs. Gretsch's desk outside his office. Due to the noise surrounding them, he walked behind her desk and spoke in her ear, directing her to send Hillary to his office.

Mrs. Gretsch nodded, then walked off among the machines.

Minutes later, Hillary knocked on Frank's door, waiting until she was told to enter. Hillary closed the door, then advanced to his desk, waiting for him to speak.

"Sit down," he said, displaying a friendly smile. "I'm sorry to hear about your mother's illness. Is it true she's not able to work?"

Hillary was looking down at her lap. "Yes," she answered, timidly.

"If she isn't working, how will she pay your rent, or buy food and medicine?"

"I don't know." Hillary's lips began to quiver, as she fought a flow of tears.

"Fortunately, I could buy these things for you," Frank said, concentrating on Hillary's emotions. "I know excellent doctors who could help your mother, but these doctors are expensive. Would you like me to arrange for a doctor to help your mother?"

Hillary raised her head and became more attentive. She recalled her conversation with Father Adams after a Sunday mass, telling her to accept any help that came her way and be thankful.

"What I say to you now must be kept a secret," Frank insisted. He leaned over his desk and looked deep into her eyes. "Agreed?"

Hillary agreed, eagerly. She was willing to agree to anything, if it could help her mother. She smiled, waiting to hear his offer.

"If you repeat anything we discuss now, I'll stop helping her. I'm sure you don't want to be an orphan." Frank knew that statement had impact. He chose his words carefully, while continually stressing the importance of her silence.

Hillary's enthusiasm waned, as Frank continued. "You are a young woman now, old enough to be alone with a man, to undress and touch each other in an adult way. Do you understand what I am saying? If you do that with me when I send for you, I'll help your mother."

Conflict of right and wrong tore at Hillary, yet she knew she had to save her mother. She wasn't presented a choice, only a price. She thought of Sarah and the two girls at the market place, selling their bodies to men. Her surroundings blurred away, as her full concentration centered on Frank. She began to feel as if she was suspended in a cocoon, with only Mr. Dragus's face leering at her, his voice explaining what she didn't want to hear. She was terrified and confused. This is what she would have to do to help her mother, her last parent. Hillary believed there was no way to refuse him. She didn't want to be an orphan. She clasped her hands together, tightly. "I want you to help my mother. I promise I won't tell anyone."

Kate returned at one o'clock, cradling Frank's leather pouch in her arms. "He sure was slow signing them papers. Sometimes Mr. Kerner signs papers straight away, then other times it takes him forever."

"Complain to Bernie, when he comes to play cards Thursday," Frank suggested, sarcastically.

Frank had an arrangement with Bernie Kerner to keep Kate at the bank when he wanted her out of his office. He accomplished this by sending bogus papers to Bernie, signifying he should stall for time. It worked perfectly.

Frank rose from his desk to lock the safe, telling Kate he would return about 2:30. He intended to call on Mr. Thompson to arrange payment of Laura's rent and food bills. Frank left through the rear stairwell that led to a gravel courtyard and small coach house behind the mill. Emo, his coach driver, was carrying a bucket of water and rags to wash the coach windows. He was a tall, muscular man, with black hair and dark complexion. He spoke with an Eastern European accent that was difficult for most people to understand. His dark, sinister appearance inspired many jokes about him being from Transylvania. Emo's most menacing feature was his huge, powerful hands, which could put fear in most men. People believed he was more Frank's bodyguard than driver.

When Emo saw Frank come out of the building, he knew Frank wanted to go somewhere. Emo changed direction and returned the water and rags to the coach house. Frank climbed into his coach and lit an expensive Caribbean cigar, imagining his upcoming encounters with Hillary, as he rode to Thompson's Grocery Store. He enjoyed his bachelor life.

Frank entered the store, walking up and down the aisles, looking at the canned goods, boxes of crackers and cereals. He was curious to see what poor people ate.

Avery Thompson pushed aside the blue curtain that separated the back room from the store and walked toward Frank. He was surprised to see such a well-dressed man in his store, and the beautiful coach outside. "May I help you, Sir?"

"If you are Mr. Thompson you may."

"I am," Avery responded, with a puzzled look.

"My name is Frank Dragus. I own the Alton Textile Mill. I came here to discuss private matters concerning Laura Cook. Since you are a friend of hers, I'm sure you're aware her illness has taken away her ability to work."

"She is more than a friend," Avery replied. "My wife and I love her, as if she was our daughter. My wife, Sari, is upstairs feeding her now. We're very concerned about Laura."

"I'm concerned about Laura and Hillary, too," Frank said in a convincing manner. "They're lovely people and I would like to help them. But in doing so, I want you to keep my help confidential. I'm sure you can appreciate my position. If others were to hear about my generosity, I would be inundated with appeals for help. Alton is full of poor people and I can't help them all."

"What do you have in mind?" Avery asked. "I'd offer you a seat, but all I have are cracker barrels. Unless you care to go in my back room?"

"That won't be necessary," Frank said, waving Avery's suggestion off with his hand. "I'm offering to pay the Cook's rent and grocery bills each month, without Laura or anyone else knowing about it. I want you to pretend a 'pay-me-later' attitude with Laura, so she thinks you are deferring payment of her debts. I can't stress enough, the importance of keeping this arrangement to ourselves. Will you agree to that?"

Avery looked shocked. "Absolutely. I certainly wouldn't hinder a generous offer like that."

"Good," Frank responded. "I guess our business is completed, so I'll leave you to your work." He looked directly into Avery's eyes. "You said your wife is upstairs, feeding Laura. Obviously, you and Sari are kind people. Together, we can make life a little nicer for Laura and Hillary."

They walked side-by-side towards the front door when Frank noticed glass jars of licorice on a display cabinet. He changed his course and went to the candy counter. "I'd like a licorice stick. How much are they?"

Avery went behind the candy counter. "Two for a penny. How many do you want?"

"One will be enough. It's been a long time since I enjoyed one of those."

Avery removed the lid from the round glass jar and tilted it toward Frank, so he could select his own.

Frank removed one and smelled it. "It brings back memories. How much do I owe you?"

"Forty years of rent and groceries will be enough," Avery said, with a smile.

"I can appreciate that statement," Frank said, with a chuckle. "I'll have my coach driver here every month to make a payment. He will come without the coach, of course." Frank nodded and waved his licorice stick, as he went out the door.

Frank Dragus's friend, Dr. Reaf, visited Laura twice that week and realized there was nothing he could do, so he, too, gave her placebos, pretending they might help. He continued to visit Laura twice each week, as a favor to Frank.

Laura's condition became such that Hillary could no longer share her mother's bed. Mr. Thompson brought a cot and additional blankets to the apartment. Hillary had him put the cot next to her mother's bed, so she could hear her mother breathing in the dark. There were many nights Hillary awoke, finding herself drenched in sweat, fearing for her mother, and crying herself to sleep.

Hillary's depression grew, watching her mother's health decline. Laura's cheek-bones became more prominent, as she continued losing weight. Hillary also noticed the loss of strength in her mother's arms when Laura tried brushing her hair. She observed all who came to visit, studying their behavior and listening to conversations. The outcome was obvious. Hillary's ceased to believe that Frank Dragus's friend, Dr. Reaf, could help her mother.

In mid-May, the colors of spring were beginning to grace the landscape. Laura suggested that Hillary go to church and school, and join her friends to inspect the wildflowers, especially on such a pleasant day.

Again, Hillary chose to stay home. She hadn't shared a Sunday with Iris and Vera for three weeks; afraid something might happen to her mother while she was away.

Laura was fully aware of Hillary's reasoning and accepted her decision.

Kate arrived an hour earlier, to visit and comfort her friend. She set a glass and pitcher of water on a small table next to Laura's bed. She smiled at Laura, "She isn't going anywhere. She loves her mother."

A sudden burst of unsynchronized knocks resounded on the door, obviously made by more than one person. Kate went to the door and opened it, just enough to see who was outside, then backed up to let the visitors come in.

Iris and Vera stepped into the room, displaying controlled smiles, not knowing what circumstances they would find in the apartment. "We haven't seen you for such a long time, we decided to stop by and visit. Do you mind?"

"No. I'm glad you did. I've been wanting to see you."

"It's a pleasant surprise," Laura said, with difficulty. "We've missed you girls and talk about you all the time."

Iris cradled a blue-knitted hat in her arms, walking to the bed. Everyone could see the hat was filled with something, but couldn't guess what it was. Iris set her knitted hat on the bed, letting it collapse against the blanket. A tiny gray and white kitten sat in the middle of the soft blue hat. It looked around the room and let out a tiny "meow."

Hillary smiled for the first time in weeks and reached for the kitten. "She's beautiful," Hillary said, cuddling it against her cheek.

Laura and Kate looked at each other, pleased to see Hillary smile once again. Everyone was amused by the faint, "meows" coming from the kitten.

"It was very nice of you girls to bring the kitten," Laura said, weakly. "It's been rather dull around here."

Iris and Vera were astonished by Laura's emaciated appearance and frail voice, but pretended not to notice. Their parents told them that Laura might have changed drastically, and they should be prepared to smile under any circumstances.

Vera removed a few wildflowers from her dress pocket and handed them to Hillary. "They haven't bloomed yet, but you can see they're budding. If you put them in a bowl of water, they may blossom in a few days."

"Thanks!" Hillary pointed to the wall across from her chair. "See the wreath I made from the wildflowers you girls gave me for my birthday?"

"It looks nice," Vera said, stepping close to the wreath. "I think I'll make one, too."

Hillary handed the kitten to Laura, so she could play with it.

Laura laid the kitten on its back and began scratching its stomach with her fingernails. The kitten pawed at Laura's hand, enjoying the massage.

Kate went to the foot of Laura's bed. "Do you want me to help you sit up?"

"It's not worth the struggle. I'm fine like this," Laura replied. "You can help me later, if I decide to read."

Sari entered the apartment to see if Laura needed her. She saw the kitten, but was more concerned about Laura than the animal. "Do you need anything?" she asked.

"I'm fine for now, thank you." She handed the kitten to Hillary, watching her cradle it in her arms and pet it.

"Where did you get the kitten?" Hillary asked Iris.

Iris sat on the edge of the bed next to Hillary and played with the kitten's paws, while Hillary continued to pet it. "They were born under our back porch. My neighbors across the hall, Eva and Charlie Geroux, found them last Sunday, while playing ball in the yard. Eva chased a ball that rolled under the porch and she found a cat and four kittens. Her parents said they were outdoor cats and should stay that way."

Sari and Kate stood at the foot of the bed watching the girls play with the kitten. Vera was on her knees next to the bed, eye level with the kitten. She removed the belt from her dress and dragged it across the top of the bed, so the kitten would paw at it.

Iris put her arm around Hillary's waist. "We miss sharing our Sundays with you. It's not the same when it's just Vera and me. Come with us next Sunday, so you can play and get some sunshine."

"I'll have to see how my mother is feeling." Hillary decided to change the subject, for she knew she would be with her mother every Sunday. "What's the kitten's name?"

Iris stroked the kitten's back. "It hasn't got a name, yet."

Laura began to cough. Kate and Sari looked at one another, wondering if it was another severe coughing spell. Calmly, they moved to both sides of the bed. The coughing increased and Laura began gasping for breath. Kate and Sari turned Laura onto her stomach and Sari started hitting Laura on her back, to loosen the phlegm from her lungs. Sari suggested that Iris and Vera leave and come back another time.

The girls were frightened by what they saw and were happy to go. They gave Hillary a hug and kiss, promising to stop by again. Iris picked up the kitten and said, "good-bye" to Laura, even though she knew Laura couldn't answer.

Sari devoted herself to Laura daily, giving her baths, feeding her, reading to her well into the evening hours after Hillary returned from work.

All three women agreed it was better for Hillary to continue working at the mill, to minimize her exposure to conditions at home. Realizing Hillary's depression, Kate arranged to have her do work at the mill that didn't involve dangerous machinery.

Laura's condition declined rapidly over the next two weeks. She began to vomit more often, and her bowel movements became more intense. The occasional abdominal pains that were her original warning signs were now habitual.

One evening, Kate arrived at Laura's apartment, while Sari was feeding her. Kate sat in Hillary's chair by the window and looked down on Union Avenue. She recalled the night she had met Biff and brought him to Laura's apartment, and how attracted they were to each other upon meeting. Suddenly, it occurred to her. *My God! Biff! He doesn't know anything about Laura's condition.* For him to see her without being prepared would be devastating. Immediately, she began figuring the number of weeks since his last visit. It was almost six weeks. *He could arrive any day, or was he here now?*

Kate had to figure a way to intercept him. She realized the logical answer was Schmidt's boarding house, his first stop from the train station. She needed to see Mrs. Schmidt right away.

Kate looked at Laura resting on the bed. Hillary was sitting in her chair next to her, holding a book she'd never read. Kate went to Mrs. Thompson sitting at the kitchen table and informed her she would return within an hour, then headed straight to Mrs. Schmidt.

Chapter
Twenty-Two

Biff arrived three days later, on a Wednesday, so he would have two extra days to arrange a date with Laura on the weekend. He brought Hillary an Indian doll dressed in buckskin, with a feather standing in the back of its braided black hair. Biff believed Hillary had never seen one like it and would love it. For Laura, he had a box of premium chocolates in a fancy blue box wrapped with a wide red ribbon. He even had a surprise for Kate. He was going to take her to John. Biff was eager to reveal the news and witness her happiness. Overall, he expected this to be an exciting visit. He arrived at the rooming house, filled with enthusiasm.

Glo greeted him, as if nothing were wrong, gave him his room key and told him she would bring towels directly. She intended to talk to him in the privacy of his room.

Biff took the stairs two at a time, anxious to bathe and see Laura. He placed his leather bag on the bed and set the box of chocolates on the edge of the dresser. He leaned the Indian doll against the oval mirror. He was removing his boots when he heard Glo's footsteps coming toward his room. He jumped up from the bed and opened the door.

Without a word, she draped two towels over the brass bar mounted on the inside of the door. She was nervous. Telling him was going to be difficult. "Sit down," Glo suggested. "I must tell you something, and it won't be pleasant."

Biff sensed what she had to say was important. He thought she might be having financial problems that would cause her to lose the boarding house. He sat on the bed with his arms crossed, listening to the worst nightmare possible.

When Glo finished, Biff was staring at the floor, his face pale. She removed a silver flask of whiskey from her apron pocket and laid it on the bed next to him. "Take this. It will help. I'm sending a boy to tell Kate you're in town. She will go to Laura immediately, so they will expect you anytime after seven."

When she closed the door, Biff stretched out on the bed, leaning against the brass headboard. Slowly, he twisted the cap from the flask, passed it under his nose and took a long drink. He paused, and drank again. His eyes strayed to the box of candy, then to the Indian doll leaning against the mirror. Behind the doll, the mirror reflected the windowpanes across the room, and the endless blue sky he had previously interpreted as a good omen. His chest tightened and the images began to blur.

Two hours later, Biff climbed the stairs to Laura's apartment, imagining unrealistic miracles that would save her. Except for a battered wooden bench standing against the wall, the dimly lit hallway was empty. Obscure conversations and whining children could be heard from different rooms. Biff stopped in front of Laura's door, knowing what he was about to see would be difficult to accept. He knocked and waited until Kate opened the door. He entered the apartment, giving Kate a passing glance. The expression on her face confirmed the worst. Hillary was sitting on a chair at Laura's bedside, her eyes red from days of crying. Dr. Merges and Sari were standing at the foot of Laura's bed.

Wearing a forced smile, Biff moved closer to Laura, pretending she would eventually recover. Her gaunt appearance left no doubt as to the inevitable, causing his world to crash around him. He refused to look at anything but her eyes and the newly set curls at her temples.

"You have new boots," she said, weakly.

Biff wondered how she could notice something so insignificant under the circumstances. He leaned toward her and replied, "I hoped new boots would get me here faster."

"Good response," Laura murmured. The corners of her mouth curled slightly in an attempt to smile, demonstrating the limit of her energy.

Biff turned and kissed Hillary on the top of her head. He tried consoling her by telling of the dinners and travel the three of them would share when her mother recovered. Hillary continued to sit expressionless, staring at the floor, as if he had never spoken. He turned back to Laura, as she raised her arm. Taking her hand in his, he looked directly into her eyes, thinking of what could have been. The pain that masked his face belied his casual manner.

Slowly, Laura slid her other hand from under the pillow, clutching a small bouquet of three paper flowers. "One red, one white and one yeller," she said.

Dr. Merges could see Laura was getting weary, and suggested that Biff leave and come back in the morning.

Biff was torn. He didn't want to leave. Yet, he didn't want to drain what little energy Laura had. He squeezed her hand gently and laid it on the bed. He told Laura he would be in Alton for a few days and kissed her pale lips, realizing it might be his only opportunity.

Laura smiled again, then raised her hand, signifying "goodnight."

Kate said she was staying the night. She walked Biff and Mrs. Thompson to the door. Mrs. Thompson told Biff she would give Laura a bath and breakfast by ten o'clock in the morning. He could return after that.

Biff glanced back to find Laura's eyes already closed. He asked Kate how Hillary was coping with the stress all these weeks.

Mrs. Thompson understood they wanted to talk privately, so she moved on.

"She hardly says anything," Kate answered. "Occasionally, Hillary says something to Laura, but mostly, she just sits and stares. When we speak to her, she rarely responds. Hillary's withdrawn from everyone, but her mother."

Biff wanted to do something for Hillary, but he couldn't decide what. He kissed Kate on the cheek and headed back to his room.

When Glo heard Biff return, she watched him pass her office, letting him decide if he wanted companionship.

He lay on the bed in total darkness. Except for his boots, he was still dressed. Time seemed to pass quickly, as he pondered this nightmare and Hillary's future. It was almost midnight when he heard knocking at the front door. Soon, the knock was repeated. He heard the familiar shuffle of Glo's slippers across the hall floor. Immediately, after opening the door, Biff heard a man talking hurriedly, but was unable to decipher what was being said. The conversation was brief and he heard the man run down the porch steps. Glo quietly closed the door.

Soon, the staircase squeaked, and the sound of Glo's soft slippers came straight to his room. Light from her kerosene lamp penetrated his room from under the door. She rapped lightly, trying not to wake other guests. "Biff, are you awake?" she whispered.

He rushed to the door and turned the key.

Glo was upset and talking fast. "A man came with a message. I would like to be more delicate at this time, but this is an emergency. I'm sorry, Biff. Laura died a few minutes ago and Hillary is gone. They need you, immediately."

She realized that Biff hadn't heard the total message. She put her hand on his shoulder and looked directly into his eyes. "Biff, listen to me," she demanded. "Hillary is gone. They don't know where she is, and they need you. Go to Kate, now."

"Hillary is gone?" he repeated. He grabbed his boots next to the bed and jammed his feet inside.

Glo continued talking, as she stood in the doorway. "Kate and the doctor were tending to Laura when they realized Hillary was gone. They have no idea where she went."

At the west end of town, Hillary entered St. Paul's garden, keeping in the shadow of the church. She was exhausted, her strength drained from weeks of watching her mother languish until her death. Hillary was terrified, now that she was an orphan. She was confused and incensed as to why God had chosen to take her parents.

She walked to the stone saints, their whiteness illuminated by moonlight. "I've come to you for the last time," she said, angrily, "and I'm not going to kneel. I prayed to you. I begged you to save my mother and you did nothing. You let both my parents die, and now I'm alone." Her voice got louder, as she continued. Tears streamed down her face, as her anger and frustration increased. "We were good people and you let this happen. Did you take my mother to punish me for being with Mr. Dragus? He was the only person I thought could help." Hillary raised her apron from under her coat to wipe her eyes. "I would have done anything to save her. I didn't want to be with him. It was the only way I could help. Now, I'm nothing and you did nothing!" she screamed.

As her anger turned to rage, Hillary could barely see through her tears. She charged the statue of the Blessed Virgin, yelling, "You did nothing to help us!" She pushed hard, knocking the freestanding statue from its pedestal. It hit the soft ground without breaking. Next, she attacked a larger statue of the Holy Family. It was too heavy to move. She hammered on it with her fist, screaming, "You did nothing!" She ran to St. Paul, pushing the statue off its pedestal with ease. "Why?" she cried. "Why did you let this happen?" Realizing the futility of her words, she walked to the front of the garden and stopped at the gate. Before departing, she stood glaring at the fallen statues, her body and mind spent. "You are nothing but a lie!" She walked through the gate, shouting, "I am not going on an orphan train." She walked toward the Clarion River, filling her coat and apron pockets with stones.

Kate was pacing in front of Thompson's building when Biff ran up to her. "How long has she been gone?" he asked, frantically.

"Almost an hour," Kate replied, looking in both directions on Union Avenue. "Their neighbor, Mr. Kaffer, knows where her father is buried, so he's looking for her at the cemetery. Go to St. Paul's and see if she's there. If not, look for her at the pond. I'm going to Iris and Vera's apartments."

"What about Laura?" Biff asked, holding Kate's arm, so she couldn't run.

"Dr. Merges is still upstairs. Meet you here later."

They ran in opposite directions, looking in doorways, under porches, behind bushes and fences. The weak gaslights along the streets were too dim to be of much help, so they lost precious time searching possible hiding places.

When Biff arrived at St. Paul's, he tried opening every door, hoping to find one unlocked where Hillary could be hiding. All were locked. He entered the garden from the back, sidestepping between the tall bushes. Immediately, he saw two statues lying on the ground. Biff sensed that Hillary had been there, venting her anger. He realized that she was deeply troubled and he had to find her in a hurry. The logical place now was the pond, the one location where she could feel close to her parents. It had been "their place."

Biff left the dim lights of Alton behind, running through the dark prairie, aiming for the black silhouette of trees standing before the river. Weeds whipped against his boots and legs with each stride, as his eyes scanned the moonlit riverbank. Images of Laura and Hillary constantly alternated in his mind, driving him onward.

He searched carefully around the pond, among the trees and along the riverbank. He felt Laura watching, coaxing him to find Hillary. After a thorough combing of the area, he was disappointed and frustrated at his failure to find her. He decided to return to the apartment, hoping someone had been successful.

It was after 3:00 a.m. when Biff returned to Laura's apartment, tired and discouraged. An hour earlier, Dr. Merges had Laura removed from the room. To Biff, despite everything being in place, the room seemed so empty without Laura.

Kate was sitting in Hillary's chair, looking out the window, contemplating Hillary's and her own future. She turned to look at Biff, surveying his emotional state, as he walked across the room.

"Has anyone found Hillary?" he asked, running his fingers through his hair.

"Not yet. Mr. Kaffer isn't back from the cemetery. Maybe he found her and is trying to console her." Kate walked over to Biff and embraced him. They remained silent, sharing a measure of comfort in each other's arms.

"It's amazing how someone's life can change so quickly," he whispered. "I came to Alton to deliver messages. Now my world is upside-down."

Kate looked up at Biff, while holding him. "Laura cared for you, too. She cared very much."

"Thank you," he replied. "By the way, I'm taking you home with me Sunday morning. Soon you'll be in your new home and you can be a June bride. Seems like Alton is going to be but a memory for both of us."

Kate backed away, still holding his arms. "Finally. But excuse me if I delay my excitement for another time."

They were interrupted by footsteps in the hall. Mr. Kaffer walked in, panting. "Anyone find Hillary?"

Biff stepped away from Kate. "I can't just stay here and wait. I'm going back to the pond." Biff raced down the stairs and into the street. Union Avenue was deserted, except for two stray hounds searching for food.

A thin line of yellow and pink light streaked the horizon as he entered the cool prairie. Black silhouettes of small birds darted above, snatching insects from the air. He hurried through the eerie morning mist, closing in on a man walking toward the pond. As he gained on him, he realized it was Avery Thompson. "Any sign of her?" Biff asked.

Avery turned his head, as Biff arrived next to him. "No! We must find Hillary. She's alone and frightened. She shouldn't be alone—not now."

"I was here earlier," Biff explained, looking in all directions. "I want to try again. It's the logical place."

"You're right," Avery agreed. "I want to see for myself. I don't know where else she would go?"

As they approached the oak trees, a pair of ducks flared from behind the riverbank, startling the two men. They watched as the birds raced over the course of the river, settling by some reeds further west. The sound of someone walking through weeds could be heard from where the ducks erupted. It was a boy walking backwards up the riverbank, slowly rising into view, throwing stones down at the water. When he got to the top of the riverbank, Biff recognized him by his long coat. It was the boy called, "Pocket Merchant."

Avery tapped Biff's arm to get his attention. "Quick! Let's ask him if he saw Hillary." They started walking faster toward the boy, hoping he wouldn't run away.

The boy turned and saw the men coming toward him. He dropped the stones he was carrying and slid his hands into his coat pockets.

"Good Morning," Biff shouted, wanting to appear friendly. "Can you help us?"

The boy stood in place until they stopped in front of him. "I'll help, if I can," he answered, wiping his nose on his coat sleeve.

Biff took another step closer to him. "We're looking for a blond girl about your age. Her name is Hillary Cook. Do you know her?"

"Yeah. I know Hillary, but I ain't seen her for weeks."

"You didn't see her here tonight?" Avery asked, hoping he would recall differently.

"No. She mighta come by when I was sleeping down by the water, but I didn't see her. Why would she be here at night?"

Biff ignored the boy's question and reached into his pocket for a silver dollar. "Here, take this. If you see her, take her home immediately."

"Thanks, Mister," the boy said, looking at the coin in his palm. "If I see her, I'll drag her home, if need be."

It was almost 6 a.m. when the men turned from the boy and started walking back to Laura's apartment. When they arrived, Kate was sitting on Laura's bed facing the windows, warming herself in the early morning sunlight. She turned toward the men entering the apartment without Hillary. Kate looked tired and worried. "No luck, I see," she mumbled. "Sari said she would make breakfast when you returned. Go ahead, I'll be there in a few minutes." Kate looked pointedly at Biff, so he would understand what she was about to say. "There are things I have to do, before I leave this apartment."

Biff returned her look. "I understand. We'll go ahead, but come soon, so we can eat together." He laid his hand against Avery's back and they walked out of the apartment.

Kate walked over to the wall where Hillary had hung her wreath of wildflowers. She lifted it from a nail in the wall and laid it on the dresser next to Laura's brass cathedral clock. Kate went to the windows and looked down on Union Avenue, hoping to see Hillary. Across the street, Mr. Brummer was sweeping the sidewalk in front of his shop. Two men with lunch pails under their arms were walking on the red brick street, talking feverishly with their hands in motion.

"I'm sorry, Kate," came a voice from behind her.

In the glass windowpane in front of her, Kate could see a reflection of Hillary, standing in the doorway. She spun around and rushed to Hillary, engulfing her in her arms. "You scared us to death. Where have you been? People have been running around town looking for you." Kate was angry with Hillary, but she was so delighted to see her, that all she felt was relief and love.

Hillary found it difficult to begin explaining, ashamed for what she did. "I went to the cemetery and told my father that his wife would be with him, and I would join them soon." Her lips began to tremble, as she continued. "Then I went to church to tell the saints how angry I was with them for taking my parents from me." Tears gushed forth, as she flung her arms around Kate's neck, confessing what she had planned to do in a continuous rush of words. "I went to the pond and filled my coat and apron pockets with stones, then I was going to walk into the water, so I could be with my parents. I saw a boy I knew, so I hid, knowing he would stop me." Tears collected on Kate's shoulder. "I went to Mr. Schert's stables to hide, until I could go back to the pond. While thinking about what to do, I fell asleep on the straw. I decided I didn't want to die. Yet, I want to be with my mother and father. What will happen to me? Where do I go?"

Kate held her, stroking the back of her head. "Hush, my dear," Kate whispered. "The first thing you're going to do is make some people very happy that you're home. We've been out of our minds worrying about you." Kate pulled a handkerchief from inside her dress sleeve and wiped tears from Hillary's face, then kissed her on the cheek. "Don't worry about your future, my dear, your mother and I discussed that months ago. John and I are getting married and you're going to live with us on a farm. As you know, he's been out west getting our farm ready. Now it will be three of us."

Hillary lifted her head from Kate's shoulder and looked into her eyes. "Why would you and my mother have been talking about me living with you and John? How long have you known she was dying?"

Kate took Hillary's hand and walked her to the bed. "Biff is at the Thompson's apartment eating breakfast, but before we join them, let's sit here and talk—just the two of us." Kate continued to hold Hillary's hand, sitting side by side on the edge of the bed. "One Sunday afternoon, your mother and I were resting on a bench on Union Avenue, warming ourselves in the sunlight. I mentioned to her how much I love you, and that if anything ever happened to her, I would take care of you. Neither one of us believed anything serious would happen to your mother, but I wanted her to know how I felt about you."

Hillary laid her head against Kate's shoulder and continued to listen.

"When your mother and I found out how sick she was, I repeated my promise to her. And as for John, he loves you as much as I do, and he immediately agreed to you living with us. He said you could help us raise our babies."

Hillary liked that idea. She giggled and smiled, then wiped her nose with Kate's handkerchief. "You and John are the only people I'd want to live with, and I promise you won't be sorry you took me." She paused a moment before continuing. "I thought I would be sent away on an orphan train."

Kate gave Hillary's hand a gentle squeeze. "I would never let that happen to you. When we get to the farm, John and I will take you to a livestock auction and buy you a pony." Hillary smiled again. "Then, when you become a good rider, we'll buy you a horse."

Hillary's eyes revealed her excitement. "Where is the farm?"

"I don't know. Biff will tell us Sunday." Kate pointed her finger at Hillary. "Right now, I'll tell you what you need to know, but you must keep it a secret—even from Iris and Vera. Promise?"

Hillary agreed by nodding her head, then asked, "Is this a secret because some people believe John killed a man?"

Kate straightened her back and took a deep breath. "So, you heard about that. Where did you hear—Well, never mind. It isn't important. What is important is, do you believe John killed someone?"

"No!" Hillary said, with conviction. "People are just guessing. If they knew John like we do, they'd know better."

Kate assured her that John didn't kill anyone. "His friends at work and our friends at Doyle's don't think he did, either," Kate added. "Sometimes people go to jail for crimes they didn't commit. The law isn't perfect. John knows this, so he felt the safest thing to do was to go where he couldn't be found. John and I already planned to move west and live on a farm, so he went sooner than expected." Kate winked at Hillary and said, "What you didn't know, was that you and your mother might have come with us. She seemed interested."

"I don't think she would have gone," Hillary said, staring at the floor. "She would have to leave my father to do that."

Kate lied and said what she thought Hillary wanted to hear. "Laura did say that it would be difficult for her to leave Jeremiah. You're probably right."

Hillary looked at Kate. "What is the secret you wanted to tell me?"

Kate stood and faced Hillary sitting on the bed. "Since you know about John, I guess it's quite simple. Don't tell this to anyone, but Sunday morning, you, Biff and I are taking a train to the farm. No one should know we're leaving town because if we were followed, they would find John. Sometime today, you must take that suitcase under your bed and pack it with enough clothes for five days. You'll sleep at my apartment tonight and tomorrow. Sunday, I'll leave the Thompson's a farewell note before we leave town. Otherwise, they won't know what happened to us. Now, let's join the others for breakfast."

Hillary began swinging her legs, "I'd like to come back and visit my parents sometime."

Kate extended her hand to Hillary. "So would I."

That afternoon, Biff met with Robert Grast, making funeral arrangements, insuring Laura a respectful burial. He pretended to be Laura's cousin to protect his true purpose for being in Alton. The visitation was set for Friday, from 4 p.m. until 10 p.m. A funeral mass was scheduled for eleven o'clock Saturday morning at St. Paul's before proceeding to the cemetery. Biff and Kate would engage in a game of deceit, until Sunday's 10:47 a.m. train.

At five o'clock, Biff left the funeral parlor hungry and exhausted, hoping to eat a good meal, then sleep until morning. He examined the eating establishments along Howard Street, but most looked uninviting. Glo's dining room seemed the better choice.

When Biff arrived at the boarding house, Glo surprised him by stepping out to the porch, neither expecting the other. Tall bushes on both sides of the porch swayed in a gentle breeze from the bay. "Good timing," Glo said. "Dinner is just about ready." She could see in his eyes his courage was wearing thin and pain was taking control.

Biff was reluctant to dine with the other boarders, but decided it would be easier to eat at Glo's and go directly to his room. After washing off a day's accumulation of dirt, he joined the other guests in the dining room. A variety of questions were asked by other boarders: "Where are you from?" and "What do you do for a living?" Biff directed much of the conversation from himself and lied when he had to. When he finished eating, he excused himself and went to his room to sleep. At the end of an hour, Biff was still lying awake, watching the light of the kerosene lamp flicker on the wall.

CHAPTER
TWENTY-THREE

A polished mahogany casket lay in front of an array of tall palms and mixed flowers.

Heavy burgundy drapes covered the chapel wall, providing a rich background highlighting two gold candelabras. Potted palms stood between fabric covered chairs and sette'es lining the walls.

Biff was wearing a tan dress coat, black shirt and black tie. He greeted people entering the chapel, receiving sympathies and solemn utterances, as people took his hand to certify the sincerity of their words. He continued to smile and be gracious, portraying the character of "Cousin Biff." He was grateful for the large turnout during the early hours, protecting him from long conversations that could become embarrassing.

Kate waited until seven o'clock to bring Hillary to the chapel, believing it wasn't necessary for her to be there for six hours, listening to comments from people she didn't know. Kate bought Hillary a new pair of black shoes and a gray dress with a wide black belt. Kate was dressed in black.

The hum of conversation dissipated, as everyone watched Hillary walk through the chapel, staring ahead at her mother. Kate held her hand, guiding her through the crowded room. Women burst into tears when Hillary knelt next to her mother and began crying. Kate's eyes filled with tears, putting her arm around Hillary, trying to console her.

Throughout the evening, friends and neighbors filed into the chapel arm-in-arm or holding hands, recalling their relationship with Laura. Crying and moaning could be heard among words of comfort and mumbled prayers. Iris and Vera arrived at the parlor minutes after Hillary, huddling together and embracing each other, giving Hillary the tender support and companionship she needed.

When the chapel closed, Biff walked Hillary and Kate to their apartment. They decided to meet at the church at 10:30, then hugged and kissed before Biff walked on. When Biff arrived at his room, he found a white envelope in the side pocket of his jacket. Inside was a bouquet of three paper flowers. "Thanks, Kate."

After mass the next morning, forty people gathered at the cemetery. A cool breeze sent dry leaves skipping over the ground, some sinking into Laura's grave. Tall trees spread shadows across the assembly, as Father Adams finished his prayers. "Whether in life or death, we belong to the Lord, and she shall have life everlasting in heaven. Amen." With heads bowed, all tried to accept the unacceptable.

Iris and Vera's parents had to go to work, so the girls attended the funeral mass with the Thompson's. As Sari wiped at her tears, Avery and Sari clung to each other. Father Adams stepped back into the crowd, when Hillary walked forward to drop her wreath of wildflowers onto the casket.

Biff looked to Jeremiah's headstone. "You have her forever."

Robert Grast led the assembly away from the grave and down the gravel path, exiting the cemetery at a calculated pace. Iris, Vera and the Thompsons followed Kate and Biff to the narrow street beyond the stone columns. Kate turned to the three girls and asked if they wanted to go to her apartment. Hillary's pleading stare was all Kate needed to understand she wanted to spend her last afternoon in Alton with her two friends. Kate leaned forward and kissed Hillary. "Be at my apartment before dark."

The Thompson's accompanied Kate and Biff for the walk home, each person meditating more than talking. Biff discretely reminded Kate to remove her money from the bank before it closed, then suggested she and Hillary arrive fifteen minutes before the 10:47 a.m. train the next morning.

At Union Avenue, they stopped on the corner. "I'm going to my room," Biff said. "I'm still short on sleep."

Avery stepped up to Biff, with his hand extended. "It was a fine thing you did for Laura. She deserved a nice funeral and none of us could have given it to her."

Biff shook his hand, while nodding to Sari. "She was a special lady. I couldn't let it be any other way."

Sari came forward to take Biff's hand. "Thank you," she said, with tears in her eyes. "God bless you for all you've done."

Biff smiled, appreciating her kind words, and thanked her for all her work attending to Laura during her illness.

Biff gripped Kate's upper arm. "I'll see you tomorrow," he said, with a knowing stare, then crossed Union Avenue.

"I like him," Avery said. "He would have been good for Laura and Hillary. We can thank Mr. Dragus, too."

Kate was dumbfounded by the kind words for Frank Dragus. "Mr. Dragus?" she questioned, raising her voice. "Why Mr. Dragus?"

The Thompson's were perplexed by Kate's reaction. "He helped them, too," Avery answered. "He paid their rent and food bills since Laura was unable to work. I shouldn't have mentioned it, because he wanted to keep it private."

"I'll bet he did!" Kate said, angrily. She knew Frank didn't do anything for anyone unless he got something in return, and Hillary had only one thing to give.

The Thompson's were disturbed by Kate's reaction, watching her become increasingly upset. Kate excused herself by feigning an appointment, then headed for the prairie at a fast pace. She wanted proof that Frank had been with Hillary, and there was one person who would know—Mrs. Gretsch!

Kate didn't want to believe what she was thinking. She hoped she would uncover another reason why Frank helped them financially. When Kate arrived at the mill, she went directly to the second floor. Mrs. Gretsch was sitting at her desk outside Frank's office, reading sheets of work orders.

Mrs. Gretsch looked up and smiled, as Kate walked directly toward her. Kate needed to get close to her, so they could be heard over the noise of the machines. She leaned over the desk, glaring into Mrs. Gretsch's eyes. "I'm going to ask you a question," Kate yelled, "and I want an honest answer."

Mrs. Gretsch leaned back in her chair, fully aware that Kate was angry. "Ya, sure," she responded, still clutching papers in both hands.

"Did Frank have Hillary in his office, like some of the older girls?"

Mrs. Gretsch stiffened. Without responding, she began flipping through the papers she was holding.

Kate became impatient, waiting for her answer. She repeated the question louder than before.

As though Kate wasn't there, Mrs. Gretsch continued looking at the papers.

"It's obvious the answer to my question is, yes!" Kate screamed. "That's not the answer I wanted. Why didn't you protect her? She is only twelve years old and you let it happen? Hillary isn't a child of the streets. She's a lovely, innocent girl, willing to do anything to save her mother." Kate's throat was getting sore from yelling, but she had no intention of ending the conversation.

Mrs. Gretsch became defensive, stammering as she replied. "No my business. I do good work here. Don't want lose work."

"My God!" Kate hollered. "Why didn't you come to me? I would have risked my life to protect her!" Kate looked at Mrs. Gretsch, with contempt. "How come I never saw her go into the office?"

"When you go bank, she go office," Mrs. Gretsch replied, hesitantly. "Please, not my business. I no say nothing more."

Kate straightened up in front of the desk. "You don't need to say more." She stared at Frank's office door. "You bastard. You filthy bastard!" she mumbled. Now Kate understood why Frank had gone out of town for three days. He hadn't left for business reasons. He left to avoid the funeral. Kate was livid. It became clear why Hillary thought of killing herself. Her parents were gone and she felt disgraced by being with Frank, leaving her to feel there was nothing decent left for her.

She thought of the loneliness and shame Hillary must have felt. Kate wanted to give Hillary support, telling her that it wasn't her fault; that she'd been the victim of an evil man. But would she do Hillary more harm, admitting she knew the truth? She decided not to mention it now, but help Hillary heal emotionally.

Kate knew Frank would go to the office Sunday morning after being away three days. She was determined to confront him before leaving town. She looked at the clock on the wall and realized there wasn't much time to remove her money from the bank. Without another word, she turned from Mrs. Gretsch and headed for the stairs.

Kate walked through the prairie, deciding to go to the boarding house and leave a note for Biff, asking him to come to her apartment at 9:30 a.m. and get Hillary on his way to the train station. They could have breakfast together, while she was at the mill confronting Frank.

The next morning, after Biff took Hillary to breakfast, Kate snacked on tea, crackers and cheese, while packing her clothes. The last thing she put into her tan canvas bag, was the brass cathedral clock Laura asked her to keep for Hillary. She wrapped it in a hand towel to protect it and placed it in the center of her bag.

Her confrontation with Frank was the most important thing on her mind. Kate carried her bag to the door, taking a last glimpse at the apartment. "I won't miss you, either," she said, aloud, then closed the door and started for the sunlight at the bottom of the stairs.

She walked along Union Avenue, taking a final look through the shop windows before stepping out of Alton and into Mill Prairie. As she toted her canvas bag to the mill, the sun was halfway to its zenith. She turned her eyes towards the river for a lasting look of the pond and its cluster of aged oaks and sprawling patch of wildflowers. It was all she wanted to remember of Alton.

She placed her bag on the ground and unlocked the door to the mill. Kate entered, closing the door quietly behind her. The silence was overwhelming. Six days each week, the machines rattled with pulsating noise. Today, they only cast shadows onto the floor. The eerie silence was ghostly.

When Kate reached the second floor, she saw Frank's silhouette pass the frosted glass of his office door. She hid her bag under a bench, so Frank wouldn't become suspicious. Kate entered the office, ready for a battle.

Frank saw fire in her eyes, but pretended not to notice. He turned his back to her and began moving papers in and out of the safe behind his desk. "Was it a nice funeral?"

His manner was casual and insincere, which infuriated her more. "You should have been there," Kate replied, slamming the door shut. "You could have seen your victim sobbing at her mother's casket."

Frank turned slowly, looking at her. "Victim? What the hell are you talking about?" His frown was deep and intense.

"You've had Hillary Cook in here, haven't you?" she snarled. "I don't want to know how often. I just want you to admit it."

Frank turned his back to her again, continuing to shift papers in the safe. "You seem to have quite an imagination."

"God damn liar!" she shouted, walking behind Frank's desk "I talked to Mrs. Gretsch. She didn't tell me anything, but I knew by the way she acted, I was right. You didn't pay the Cook's food and rent bills just to be nice. You did it to take advantage, like you did with other girls." Kate glared at Frank. "She's only twelve! How could you think of abusing a girl that young?"

"They enjoy themselves, too," Frank hollered, not wanting to be outdone in volume.

"Enjoyed?" Kate screamed. "Are you really stupid enough to believe those girls wanted a piece of shit like Frank Dragus? They needed help and you took advantage, as always. Hillary was a scared, innocent child, trying to save her mother." Kate began trembling with hate. She turned from Frank and found herself facing the black leather sofa. The thought of Hillary being there with Frank made her sick. The contents of her stomach erupted like a fountain, spraying the sofa.

Frank responded quickly. "You bitch, clean that mess now!" he yelled.

Kate ignored Frank's demand and walked up behind him, steadying herself against the desk. "Hillary is only a child. How young will you take them?"

Kate looked down at his desk, her hand inches from Frank's silver letter opener.

At that moment, Frank snickered and responded, sarcastically, "Old enough to bleed, old enough to breed."

Kate gasped, at his insensitive remark. "You took Hillary, because she was old enough to bleed?" Kate's trembling hand gripped the letter opener tightly and raised it high, then rammed it into Frank's back, screaming, "You raped *my* Hillary."

Frank groaned, stiffening to a full upright position. Motionless, his eyes rolled toward the ceiling and the papers he was holding scattered to the floor. Frank staggered to his left, collapsing between his desk and the safe.

Kate stared at Frank, waiting for him to move. She stepped back, shaken by what she had done. Her heart pounded, as though it was trying to escape from her chest. Her pulse throbbed at her temples and breathing became difficult. She watched Frank a few moments then approached him to feel for a pulse. He was dead. Kate rose to her feet, hoping to get out of the building without being seen.

Frightened, she listened for another presence, someone who could find her with Frank. She didn't hear anyone. Kate looked at the clock on the wall: 10:13 a.m. She had to leave, immediately.

Kate knew no one would enter the office until morning, giving her plenty of time to leave town. She took water from the pitcher on Frank's desk to rinse her mouth and remove bits of vomit from her clothing. Satisfied with her appearance, she moved toward the door, opened it slightly and looked in both directions. No one was in sight. She began to relax and her breathing came easier. She locked the door and retrieved her canvas bag from under the bench. She gripped the leather handles firmly and quietly descended the stairs.

Kate hurried through the prairie on a direct course for the train station. She could see black smoke from the train engine rising in the distance. At the station, Biff and Hillary were standing on the platform waiting for her. Kate was anxious to get on the train and leave Alton behind. "Do you have the tickets in hand?"

"Yes," Biff replied. "Three tickets to New York."

Kate was confused. "New York?"

"Right. We get off the train in Philadelphia where we buy three tickets to Galena, Illinois. That's how we cover our trail."

Kate smiled. She definitely wanted to cover their trail.

Hillary rushed up to her and gave her a hug. "It was getting late and I was afraid you would miss the train."

"I'd never miss this train," Kate replied, kissing Hillary.

The train came to a slow stop, belching black smoke from above and white steam from below. A porter jumped from the car in front of them and placed portable stairs on the ground, so passengers could disembark. Most had luggage, boxes and children. No one was in a hurry.

Kate was nervous, wanting to board the train and get away as fast as possible. The moment the last passenger dismounted, she took Hillary by the hand and led her into the car for a seat by a window.

Biff followed, placing their luggage in the overhead rack before sitting behind them.

Kate settled back in her seat, picking nervously at her fingernails, waiting for the train to roll out of town. She looked over her shoulder at Biff. "I want to thank you for helping me and John these past months. To show my appreciation, you'll be eating many of your favorite meals in my new kitchen."

Biff crossed his legs and smiled. "That's an offer I can't refuse. I'll make a list of all the meals I like and post it on your kitchen wall."

Hillary turned and knelt on her seat, facing Biff. "And I'll make you hot tea and raisin bread, whenever you want. See, between Kate and me, you'll never have to get married, because we'll take care of you."

Biff leaned forward and placed his hand against Hillary's cheek. "You could be right. I'm very happy with my new family."

The train jerked forward and Hillary looked out of the window. The smile on her face was replaced by pensive reflection, as a jumble of thoughts and plans and memories streamed through her mind. "Look on the hill," she whispered, pointing. "There's the white cross where my parents are."

Kate rubbed her hand up and down Hillary's back, attempting to comfort her. "We're starting a new life together, but your parents will always be with us." Kate sighed, watching the cross fade into the distance. Now, she understood the guilt that Laura feared, had she abandoned Jeremiah by going west, for she, too, was feeling a measure of guilt, knowing she would never return.

OoOoO

978-0-595-42683-6
0-595-42683-2